UNTIL I MET YOU

MONICA WALTERS

B. LOVE PUBLICATIONS

DEAR MONICA,

Hey, sis.

It's B.

I wanted to really quickly let you know how proud I am of you. When I first did that Halloween challenge in 2018, I was so excited when you submitted! When I read your book, I was like... damn. I gotta get her to sign a longer contract, lol!

You are becoming the epitome of what BLP represents for/to me. You have allowed me to teach you and pour my wisdom into you, giving you a foundation solid enough for you to build a solid platform on your own. Your dedication and passion for your craft and career does not go unnoticed, and you are such an inspiration to the rest of BLP.

The sky is not even the limit for you. Your future is limitless. I'm so excited to see what all God has in store for you.

Thank you for trusting me with your career, and I am so, so fucking proud of you!

—B. Love

PREFACE

Hello, Readers!

Thank you for purchasing and/or downloading this book. This work of art contains explicit language, lewd sex scenes, some violence, and moments of depression. This is also an insta-love type novel. If any of the previously mentioned offend you or serve as triggers for unpleasant times, please do not read.

Also, please remember that your reality isn't everyone's reality. What may seem unrealistic to you could be very real for someone else. But also keep in mind that despite the previously mentioned, this is a fictional story.

If you are okay with the previously mentioned warnings, I hope that you enjoy Vance and Jennifer's story.

Monica

This book is dedicated to the Facebook reading group, EyeCU Reading and Chatting. This story was born from a Freestyle Friday writing prompt about fathers and their daughters, in leu of the Kobe Bryant incident. The prologue of this book was the freestyle I came up with.

I appreciate the opportunity they gave me to showcase my skills and gain readers. Not only that, it was FUN! LOL

If you are on Facebook, you should consider joining their group. There's the opportunity to learn of new authors and books that you may not find otherwise.

Thank you, Ebony Evans and Kaylynn Hunt for the love you've shown me!

Here's the link to join:
https://www.facebook.com/groups/67068628976084/?ref=share

There's also a page you can follow on Facebook as well.
https://www.facebook.com/EyeCU-Reading-Social-Network-106426849417809

PROLOGUE

$\mathcal{V}$ance

"Daddy, this bisque tastes sooo good!"

"I know! That's why I brought you here. I knew you would enjoy it."

Every day, my daughter, Meena, and I went to lunch. That was my baby. She was a junior in college, majoring in social work. Since I retired two years ago from the fire department, we made it our business to spend as much time together as possible. She always made sure to schedule her classes where she had a break in-between for our lunch dates. Being my only child, we were *both* spoiled, especially since her mom died five years ago. We were close before then, having an impenetrable father-daughter bond, but after that, we only got closer. The only times we weren't together was when she was at school or with her boyfriend.

As we sat, enjoying our lunch at Tia Juanita's, her phone chimed. Normally, we didn't bring our cellular devices to lunch because we didn't want to be tempted to use them. This was our time. But I had to face reality that Meena was no longer a little girl. She was my twenty-one-year-old daughter, who I'd raised to be a responsible adult. "Sorry, Daddy. You know Chop can get thirsty sometimes. We're going out tonight, so he was making sure we were still on."

I slightly rolled my eyes. I couldn't stand that nigga. It was something about him that rubbed me the wrong way. I refused to call him Chop, and I could tell that irritated him. His name was Chad and that's what I called his ass. I only tolerated him because I knew she loved him. They'd been dating for a year now, and he was a kinesiology major. I continued eating my shrimp as she stared at me. "Daddy, what's wrong?"

Refusing to ruin lunch and express my disdain for Chad for the umpteenth time, I said, "Nothing, sweetheart. How's classes going?"

"They're great. I should have a 4.0 this semester. Can you believe that?"

"Well, of course I can believe that. I have a very intelligent daughter. I mean... she has a very intelligent dad."

She giggled as I smiled at her. I wouldn't let my issues with Chad keep me from enjoying lunch with my world... my sunflower... my greatest accomplishment. Meena was a reflection of everything I'd done right in my life. She was perfect: beautiful, smart, creative, and she cared about people. That was her reason for wanting to be a social worker. We continued eating so I could get her back to the school.

Once we got to Lamar, I kissed her cheek and told her I loved her, then watched her walk away, socializing with other students on her way to class. Madelyn and I had showered Meena with love. Not that our household was perfect, but I'd like to think that we gave Meena the best upbringing we could provide. She was a reflection of that. Everyone loved her and seemed to gravitate toward her. Her energy and aura were attractive, and it was why

I was somewhat protective. Some people didn't mean her any good. But because her heart was so pure, she didn't always peep game. But that was what I was here for. I tried to enlighten her, but her response was always, *Daddy, don't be negative. Everybody has some good in them. I just choose to focus on that instead of their flaws and mistakes.* I could only shake my head at her naivety.

After getting home, I began working on a training manual for the fire department. I'd taken on the task to give me something more to do, plus it would bring in extra income. Not that I was hurting for money, but my account wouldn't be angry with the extra deposit, versus the withdrawals it saw on a daily basis.

When I finally decided to look up from my outlines and plans, I'd warmed dinner and got right back to it. I wanted to finish outlining tonight, so I could start filling the detail in before the week was over. So, when I finally finished, it was practically nine o'clock. I felt accomplished, but tired as hell. After taking a shower, I planned to check on Meena, then go to bed. However, before I could call her, she was calling me. I answered with a smile, "Hey, baby girl."

"Daddy!! Please meet me on Irvin and Doucet. Chop left me here and I'm scared."

"Shit! I'm on my way now."

Why in the fuck would he leave my baby in the south end of Beaumont like she was a fucking prostitute? I slipped on a t-shirt and grabbed my nine-millimeter. Ain't no way I was going there slipping. Hopping in my SUV, I got there in record time to see my baby sitting on the cement curb. Her hair was all over her head and she had a black eye. "Shit! Meena, what happened?"

She was crying hard, and that shit made me even angrier than I already was. I scooped her up as she cried harder. When I placed her in my vehicle, I saw all the bruises on her body. Today, he would be Chop... chopped fucking beef. I got in the driver's seat and looked over at my battered baby. "What happened?" I asked, my voice extremely low, sounding deadlier than I'd ever heard it sound.

"Chop went crazy. We were arguing over what movie we would watch and ended up seeing what he wanted to see anyway. Then we argued over the restaurant we would eat at. It was like he was a mad man tonight, and I don't know why. Finally, after we left the restaurant *he* wanted to go to and we got in his car, he just started swinging on me. His fists landed everywhere, Daddy, and I couldn't stop him," she cried.

A tear dropped from my eye as I drove to the emergency room. I needed to get her checked out to be sure she was okay. "Where the fuck did he go?"

I'd never done serious bodily harm to anybody, but that would change tonight. "I don't know, Daddy. I'm so sorry. You tried to warn me about him, but I didn't want to listen."

Gently rubbing my fingers down the side of her face, I said, "Calm down, baby. This isn't your fault. Okay? You couldn't have known he would flip like this. I didn't even see this coming, but I know exactly what's gonna happen next."

When I got to the hospital, I helped baby girl out and realized that her clothes were torn, practically falling off her. Glancing down at her legs, I could see them trembling and the bruises on her thighs. Being that she was light complexioned like her mother was, it wasn't hard to see. "Meena... did he rape you?"

She cried harder and buried her face in my chest. If my fire wasn't raging before, it was definitely wild and uncontained now. I carried her inside and they brought us straight to the back. The police were called, and I had to wait in the hallway while they tried to put my baby back together. I was sure they would do a rape kit, along with x-rays. I knew that the bastard lived on campus and I knew the license plate number of his Dodge Durango by heart. He done fucked with the wrong man's daughter.

When all was said and done, Meena was physically okay, just plenty of bruises and a bruised rib. Once I got her home, I got her situated in her old room with heating pads and gave her pain medication. When she went to sleep, I headed out to find that bitch. Imagine the adrenaline that rushed through me when I saw him arriving at the school at the same time as me. I quickly parked and got out my car, approaching his.

He got out of the car, not even noticing that I was approaching. He was staggering like he was drunk. Holding my gun in my hand, I said, "Chop."

He turned around and was face to face with my nine. "Oh, fuck! What the hell? Please, Mr. Etienne, don't shoot. It was my bad. I didn't mean to hurt her," he yelled, frantically searching with his eyes for someone that could possibly help him.

His ass had sobered up quick. I supposed a gun to the face would do that. "So, you thought you would get away with harming my sunflower... my world? You know how much she means to me. I'll go to hell for her, so jail ain't shit. I hope you right with the Lord."

1

*V*ance
        Ten years later...

"DADDY!"

"Hey, my sunflower!"

Meena rushed to my outstretched arms as I made my exit from O.L. Luther Unit in Navasota, Texas. I'd served ten years to the day for murder. Because I was on the grounds of an institution for higher learning, the crime was considered a federal offense. Swinging her around in my arms for the first time in years had me emotional as hell. After putting Meena down, I followed her to her car. My twenty-one-year-old daughter was now thirty-one and a wife and mother. It killed me that I couldn't be there to give her away or even meet this new guy. She brought him to a couple of visitations, and I hoped that just by him knowing why I was in prison was reason enough to do right by her.

When we got to her car, he was seated in the driver's seat and I noticed the car seat in the back... my granddaughter. Meena had never brought her for a visitation, so I was beyond excited to meet my eight-month-old grandbaby. "Welcome home, Mr. Etienne."

"Thank you, Tyrone. I appreciate y'all coming to get me instead of letting me ride that horrible bus."

"Daddy, really? You know there was no way in hell I was gonna let you ride a bus."

"Mr. Etienne, come on now. I know we don't know one another well yet, but whatever and whoever is important to my wife is important to me."

"Thank you," I said as I got in the car and laid eyes on the most precious baby I'd seen since Meena was born.

She was staring at me with her big, beautiful brown eyes and I felt it in my heart. "Hey, Belan. I'm your PaPa."

She smiled at me and that melted my heart. "She's beautiful, just like you, Meena."

"She's the spitting image of her mama. It was like I had nothing to do with her conception at all," Tyrone said.

I chuckled as we drove away, heading back to Beaumont. My daughter had been amazing to me while I was locked up. She kept up my house and bills. Thankfully, I'd made her a signer on my account, so she could keep up with my retirement money and pay bills for me. I was able to get out and have somewhere to live and money in my pocket.

For my first year behind bars, I was depressed as hell. It was like that boy's blood was crying out to me from the grave, but he pushed me, and I snapped. He tried to crush my sunflower and that brought out the beast in me. I'd already lost her mother. I'd be damned if I was gonna let a punk like him take my daughter from me. I began looking at the situation like, had I not killed him, who was to say what he would've done next. He could have killed Meena, and in doing that, he would've killed me, especially knowing that I could have put a stop to it beforehand.

Thankfully, I'd had my career already and had retired. So, doing this time didn't really affect me at all. I was able to come home like I hadn't missed a beat. I *did* realize that it affected me mentally and emotionally, though. I wasn't nearly as talkative or approachable as I used to be or as friendly. I had to stay on-guard at all times while locked up. Always expecting something foul to happen had become habit. "So, Daddy, after we bring you home to take a shower, get dressed because we are taking you out to dinner. Wherever you wanna go."

"Thanks, baby girl. Well, I'm about ten years behind on where all the best places to go, so y'all pick."

"Not much has changed in Beaumont, Daddy. You wanna go to Cheddar's?"

"That's fine, baby. Wherever y'all take me is appreciated."

I sat back in the seat and tried to get comfortable for the two-and-a-half-hour drive. Being on the outside was gonna take some getting used to. For ten years, I'd gotten used to somebody telling me when I could take a shit, and now, I'd be able to come and go as I pleased again. Meena had sold my car, so I knew I would need to get another one after obtaining my driver's license. I wasn't sure when that would happen, though. Meena worked and her time was limited now that she had a family.

As I looked out the window, Meena said, "Oh, Dad, here's your phone. I upgraded it, of course. I went got this yesterday, so it would be ready for you. I'm not sure who you would call, but all your contacts are in there. I'm also not sure how many of them are good, but you can figure that out in time."

"Thank you, baby."

"Is there a reason you're so quiet?"

"No. I'm just taking everything in."

"Okay."

She turned back around in her seat as I glanced at my sleeping granddaughter. It would take some time for things to get back to normal. I wasn't foolish enough to think that it would just go back to normal the moment I walked out of the prison's confines. I needed to get to know my daughter as a grown woman. While she was twenty-one when I got locked up, she wasn't nearly an independent grown woman. Ten years was plenty of time to change... grow... mature. She and Tyrone had been married for three years and had dated for two years before that.

No one was the same person they were ten years ago. If they were, then they weren't living. Even with being locked up, I was different. Whereas I used to be clean cut, I wasn't anymore. The dreads on my head were a testament to that. Prison had made me darker. I wasn't the beacon of light I was before the murder. I was now rough around the edges and maybe a little rough internally as well. As I watched the scenery, I thought about Milina. The woman I'd left behind. We weren't dating, but we'd only just begun on the path to that. After having maybe three phone conversations, we'd admitted that we both wanted to get to know one another more and in person. However, before we could have our first date, I'd been arrested.

I tried calling her from prison once, and when she heard who the call was from, she declined the call. I didn't blame her. She didn't know me that well. She didn't know that I wasn't a violent person, and that this was about being there for my daughter. I knew it wasn't right to kill that boy, but it wasn't right for him to do what he did to my daughter, either. Two wrongs didn't make a right, but I sure felt better knowing he wouldn't be in my daughter's life or no one else's daughter's life, for that matter. It was one thing to break her heart... that was going to happen. But what he did to my sunflower was unforgiveable for me.

I wondered what Milina was doing now and if she was taken. I'd met her at the grocery store that we both frequented. At the time, she was in her late thirties and I was forty-three. She was a beautiful woman that had me smitten and I'd finally gathered the nerve to approach her. She was warm and friendly, and I believed that we would have had more had I not gotten into trouble.

For most of the ride back, I was in my head, but engaging in small talk as well. I was somewhat nervous to be out. Trying to fit in amongst society again could prove to be difficult amongst people that I knew. While I knew the story had been aired on all the major news outlets, I knew there would be people that would still choose to judge me and try to belittle me. I honestly wasn't ready to deal with that. Dealing with strangers would be much easier.

When Tyrone pulled in my driveway, I sat there for a moment, staring at my house. I damn near cried at the sight of it. When we got out of the car, Meena handed me my key and said, "I took off Monday, too, Daddy. That way we can try to get as much business squared away as possible, like getting your license renewed and other things you may need. I know you'll need to make a grocery store run. I tried to buy you some necessities like soap, water, toilet paper, milk, cereal, and a few snacks that I remembered you liked."

"Thank you, baby. I really appreciate it."

I pulled her in my arms and hugged her, then kissed her cheek. "Daddy, you did this time for me. I would be a fool to not make sure you were taken care of. You're still my everything. Just because I'm married, doesn't mean you're no longer on my list of priorities. You sacrificed your life for me, and I will always be grateful to have a father like you. So, whatever you need, I got'chu."

She kissed my cheek as I swallowed the lump in my throat. I smiled at her and began walking away, when she said, "Oh, and Monday, we will resume our lunch schedule."

I smiled again and nodded at her. She had me in my feelings big time. When I got to the door and unlocked it, I pushed it open and just stood there. Everything was in its place. I noticed the training manual I was working on for the fire department was still on the coffee table, but everything else had been cleaned and put away. It seemed the house had just been cleaned because there was a fresh scent that wafted its way to my nose.

Walking inside and closing the door behind me, the emotions I held hostage the entire way back overcame me. I literally fell back against the door and cried harder than I ever had, except when Madelyn died. It felt good to be back in my house. Composing myself, I walked through and noticed how Meena had kept things up. She'd even hung a family portrait of them and one of just Belan on the wall. That made my heart smile.

Walking from room to room, I appreciated her more and more. She'd been the perfect daughter and I'd kill again to protect her. Finally making my way to my room, I went to the bathroom and started the shower. I needed to visit a barber as soon as possible. Hopefully, Tyrone could take me to one tomorrow. The hot water from the shower was just what I needed. Looking in the cabinet, all my colognes were still sitting there. I sprayed just a little. Wrapping the towel around my waist, I walked to the bedroom to see what I would wear. As I did, the phone started to ring. I knew that had to be my daughter.

However, when I went to answer it, it was a number that wasn't saved in my contacts. Probably a solicitor, so I ignored it. Shortly after, it rang again, so I answered. "Hello?"

"Hey, Daddy. You busy?"

"What number are you calling from? It's not saved in my phone."

"Oh. I must've forgotten to program Tyrone's number in it. I'm on his phone."

"Oh okay. I just got out the shower."

"Okay. We should be there in an hour. The passcode for your phone is 011288."

I smiled slightly. That was me and Madelyn's anniversary date. "Thank you. Your mom would be so proud of you, baby girl. I just hate I missed both graduations, your wedding, and the birth of my granddaughter."

"I figured you would hate that. So, I have something special to show you after dinner."

"You never cease to amaze me. Okay, let me find something to wear."

"Okay, Daddy. I'm so glad you're home."

"Me too."

I ended the call and smiled at the phone. She probably had a video to show me and I couldn't wait. Pulling some jeans from the closet and a nice button-down shirt, I hoped it was still considered nice. I was getting old anyway. I'd probably get away with it. My beard was gray and so were my temples. I'd have to cover my head with a Fedora. Although, I knew I'd have to take it off at the dinner table. After grabbing some under clothes from the drawer, I proceeded to get dressed.

When the horn sounded and my phone rang, I knew my ride was here. Walking out the door, I locked it and made my way to the car. It looked like someone else was in the car, too. I didn't know how I felt about that. Trying to get comfortable again around my own daughter and son-in-law would be even more difficult with a stranger there. When I got in the backseat, Meena turned in her seat and said, "Daddy, this is Ms. Jennifer. She's our neighbor and helps with Belan."

This woman was so damn gorgeous. I was taken aback as I stared at her. "Nice to meet you. I'm Vance," I said as I reached for her hand.

If I wasn't tripping, I could have sworn I saw a smirk on Meena's face before she turned forward in her seat. "Nice to meet you as well, Mr. Vance."

And her voice... it was so smooth, like the most expensive cognac. It could be because I hadn't been in the company of a woman in a long time, but I was pretty sure that my taste in women hadn't changed. Her makeup was perfect. Pulling my gaze from hers, I looked down at Belan. "Hey, PaPa's baby. How are you?"

She smiled at me. That was what she did last time. This time, she started speaking gibberish while staring at me. She loved me already. I grabbed her hand and kissed the back of it. "That's what gentlemen do, baby. You look so beautiful this evening."

She began kicking and Meena laughed. I glanced up to see Ms. Jennifer smiling. Sitting back in my seat, I couldn't help but notice her cleavage in the pink dress she was wearing. Choosing to avert my gaze, I looked out the window as we traveled to Cheddar's. Meena was right. Beaumont hadn't changed much from what I had seen so far, except that building that read Beaumont Emergency. "Is that a new hospital?"

"Beaumont Emergency? No. It's a facility to handle minor things. If you need to be hospitalized, they transport you to Baptist or St. Elizabeth."

"Oh."

I could see Ms. Jennifer staring at me, and I hated I'd asked that question. Hopefully, she didn't ask questions about where I'd been. I remained silent the rest of the way and when we arrived, I got out and opened the door for Meena as Tyrone opened the door for Ms. Jennifer. Tyrone detached Belan's car seat from the base and carried her inside. "It's only five, so we shouldn't have too much of a problem getting a seat," Tyrone said.

I held the door open for everybody, but when I caught the full view of Ms. Jennifer, I couldn't help but scan her full-figured body. She was showing plenty of leg and they were thick as hell. I had to wipe my mouth to make sure I wasn't drooling. Damn. I could feel my third leg stiffening and I was thankful I'd worn jeans instead of slacks. When she walked past me, she gave me the eye... the eye that said, *come fuck me, daddy*. It had been over ten years and I would gladly give her what she wanted.

I followed her inside, repeatedly glancing at her ass. As we approached the hostess, she was already grabbing menus to seat us. I followed behind everyone as we were being seated at a table. The waitress brought a highchair for Belan and Meena took her out of her car seat. "Before you put her in there, can I hold her?"

Meena smiled at me and said, "Of course."

Bringing her over to me, I stood and reached out to her. She smiled but didn't reach for me, so I took her. Belan looked back at her mama, then back at me. I was sure to wait for Meena to sit before I sat to avoid Belan having a little fit. She put her hands in my beard and smiled. So that was it. She liked my beard. Tyrone didn't have a beard. "Hey, baby girl."

"Da-Da-Da-Da."

"Can you say PaPa?"

She watched my lips for a moment, then proceeded to say da-da. I laughed as did the rest of the table. "We're gonna get very acquainted. I'd love to watch you sometimes while your parents are at work."

Meena looked away as if she wasn't cool with that, so I added, "But only if they're cool with that. I'm sure you're probably learning all types of things where you go now."

"She's learning to be the perfect little lady," Ms. Jennifer said.

"Oh. I didn't mean to step on your toes. I apologize."

"It's no problem. We can take turns."

Meena smiled. That was why she'd looked away. She didn't want to step on Ms. Jennifer's toes, either. I smiled at Ms. Jennifer and continued to play with my granddaughter, getting hearty laughs out of her until it was time to order.

2

*J*ennifer

IF GOD WAS STILL in the business of hand sculpting a man from clay like he did Adam, his name had to be Vance. From the top of his dread-loc'd head to the soles of his feet, this man was touched by the holy spirit. I felt the anointing as soon as I laid eyes on him. My God. When Meena said her dad was coming along, I was expecting some washed-up looking old guy. She'd told me that he'd been in prison for ten years, but still... I wasn't expecting this level of perfection. His chocolate goodness with that white beard and that deep, raspy voice was bringing my mind places it shouldn't have been.

I was here with my babies, trying to enjoy dinner, but all I could see that was appetizing was sitting next to me, holding Belan. *Jesus, Mary, and Joseph.* That chocolate fondue was making me thirsty as hell. My ex-husband and I had gotten divorced almost three years ago and I hadn't been with anyone since. I'd had to work on rebuilding myself from where I allowed him to tear me down to. I promised myself that I wouldn't pursue another man or let him pursue me until I was completely happy with Jennifer... happy with who I was and had evolved into.

Depression had weighed me down the last few years of our marriage and I had gained a lot of weight. I wasn't a small woman when we met, but I'd swallowed my size sixteen whole years ago. I'd gotten up to a size twenty-six and had refused to go anywhere because of my size and appearance.

But finally, I was able to pull myself from the slums and divorce that lying, cheating sack of shit. I hit the ground on a mission to find myself again and began going to aerobics classes, counseling sessions, then group sessions with other abused women, and with their support, I found the strong woman I used to be before marrying Oscar's abusive ass and I lost the weight I'd gained through the depression. I was down to a size twenty-two and I loved the way it looked on me. Men seemed to like it, too.

Thankfully, I didn't have kids to drag through that turmoil. That would have only made the situation worse. I was suffering from high blood pressure and was on the cusp of diabetes but thank God, I was able to get all that under control. I was almost fifty years old and I was fly as hell, giving these young girls a run for their money. I was sure to make a statement in every room I walked in, even if I was making that statement to my-damn-self. The only person that needed to be happy with me was me. If other people weren't feeling me, they could go to hell for all I cared. I didn't live for their opinions of me.

After giving the waitress my order, I looked over at Vance. It was something about him besides his appearance that drew me to him. Knowing he'd done ten years for protecting his daughter was sexy as hell to me. He'd given up everything to make sure the man that violated her wouldn't violate another, taking the law into his own hands. Then Meena said he called the police on himself. He was a bad muthafucka and that was the kind of nigga any black woman should want on her team. Hell... I was hot. Felt like I was flashing sitting this close to him. If he looked this good fresh out the joint, I could only imagine how good he would look fresh out the barbershop.

Meena cleared her throat, so I looked at her. Everyone was staring at me. "Did I miss something?"

"I was asking what you did for a living or if you were retired," Sexy Chocolate said.

"Oh. I apologize. I retired from the State of Texas about five years ago and now I sell crafts. Mostly hair bows, t-shirts, and things like that. I made the pretty bows in your grandbaby's hair."

"Oh okay. They're beautiful. What did you do for the state?"

"I was a social worker."

"She helped me get on, Daddy."

"Oh, wow. Thank you for looking out for my baby."

I nodded and he fidgeted slightly. I assumed that Meena hadn't told him that I knew. Now wasn't the time to tell him that I knew where he'd been the past ten years, either. I only cared about where he was now... next to me. Meena came over and took Belan from him to put her in her chair and she whined a bit. "Looks like she's already getting attached to PaPa."

Shit, I wanna get attached to PaPa's fine ass, too. My hormones were raging, and I couldn't do a thing to stop them. I was a forty-nine-year-old woman that felt like she was just hitting her sexual prime and I needed somebody to work out all this energy on. Standing from the table, I said, "Excuse me, y'all. I need to go to the ladies' room."

When Vance stood as well, I knew I was in the presence of an old school type of loving. Tyrone and Meena were staring at him like they didn't know why he was standing. *Youngsters.* I nodded at him and walked away. When I turned the corner, I saw that he'd sat, but his eyes were still on me. That was why I had to go to the ladies' room. I needed to cool off. His presence had me wound tight as hell. That shit was dangerous. I'd have the man at my house for drinks after this and who knew where that would lead to.

After giving myself a pep talk, I washed my hands and headed back to our table. When I rounded the corner, Vance stood to his feet and Tyrone did the same as Meena fed Belan green beans. "Thank you, gentlemen."

They both nodded, and not long after I'd been seated, the waitress brought out our food. Looking at my catfish, I was ready to get to it. Instead, Vance reached for my hand. I slid my hand in his, immediately feeling the heat between us. Glancing over at him, he was staring at me. I quickly closed my eyes and bowed my head as he began blessing our food. Everything about him was possessing me, and for the first time in a long time, I wanted a man to inhabit me. *Hell yeah... live right between my legs.*

We all exchanged small talk as we ate and watched Belan play with her green beans and mashed potatoes. As I finished what I would eat of my food and asked for a box, Vance asked, "So, what's your last name, Ms. Jennifer? Are you originally from here?"

"I'm originally from Lake Charles, but I moved to Beaumont when I started at Lamar. My last name is Monroe, but I'm in the process of getting my maiden name, Rubin, back."

"Oh, okay. I used to work with a guy whose last name was Monroe. You know of a fire fighter with that last name?"

My face had to have gone pale. He knew Oscar's punk ass. "Yeah. My ex-husband, Oscar, is a fire fighter."

Meena quickly tried to change the subject. "The food was so good."

"Yes, it was, Meena, but it's okay. I'm over him. We've been divorced for about three years, Mr. Vance."

"I apologize. I didn't mean to make you uncomfortable."

"It's okay. How could you have known? How long did y'all work together?"

"Umm... I don't quite remember. It's been a while. I, uh..."

I reached over to grab his hand. "It's okay. You don't have to explain."

He smiled at me and Lord have mercy, I wanted to attack him at this table. That smile was bright, and his teeth were gorgeous. When I realized I was still holding his hand, I quickly pulled it away and I could feel my face heating up. I believed my gesture alone let him know that I knew what had gone down with him. At that very moment, he seemed a little more relaxed. Glancing over at Meena, I could see her wink at me. It had been weird to hear her calling me Ms. Jennifer all evening. She normally called me Mama. I knew she didn't want to do that in front of her dad, since she hadn't time to talk to him about me.

Totally surprising me, though, he grabbed my hand and said, "This evening has really been enjoyable with you here. Thank you for not making this awkward."

I nodded as my face heated up. I was sure my cheeks were red. Ugh. Although he let my hand go, he continued to stare at me as I took a sip of my water. "Well, since we've all boxed our food up, are y'all ready?" Meena asked as the waitress brought Tyrone's credit card back.

I nodded and so did Vance, so we all stood as baby girl threw a fit. She wasn't ready to go. If I had to be strapped down in a seat, I would throw a damn fit, too. Vance went over to Meena and grabbed her from her and said, "I'll carry her. We can put her in the seat once we get in the car."

Meena smiled and rolled her eyes as we headed out of the restaurant. When we got to the car, Vance walked on the side I was sitting, so I thought he'd just switched sides until he said, "Ms. Jennifer, where are you going?"

"I'm sorry. I thought you'd unintentionally switched sides."

"No. I was opening the door for you. Is that cool? Can I do that?"

"Of course. I'd never turn down a display of chivalry."

He smiled again, causing me to wet my panties. I hadn't been this turned on in a long time, but I welcomed it. It gave me hope that there were still some good men out here. Even after only one evening, I knew that about Vance. He was such a gentleman. But it felt like I'd know him for a while, because every free moment Meena had, she brought him up in conversation. She even talked about the relationship he shared with her mother and how perfect it was up until she passed away. Meena said she was only sixteen or seventeen years old when her mom died of a brain aneurism. The bond that she had with her father was admirable, especially since my daddy was such an asshole with my mother. Then I ended up with the same type of man with Oscar's trifling ass.

After getting in the car, he closed the door and walked around to the other side with Belan. She was so excited to be in his arms. It was too cute the way she held onto his beard. Tyrone had already gotten the car seat in place, so when Vance got in with her, he put her in it... no whining. "Well, I'll be damned," Meena said.

Vance looked up at her, eyebrows slightly risen. "What?"

"She's not crying and throwing a fit with you."

"Well, baby, I have years of experience. Plus, I'm PaPa. We love each other already."

"So I see."

I chuckled quietly as Belan reached up and grabbed his beard as he strapped her in. Somehow, though, his eyes ended up on me. We stared at one another for what felt like forever. I had to be losing oxygen to my brain because he stole my damn breath away. Slightly smiling, he licked his lips and I followed every movement of that tongue until it was back in his mouth. His ass was backed up, I knew that shit. He was ready to dive up in something hot, wet, and tight. I had just what he needed, too, but he wouldn't get that shit tonight. As easy and free-spirited as I wanted to be, my self-control wouldn't allow that... at least I didn't think it would. She was screaming something different tonight.

Once he got Belan strapped in, we were able to leave Cheddar's parking lot. I didn't know why I thought they would be dropping Vance home and then leaving. I was terribly mistaken. When Tyrone pulled in his driveway, he killed the engine. Taking a deep breath, I mentally prepared myself to be here for a little while. Tyrone opened my door as Vance got Belan from her seat. Meena happily bounced out of the car. "Daddy, I'm so excited for you to see this!"

"I can tell," he said quietly.

We made our way to the door and Vance gave Belan to her dad, then unlocked it. Walking inside first, he stood in front of the door, allowing us all to enter. When I did, he stared at me, his eyes begging me to stay. After caressing my curves with his eyes, he closed the door. Meena had gone to the TV and turned it on, then did something in front of it that pulled up a video. I sat on the couch and Vance sat next to me, somewhat close. I was able to smell his cologne and it was making me want to rip the clothes off him.

He was so damn fine, there was no way he was Meena's dad. No way in hell. He had to have adopted her. If he didn't have the gray beard, I wouldn't think he was over forty, let alone over fifty. "Okay, Daddy. You ready?"

"Yep. Hit me with it."

When the video started, Meena was in a black cap and gown. She said, "Hey, Daddy. I wish you were here, but I know that it's because of you that I'm able to make this journey. I love you."

Glancing at Vance, I saw him swallow hard as he watched. Then it showed clips of her graduation ceremony and her walking the stage. The video went to Meena talking again when she was about to get her master's. Then there were clips of that ceremony as well. Glancing at Vance again, I saw the tear that rolled down his cheek. The video cut for a minute, showing picture collages, then it went to the wedding. I could feel the tremble in Vance, so I grabbed his hand and held it. He glanced at me, then continued watching the TV. Seeing someone else give his daughter away was probably eating him alive.

After a few minutes of that, the last part of the video was when she had Belan. That lasted all of about ten minutes. He slid his hand from mine and wiped his face, then stood and walked over to Meena. "Thank you so much for this. Being able to see those moments has me all sensitive in here in front of Ms. Jennifer."

I chuckled. He had to know that I knew by now. As good of a father as he seemed to have been, there was no way he would have missed those milestones in Meena's life unless he didn't have a choice. After hugging her, Meena said, "Well, are y'all ready to go home?"

I didn't respond because I wouldn't have minded spending more time with Vance. He grabbed my hand, helping me to my feet. As I was about to walk off, he gently pulled me back to him. "Ms. Jennifer, I umm... feel like we have a connection. I'd like to explore that if you feel the same way."

I smiled. "I do feel the same way. But please stop calling me Ms. Jennifer." I chuckled and he did so nervously as well. "Give me your phone and I'll save my phone number in it."

He handed his phone over and I saved my information in it, wishing that I could stay at his place a little longer. Handing it back to him, I said, "Call me any time. I don't have a job to go to, so I'm usually available."

"Okay."

He smiled, then grabbed my hand and kissed the back of it. I shied away from him and he released my hand. Turning to Meena, she had the biggest smile on her face while Tyrone rolled his eyes. She'd set this up, so she was beyond happy that we'd made a connection. We all walked to the door as Vance carried Belan out. He opened my door, then went to the other side to put Belan in her seat. We stared at one another for a moment, then he buckled Belan in. "I'll call you in an hour."

"I look forward to it."

3

*V*ance

I COULDN'T BELIEVE I still had what it took to get a woman's attention. The past with Milina had been on my mind, but the moment I saw Jennifer, that shit all went out the window. Going back inside, I took off my clothes and laid in the bed. It definitely felt better than the cot I'd occupied for the past ten years. Tonight was so enjoyable, I'd forgotten to ask Tyrone about getting my hair cut. I sent him a text message, but that took me all of ten minutes. He answered within seconds, saying he'd pick me up at nine-thirty.

My skin was somewhat dry, too, so maybe they could recommend something I could use to revitalize it. As I laid in the bed, my thoughts drifted back to Jennifer. Her beautiful, medium brown skin, big titties, fat ass, thick thighs... she was a goddess. My deceased wife was a big, beautiful woman as well. Having all that extra to grab ahold to was a turn on like no other for me. And Lawd did Jennifer have it. Those thick lips were begging me to kiss them.

My dick was pitching a tent in my drawers. It didn't take much to get me excited.

Seemed like the time was creeping by. It had only been twenty minutes. I knew they were home already. According to the address Meena had given me, it should have only taken them ten minutes. Going to the kitchen, I grabbed a bottle of water, then went back to the room to channel surf. There were so many channels and the screen looked way different. It was going to take me a good thirty minutes to figure out how to navigate through this home screen with all the channels. As I did my best to figure it out and settled on a show called *Chicago Fire*, my cell phone rang. On the screen was a picture of Meena. "Hello?"

"Heeyyy. You and Ms. Jennifer really hit it off."

"She's a nice woman. I'm surprised she didn't ask any questions about where I've been."

"Daddy, I told her a long time ago. She's been so good to me. We're so close, I started calling her Mama. She's been like a mama to me over the past few years."

"Wow. That's great, Meena. If you feel comfortable calling her Mama, then I know she's the real deal, then. Things go like I want them to go, she's gonna be your step-mama. She's beautiful."

She chuckled. "And she's just as beautiful on the inside."

"I can believe that. Thanks for the hookup. I'm surprised she's okay with talking to me, knowing that I was in prison."

"She knows why. She actually thinks it's sexy that you did that for me. Ugh. I told her to never put my daddy's name and the word sexy in the same sentence."

"Don't hate 'cause yo' daddy still got it. I can't wait to call her. When I looked at her, it was like her spirit greeted mine. That's a feeling I could never let go of."

"Wow, Daddy. This is amazing. Well, Ms. Jennifer isn't the only one smitten. Your little granddaughter whined all the way home."

"See, I'm gonna have to keep her sometimes. She's already my baby. She reminds me so much of you at that age."

"I'm so glad you're home, Daddy, but I'm gonna go to bed. I'm exhausted."

"Okay, baby. I'll talk to you tomorrow."

"Okay. And Daddy?"

"Yeah?"

"Ms. Jennifer told me you can call her now."

"Good to know. Thanks."

I ended the call with my daughter, and suddenly, I was nervous to call her. It wasn't like she didn't know. I was sure she knew everything about me, thanks to Meena. There really wasn't much to tell. Grabbing my phone, I made the call and waited for her to answer. After a couple of rings, her sweet, melodic voice answered, "Hello?"

"Hi, Jennifer. It's Vance."

"Hi, Vance. I take it you talked to Meena."

I chuckled. "Yeah. Did you enjoy tonight?"

"I really did. Umm... I can't wait to spend more time around you."

"Really? I mean... I can't wait, either. I'll be at Meena's house for a little while tomorrow after my haircut."

"Okay. Well, I'll get to see you tomorrow, then."

"Yeah. If you don't mind me asking, how old are you?"

"I'm forty-nine."

"Older than what I thought. I assumed you were in your early forties."

"No, sir. How old are you?"

"Fifty-three."

There was silence between the two of us after that, but I was cool with the silence. She wasn't a chatterbox, and neither was I, so it was probably better that we did this in person. After being silent for a while, we began talking about our likes and dislikes and how we grew up. We found ourselves laughing quite a bit and that was refreshing. I couldn't remember the last time I'd laughed so hard. It was like she was put here specifically to meet me. I hadn't been out of prison a whole twelve hours yet. What were the chances that I would meet a woman like her after only being home for a couple of hours?

After talking, I got to know quite a bit about her, and I knew that I wanted to know even more. As I yawned, she said, "Vance, why don't you get some rest? We'll talk tomorrow. Maybe I can convince Tyrone to barbeque. I'll make the sides while Meena watches Belan. What do you think?'

"It's not like I have anything else to do. Sounds like a plan. See you tomorrow, beautiful."

"Okay. Bye."

I ended the call and stared at the ceiling. She was perfect. Jennifer Monroe, soon to be back to Jennifer Rubin. I hoped she was prepared to handle me. While I would like to take it slow, after spending ten years in the joint, I knew that wouldn't happen. I was coming like a freight train. Her being married to Oscar Monroe; I already knew that jackass was the reason they'd gotten a divorce. He didn't hide his philandering ways nor the fact that he was married. I felt sorry for his wife and I didn't know her and had never seen her. He never even brought her to a Christmas party.

I knew exactly how long we'd worked together... fifteen years, but I didn't wanna continue talking about his ass. While she said she was okay, I could see in her eyes that talking about him was uncomfortable for her. That was the last thing I wanted her to be in my presence. I could see the desire in her eyes when she looked at me and I wanted to fulfill every one of them. I couldn't wait until tomorrow.

I FELT SO MUCH BETTER after leaving the barbershop. My beard was shaved off, leaving me with a trimmed and lined up goatee and

I'd gotten the dreads cut off, leaving some hair on top in disheveled twists. "You wanna go home and take a shower? I'm barbequing today, so I won't be back on this end of town."

"Yeah, if you don't mind. It won't take long."

"Okay," Tyrone said, exiting the freeway.

I couldn't be around Jennifer with dead hair all over me. He had to cut off quite a bit of hair. If I decided to hug her, I wanted to do that without fear of fucking up my chances with her. "So, you and Ms. Jennifer seemed to hit off yesterday."

"Yeah. She's a really nice woman."

"Yeah, she is. She keeps Belan whenever we need her to, and she won't take payment. She said it was her pleasure since she never had any kids. Belan is like her baby. So, I think it'll be cool if y'all hook up. You'll both be the grandparents."

I gave him a one-sided smile as he drove to my house. Thinking about Jennifer made a full smile appear on my face, though. I'd texted her this morning, wishing her a great morning and hopefully a great afternoon when I saw her later. She'd responded almost immediately, saying the same and sending a heart emoji. She had me feeling more confident than ever. It had been a while since I'd pursued a woman. I thought I was rusty. Maybe I was, but she just knew that she wanted me, despite my weak game. Lowering my head, looking at my phone, I almost wanted to text her again, but I couldn't be acting all clingy. I'd see her within the next hour.

When we got to my house, I hurriedly showered and washed my hair, then put on some khaki shorts, Sperry's and a plaid button-down. I didn't wanna look like an old man. Jennifer seemed to have it together when it came to style, so I couldn't half-step. Once I moisturized my goatee with the beard butter the barber gave me, I went to the front room. "You know we barbequing, right?"

"We? I thought you were barbequing," I said with a serious face, but dying on the inside.

"I mean... I thought you would be helping me."

I chuckled and said, "I'm just messing with you. I planned to help."

"Whew. Good, 'cause Meena went bought ribs and I'm not the greatest at barbequing ribs. Shit... I'm not the greatest at barbequing, period."

I shook my head slowly, and said, "Well, come on, so I can show you a few things. Hopefully, I remember or the barbeque 'bout to be fucked up."

Tyrone laughed and said, "Oh well. They shouldn't have volunteered me to do this shit."

I laughed with him as we headed out the door. Once we were in the car, my phone alerted me of a text. Pulling it from my pocket, I saw it was from Jennifer. I smiled as I read, *Can't wait to see you.*

"You smiling all hard, that must be Ms. Jennifer."

"You got some business?"

"Huh?"

"Go mind your business. Let me mind mine."

He chuckled, then held one hand up in surrender as I turned my attention back to my phone. I replied, *Can't wait to see you, either, beautiful. We're on our way.*

As I slid my phone back in my pocket, Tyrone looked over at me and smirked. I rolled my eyes. "So, Mr. Etienne, I was thinking. Maybe I should find something else to call you, since we're establishing this father-son relationship. I don't know, like, maybe Pops or something like that."

I just stared at him. "Or maybe not," he mumbled.

"It's cool, Tyrone. I just don't know how cool I am with being called Pops."

He chuckled. "I was just using that as an example. I'll come up with something and run it by you."

"A'ight. Make sure you run it by me before you call me that."

"Listen. I probably shouldn't joke about this, but umm... you ain't gotta worry about that. I know why you were in prison. I'm walking the straight and narrow."

I stared at him muthafuckerly, making him nervous for a moment, then laughed. "Relax, man. You too uptight. Long as you treating baby girl right, we ain't got problems. That nigga she was with before put his hands on her, then left her stranded in a dangerous neighborhood, known for prostitution. So, you good. Plus, I can't take Belan's dad from her."

"Thank God."

Shaking my head slowly, I chuckled silently as we continued to their house. When we turned in the driveway, Meena was outside, pushing Belan in a swing. Before I could say anything about my babies, this bad-ass woman walked out the door. "Shit," I said quietly.

Tyrone evidently heard me because he chuckled. Jennifer had a pan in her hands as she walked off the porch. She had on a low-cut halter and some capri pants. Jesus was gon' have to be a fence today, because if I had my way, some shit was gon' go down... tonight. Her capri pants were baggy, but with those titties on display, she would have given me a heart attack if the ass would have been on display, too. Nothing about this woman said forty-nine years old. There was a nice breeze outside and her hair blew from her shoulder. "You gon' get out?" Tyrone asked, ducking his head inside the car, then laughed.

"Shut up."

I didn't even see him get out. Jennifer had me mesmerized. When I opened the door, she looked in our direction. Her lips parted when she laid eyes on me. I assumed she was admiring my hair cut. As we walked toward them, I could feel my nature rising. The closer we got, the better I could see her cleavage. Tyrone went over to Meena and Belan while I stood silently in front of Jennifer. She licked her lips, then tucked her hair behind her ear. "Hey, Jennifer."

"Hey, Vance."

I grabbed her hand and kissed it, then pulled her closer to me. Glancing down at her pretty-ass titties, I said, "Listen. I was locked up for ten years... day for day. I don't know if I'm gon' be able to control myself, looking at all that."

"Maybe I don't want you to control yourself."

Oh, shit. My dick only got harder. She brought her hand to my face and rubbed it across my cheek, letting it linger when she got to my goatee. "Your cut looks really nice."

"Thank you. But I need you to be sure about what you're saying. Won't be no going back once it's going down."

She stepped closer to me and I glanced down at her titties again. "Vance, I'm a grown woman who knows what she wants. I don't have time for games. So, make sure you aren't playing any."

"Who would be able to play games while looking at these pretty-ass titties you got on display?" She frowned slightly. "Shit, I'm sorry. I didn't mean to be disrespectful."

"Vance, what are you talking about? I was just wondering when that was gonna come out of you. If anything, you talking to me that way is a turn-on."

She slid her fingertips over her cleavage, teasing me. "Jennifer, I'm already on edge. We can't leave them on their own for this barbeque, but I will. I'll just have to apologize later."

She blushed. "You're right. I can't leave my babies high and dry. Neither one of them know how to cook."

I chuckled. "What do they eat during the week?"

"Shit, I don't know, but that's probably why they're both skinny."

I laughed loudly, then grabbed her hand, leading her to Meena, so I could kiss her and Belan. "Hey, Daddy!"

"Hey, baby girl."

"Don't you look handsome. I love your hair cut."

"Thanks, baby. Let me kiss my princess so I can go light this barbeque pit. Is the meat already seasoned?"

Meena frowned and shrugged as Jennifer rolled her eyes and said, "I seasoned it, Vance. Just let me know when you're ready for it."

She turned completely red when she said that, so I knew where her mind had gone. I bent over and kissed Belan as she screamed in excitement, then walked over to Jennifer. I licked my lips and said, "I'm ready now. You gon' help me?"

I slid my fingers down her arm and I could see the goosebumps that appeared on her skin. "Mr. Etienne!"

I turned to Tyrone to see him with the charcoal and lighter fluid in his hands. "Let me go help this boy before he sets himself on fire."

She giggled and said, "Okay. I cleaned the pit earlier, so you don't have to worry about that."

"You have them spoiled."

She giggled as I kissed her hand again, then walked away to go help Tyrone.

$\mathcal{J}$ennifer

As I WENT INSIDE, I could feel the heat between my legs. *Shit*. I knew it was gonna be impossible to hold out. The moment he stepped his fine ass out that car and I caught a glimpse of that faded haircut, my shit started talking to me. He was fine like he was before, but now... that nigga could take me in front of the kids. I was starting to sweat, and it wasn't even that hot outside, only eighty degrees. Watching them from the kitchen window, my mind was imagining all the shit he could do to me tonight. He glanced back at the house as if he knew I was watching him. I guess that prison-mentality always had a nigga looking over his shoulder.

I began putting meat into a pan to bring out to them. Tyrone's parents were supposed to be coming over, too. As I put the two slabs of ribs in the pan and the chicken and sausage in another pan, my phone rang. Seeing Vance's number, I answered, "Y'all ready?"

"No. I just wanted to talk to you."

"Really?" I asked while laughing.

"Uh huh. You must didn't look in the mirror. You fine as hell, baby."

"Mmm... just promise that you'll show me later."

"I'll show you whatever you want."

I cleared my throat because I was progressing too quickly. "Well, right now, you gon' have to show me your skills on a pit."

"You crawfishing?"

I laughed at his country terminology. I'd met someone from up north when I was in college that didn't have a clue that was even a word. I literally had to look it up and show them that it was indeed a term in the dictionary that meant to back out of something. "I'm trying to cool myself off. We got a few hours to go. I can't be at the point of orgasm all day."

"Oh, it's like that? That's good to know. We're in the same boat, but of course, I'm in over a ten-year hiatus."

"Right. Well, it's been almost five for me."

He was quiet for a minute and I was sure he caught what I'd said. The last year and a half of our marriage, Oscar didn't have sex with me. He said that I'd gotten too damn big and I believed him. I was so happy that I'd gotten the help I needed to see myself as the beautiful woman that I was. Because of that, my confidence was through the roof now. I knew I had the shit that men wanted. Just because I was a big woman didn't mean shit. "I think we are just about ready for some meat. Bring the ribs first, if you don't mind."

"Of course not. On my way."

I ended the call and grabbed the pan, being careful not to drop anything. Meena had bought the flimsy-ass aluminum pans from the dollar store that couldn't hold much weight. I rolled my eyes when I saw them. These poor kids. Vance and I had a lot of work ahead of us. Wait... *Vance and I?* I needed to slow down, but that was hard to do when the man that did unspeakable things to me just from the way he looked at me, was staring at me as I walked to him. I just needed to feel his lips on mine. The anticipation was taking a toll on my mental. It was like I couldn't focus on anything but him. Thankfully, the sides were done. I'd finished the potato salad last night because I couldn't stand hot or room temperature potato salad. It had to be cold. The rice dressing and beans were done a couple of hours ago... before Vance got here.

When I got to him, he smiled, then took the pan from me and said, "Thank you, baby."

I knew I had to be blushing. *Jennifer, calm your hot ass down.* Even though he'd been locked up for ten years, he wasn't the man that the system had caged. He was educated, established, and successful before his run-in with the law. Vance Etienne was everything I'd been longing for and yes, I knew that immediately. The moment he got in the car last night and spoke to me... his eyes said things Oscar's never had. The intense connection was more than lust, although that shit was pretty strong, too. "You're welcome, Vance."

I was dying for him to hug me... kiss me... anything other than a kiss on the hand. At this point, I'd be okay with him popping my ass when I walked away. But he was a gentleman. I knew not to expect that, but I also knew that he would at least be watching. As I walked over to Meena and Belan, I turned to look back at him and saw him watching with his bottom lip tucked in his mouth. Damn. I almost ran back to him and put my tongue down his damn throat.

When I got to Meena, she had a big smile on her face. Sitting on the blanket next to her, I instantly regretted it. "Shit, you gon' have to help me up from here."

"Oh, I'm quite sure Vance Etienne will gladly help you up."

"Girl, shut yo' mouth. Yo' daddy fine as hell."

"Ugh."

I shrugged my shoulders as I looked over at him showing Tyrone what the hell to do. "Don't hate on his swag. That's why you here."

"I'm not hating. I just don't wanna hear about it. But I'm happy you guys are feeling each other. You may end up being my mama after all."

"Shiiid, ain't no may about that, boo. I'm gon' be yo' step-mama. Mark my words."

"Well, I can't wait to see how this develops," she said, lifting her gaze.

I turned to see who she was looking at and saw Vance standing over me. "Jennifer, can you show me where the other meat is?"

"Yeah. Sure."

He grabbed my hand and helped me from the ground, pulling me close to him. I couldn't help but stare into his dark, lust-filled gaze. *Jesus Christ of latter-day Saints!*

After clearing my throat, I pulled him inside the house as Meena yelled, "Bet' not be no funny business in my house!"

I laughed, but I was so embarrassed. Vance only shook his head. The minute we walked through that door, though, he grabbed me by my waist and pressed that hard-ass dick against my ass. *I think I just creamed... naw, for real.* I could feel his breathing on my neck when he grabbed a handful of my hair and mumbled against my neck, "Damn, Jenn. You so damn sexy."

He spun me around and kissed my lips and I thought I was gonna melt to the fucking floor. His touch... his kiss was everything I knew it would be. Vance slid his finger down my cleavage and said, "Tonight is gonna be amazing. Is it okay that I called you, Jenn?"

"You can call me whatever the hell you wanna call me."

He chuckled, then brought his lips to mine again and his hand went to the back of my neck, holding me close. When his tongue slid inside, I briefly died, went to glory, and came back. My hands went to his face as I moaned in his mouth. As he pulled away slowly, he rested his forehead against mine, and said, "Damn."

"I know. Let's get this meat before Meena carries her ass in here, checking on us."

He chuckled, then released me to go to the kitchen. "So,

besides the fact that my daughter can't cook, she turned out okay in my absence, huh?"

I turned to him with the pan of chicken and said, "She's amazing... a caring person and sweet as they come. I was proud to help her get that job. Meena's the kind of person that the state needs. I believe she can really make a difference in someone's life."

"I always worried about that. When I left, she was totally dependent on me. I wasn't completely sure that I'd given her all the tools to navigate through this world without me."

"You taught her well, Vance. You only missed one thing and that was teaching that girl how to cook. She invited me for dinner one time, and I promise you, it took everything in me to smile while I ate those dry steaks, overcooked baked potatoes, and bland green beans. She tried, though, so I somehow got it down. After she tasted my cooking the next weekend, baby girl ain't try to cook no more. The most she'll do is nachos, hotdogs, or burgers. You have to be horrible as hell to mess those up."

He laughed and said, "A'ight, enough on my baby. What about Tyrone?"

"He's sweet. He's caring just like Meena is. Maybe a little soft for a man, but if she likes it, I love it. I just like my man to be a little rougher around the edges."

"Oh, like a nigga that did ten years for fucking his daughter's boyfriend up?"

"Shit... just like that," I said, then handed him the pan of chicken.

My eyes stayed on him as I bit my bottom lip. "Keep that shit up and my daughter gon' see more than she bargained for. What about Tyrone's parents? Is there anything I should know? Do they know where I've been?"

"They're nice... somewhat quiet. His dad is more talkative than his mom. Mr. and Mrs. George Mills. I'm not sure what his wife's first name is. They told me but I forgot. She never really engages in conversation. You get Mr. George liquored up enough, he's extremely fun... sings and dances and shit. It's quite hilarious. I can tell his wife gets embarrassed, though. I like him better under the influence. It livens up the party."

"Okay, well good. Do we have any alcohol here?"

"Always. Like father, like son. But he only indulges when he doesn't have to work. Thankfully, they aren't violent drunks."

He laughed again. That laugh was so damn infectious. I could listen to it all day and giggle like a young schoolgirl. Whenever he laughed, I found myself smiling big. "Well, let me get outside before these ribs dry out." He glanced out the window and smiled. "Looks like they're here. Oh... you didn't answer my other question. Do they know about me?"

"Yes. They may be a little uptight at first. They know why you were there. So, as the parents of Meena's new beau, I could see their discomfort. I tried to assure them that Tyrone was nothing like her ex and they didn't have anything to worry about."

He nodded, but I could see the wheels turning in his head. I didn't think this would be good. It was like I could see that he was gonna fuck with them. He didn't seem like the petty type at first, but I could clearly see it surfacing. "Okay. Cool," he said, then turned and walked out the door.

Maybe I told him too much. *Shit.* I only told him that so he would understand if they were a little standoffish. I grabbed three beers from the fridge and brought them outside, only to see that Mr. Mills had brought his own cooler. After chuckling, I noticed that they had someone else with them. Frowning slightly, I wondered who this man was. He looked to be around Tyrone's age and Tyrone seemed to be excited to see him. Going back inside, I grabbed another beer and headed outside.

When I got to them, I handed the beers to Tyrone, Vance, and Mr. George and spoke to the Mills as I did so. As I handed the beer to the unknown man, he scanned my body and his eyes landed on my cleavage. "Ms. Jennifer, this is my cousin, Alex. I haven't seen him in at least five years."

"Wow. Okay. Nice to meet you, Alex."

He took my outstretched hand, and lifted it to his lips and said, "It's very nice to meet you, too."

My cheeks heated up as I took my hand from his and glanced at Vance. He had a hard expression on his face, but he didn't say a word. I walked away from him, then went to Vance and kissed his cheek, giving this Alex guy a clue. I didn't belong to Vance, but I couldn't tell my body that. She was surrendering everything to him and seeing that rough expression on his face only turned me on. It was that bad boy persona that was doing me in. Vance was a nice man, but I could see that whenever he felt threatened by someone or their presence, he was a totally different person. Pulling his attention to the barbeque pit, I asked, "How are the ribs coming along?"

Turning his head to me, he smiled softly, then lifted the door of the pit. "They're coming along great. I see what you're doing. You aren't my woman, Jennifer, but you will be. But I like that you're claiming me already. That got a nigga's chest puffed out and I'm gon' show you how much I appreciate you tonight."

Leaning over, he kissed me on the lips as Meena cranked the music up. She had Anthony Hamilton blasting from the speakers and Vance twirled me around. "Oh, you know how to swingout?" I asked.

"Sure do. You like to dance?"

"I love to swingout. That's a good thing. Maybe I can plan us a date night."

"I'd like that."

I winked at him, then walked over to Meena. I noticed Mr. Mills was on his second beer. He'd already killed the one I gave him. I smiled, knowing we were gonna be in for a time. Before I could get to Meena, he yelled, "Meena! What's that you playing? You ain't got no Marvin Sease?"

I damn near choked. Vance was cracking up and so was Tyrone and his cousin. Oh, this shit was about to be lit. Meena was frowned up as I approached, practically doubled over. "Who is Marvin Sease?"

"Don't worry about it, boo. 'Candy Licker' too vulgar for your virgin ears."

She rolled her eyes and said, "Umm... I have a daughter, remember?"

"Girl, you don't listen to vulgar shit. Marvin will have yo' ass running in the house with some of the shit he say."

Mrs. Mills was sitting next to Belan on the blanket, playing with her like only the two of them were out here. Walking over to them, I sat on the other side of Belan and she scooted over to me. "Hey, sweetie pie. NaNa Jenn just taking a break. Go play with your GiGi."

Mrs. Mills smiled slightly. "It's okay," she said softly.

Belan pulled herself up by holding on to my arm and climbed into my lap and started whining. Meena walked over with a bottle and that killed that. Glancing over toward the men, they were all seated near the barbeque pit when Mr. Mills stood and swayed to the music a lil bit. He was already feeling good. He must have started drinking before he got here. As I chuckled, I could see Mrs. Mills in my peripheral, rolling her eyes. Turning my attention to her, I asked. "You okay?"

Her face reddened slightly, and she said, "I'm just tired. He's like this almost every day now. The man I married is gone."

My eyebrows had risen in surprise because I was shocked she'd even told me that much. "I'm sorry, Mrs. Mills. I guess I just see him as being fun."

"My name is Donna. You don't have to call me Mrs. Mills. It's not so fun when he's like that every day. We can't even have adult conversation anymore. I was actually looking forward to coming here today because you've always been nice. I know I'm usually quiet, but I'm at my wit's end. I'm sorry. It probably feels like I'm dropping all my weight on you."

You are dropping all your weight on me. Shit. I had enough weight on my own. But being the nice person I was, I asked, "Have you tried talking to him about it?"

"When he's sober, he's asleep. I can't expect to have a serious conversation with him while he's drunk."

"Well, at least try. If it gets you nowhere, then try something else. He seems like a nice man."

"He is, but his drinking has gotten out of hand these days. I don't know if something he's going through is causing him to drink that way, but I'm tired."

If she was tired, there wouldn't be much I could say to make her feel better. So, I stopped talking about it. I glanced over at the men to see him singing "Nobody's Supposed to Here" by Deborah Cox. I couldn't help but to chuckle, but quickly silenced it so I wouldn't offend Donna. The shit was hilarious, and all the men were laughing. Even Meena had walked over to them to laugh and clown right along with him. They were dancing and singing together. As I watched them, I caught Vance's gaze. He licked his lips and winked at me. I smiled in return. "Are you dating Meena's dad?"

"We just started talking. I wouldn't say we're dating just yet."

"Oh. It doesn't bother you that he just got out of prison?"

"Not at all. If someone did the things to Belan that someone did to Meena, I would find myself in the same position."

"I suppose I understand. I didn't mean to pry. He seems like a nice man."

"From what I can tell, he really is."

I looked back over at him to see him dancing with Mr. George. Yeah, he was just my type.

$\mathcal{V}$ance

THIS BARBEQUE COULDN'T BE OVER FAST enough. All the eye-fucking me and Jennifer had been doing was taking a toll on me. Tasting those lips of hers only heightened the severity of my craving for her. If I didn't have her tonight, I knew I would turn into a wild animal. And that was if I didn't turn into that shit anyway. Tyrone's dad, George, had livened the party all the way up. We were dancing and singing, laughing at each other the entire time. We were all pretty lit, too, except Meena and George's wife. Jennifer had eventually left her side and came and had a good time with us. When she put all that ass against me when "Back That Azz Up" came on, I could've fucked the shit out of her.

Although Tyrone's cousin, Alex, had apologized for flirting with Jennifer, I could see him watching her... hard. Like the nigga was practically drooling. For that reason, I kept her close. I didn't want to have to fuck nobody up and I was only twenty-four hours out. As the evening progressed, it seemed me and Jennifer only got more affectionate. I spent a lot of time holding her in my arms, kissing her in various places, and just touching her in general. Holding her around her waist from the back was my favorite. Being able to mumble sweet and sexy shit in her ear was getting her ripe for what I had in store for her later, not to mention the soft kisses to her neck and shoulders.

Once we'd gotten everything cleaned up and food put away, Tyrone asked, "You ready to go home, Mr. Etienne?"

"I got him, Tyrone," Jennifer said before I could respond.

Meena lowered her head and lifted her eyebrows with a cynical grin on her face. I rolled my eyes, then kissed her goodbye, making her promise to see me tomorrow. After kissing Belan's head and shaking Tyrone's hand, I followed Jennifer out. We walked over to her house and she turned to me and said, "I'm gonna take a shower, then I'll be ready to go to your place."

"Why don't you just pack a bag and take a shower at my place?"

"Okay. I'll do that."

When she walked away, I sat on her couch. She had a nice house. At least she'd benefitted in some way from being married to Oscar. Although, I was sure she would have rather gone without than to have to go through the heartache he'd put her through. As I sat trying to be a gentleman, my mind was taking me through it, wanting me to go back there and help her 'pack' a bag. The only thing that kept me from doing so was that we both had that outside stench on us. We'd been out there for hours and had a great time, despite me having to keep my eyes on Tyrone's cousin.

After a few minutes more, she came back into the room with her duffle bag. "You ready?"

"Mmm hmm."

I stood and followed her out through her back door to her garage. I was sure her question had more than one meaning and so did my response. She hit the button on the wall to open the garage door, then I opened her car door for her. She smiled and said, "Thank you, Vance."

I licked my lips as I glanced down at her cleavage. "Of course."

Once she got in, I closed the door, then walked to my side. After getting in, I grabbed her hand and kissed it. "You still remember how to get to my house?"

"Yeah, I think so."

She backed out of the driveway and we took the ten-minute drive to my house. As she said, she remembered *exactly* how to get to my home. My dick had been on one all day and it was throbbing at this point. Getting out of her car, I walked around and helped her out, then grabbed her bag and her hand. After unlocking the door and disabling the alarm, I said, "It doesn't seem real that you're here."

"I know," she whispered as I pulled her close.

I kissed her forehead and asked, "Would you prefer to shower alone?"

"Can I? My nerves are starting to heighten."

"It's okay, baby. I'll help you relax when you get out. I'll shower in the other bathroom."

I led her to the hallway bathroom, and I continued to the master bathroom, begging my dick to stop anticipating so hard. I was gon' mess around and nut before I even entered her. Not having sex in over ten years had my ass nervous, too. When I got locked up, it had been months since I'd felt the warmth of a woman. All I could think about was what if I didn't please her or go long enough. What if I nutted and the shit wouldn't come back up? While those thoughts plagued me, it didn't make my dick deflate.

After washing up thoroughly, I dried off and put on some shorts and a t-shirt, then slid on my flip flops and went to the kitchen to see what I had. *Nothing*. I forgot to go to the store. *Shit*. All I had was water and milk. What the fuck? I was fiending for the pussy so bad, I couldn't think about anything else. When Jennifer came out of the bathroom, she walked into the front room wearing a long t-shirt and flipflops. Walking over to her, I inhaled the scent of her body wash as I stood close to her. Her breathing had gotten ragged. Grabbing her hand, I led her to the couch.

The tremble in her hand made me think twice about how she might be feeling. She just met me yesterday, maybe she was forcing herself to do this because she thought I would be upset if she didn't. Moving her hair from her shoulder, I said, "Jennifer, you're so beautiful."

"Thank you," she said as she turned to me. Putting her hand to my face, she said, "You're extremely handsome."

"Can I ask you a question?"

"Of course."

"What is it that you see in me that's making you want to give me your most precious gift? You don't really know me."

I slid my fingers down the side of her beautiful face and waited for what she would say. "Vance, as much as Meena talks about you, I felt like I knew you a long time ago. Knowing what you did for your daughter... it just sparked something in me. Although I know murder is wrong, I think every woman wants a man in her life that she knows would kill to protect her. I was definitely infatuated with you just from your pictures and what she told me about you. But when we met yesterday evening, it was so different."

She rested her palm on my cheek and continued, "It was like I felt you deep. When you stared into my eyes, I felt a connection like never before, So I feel like I *do* know you. Although I'm nervous, it has nothing to do with you. I haven't had sex since before I divorced Oscar. So, I'm nervous about that. What about you? You don't know me."

"I don't know you, but what I feel from you is magnetic. I mean, at first, I thought it was just sexual, because it's been sooo long for me. But the way my daughter dotes on you, I know you are amazing. Just the fact that she calls you mama tells me a lot. My grandbaby adores you. I can tell that you're just as beautiful inside as you are on the outside. Just to tell you how much I'm feeling you, I'm willing to wait if you aren't ready or sure."

As I got the last word out, Jennifer brought her lips to mine and kissed me sweetly, then slid her tongue to mine. I was doing my best to go slow, because everything in me wanted to just get to it. *Shit!* I didn't have any rubbers. *Fuck!* I slowly pulled away from her and lowered my head. She moaned slightly, so I lifted my head to look at her. Her eyes were still closed, and her head was tilted back. God, she was so beautiful. I gently kissed her neck, then said, "Jennifer, I'm sorry. We can't."

Her eyes popped open and she stared at me as she brought her head back down from its tilted position. After clearing her throat, she looked down at herself and seemed uncomfortable for a moment. "Okay."

"It's not because I don't want you, because my dick is so fucking angry at me right now. But I didn't get any rubbers. So, if you're okay with me just being intimate with you tonight, then I'll do my best to please you in other ways."

She smiled at me, then pulled me back to her, kissing my lips. Her nipples were calling me, so I slid my hands up her thighs as she broke our kiss. They were rubbing against me as we kissed, and I couldn't take it anymore. When my fingers reached them, she moaned, then bit her bottom lip. Lifting her shirt, I realized she wasn't wearing any underwear, either. I could knock my-own-self out for forgetting to go to the store. Before I could put my mouth to her nipples, she straddled my lap. "Jennifer, damn. I don't know if I can handle going so far, knowing I can't dip into that honey pot."

I grabbed her ass, not being able to help myself, and squeezed the fuck out of it as she grinded her hips against me. My dick felt like it was gonna burst through my clothes to penetrate what I knew would be good as hell. "I guess you've suffered long enough, Vance."

"What'chu mean?" I mumbled, then took her nipple into my mouth.

She held my head with both hands for a moment, then pulled her shirt off. "I have condoms in my purse."

I immediately laid her on the sofa and went to my knees to taste her fruit. She'd said the magic words. The moment I spread and lifted her legs and saw the light pink flower bloom for me, I was ready to sip its nectar. When I softly kissed her pussy, she moaned, and her shit instantly became juicier. I hummed in satisfaction as I tongue kissed her, then began slowly sucking up her juices. Damn, her taste was succulent like the most decadent dessert, smooth like the most expensive cognac, and sweet like a sugar cane from the fields of southern Louisiana.

The hair around my mouth was soaked and I could feel her juices soaking the length that hung from my chin. Slowly gliding two fingers inside of her, it was like a suction pulled my fingers inside. "Oh, God, Vance... yes."

Coming up for air, I said, "Shit. You taste so fucking good."

Going back in, I began sucking her clit and could feel the tremble in her legs. Reaching up I flicked her nipple back and forth with my finger. As I massaged slow circles on her G-spot, Jennifer screamed. "Fuuuck! I'm cumming, Vance! Fuck!"

I damn near came with her. Her screams of passion were so sexy. I continued slurping up all her vitamins that promised to heal my soul and make my transition back into society a lot easier. Her thick legs wrapped around my neck, nearly cutting off my air supply, but I was willing to die for this shit. That was how good it was to me. I hadn't felt a deep connection with anyone since Madelyn died almost fifteen years ago. When Jennifer's legs loosened, I lifted my head as she panted. "I'm sorry. Your head game is so damn good, I almost suffocated your ass."

I chuckled. "I'm a retired firefighter. I know how to survive for a while on limited air supply. And I'd definitely utilize those skills anytime I indulged in your flavor, baby."

She turned slightly red, then sat up on the sofa and kissed me like she needed to see what that flavor tasted like. As we kissed, her hand found my erection and she began stroking it through my shorts until I stretched the waistband and freed him. She pulled her mouth away from mine and almost whispered, "If that ain't real big dick energy, I don't know what the fuck it is. Damn, Vance."

She immediately stood and I followed her to her purse. After snatching it up, I led her to my bedroom. She sat her purse on the dresser and I pulled her to me. "So, umm, listen. I ain't used this shit in over ten years. I don't know what to expect. I don't want to disappoint you. I'm extremely turned on and I might cum in two point two seconds."

"Shhh... we'll take it slow," she said as she put her finger to my lips.

Turning to her purse, she took out a Magnum XL and a Durex XXL. She looked down at my dick, then dropped the magnum on the dresser. Approaching me with a smile on her face, she grabbed my dick and was about to go to her knees. I quickly pulled her up. "Not until I get checked to make sure everything is good."

Her eyebrows went up, so I knew I had to explain. The only thing wrapped around my dick had been my hand. "You never know what you're coming in contact with whenever you go to a toilet, especially in there. I promise you, I haven't had sex in almost eleven years."

"You remember how to put these on?"

"I should."

She handed the condom to me and went and laid on my bed. After opening it and getting the condom on, I realized how perfect the fit was. Magnums had always been slightly snug, but I'd made them work, because I didn't know about these. Either that or they weren't making them eleven years ago. I made my way to the bed and got in with Jennifer, immediately kissing her. Getting lost in her was what I wanted, and I hoped she felt the same way. I eased my body on top of hers as she opened her legs, staring at me. Positioning the head where it needed to be, I slid into her wetness as she gasped.

I lowered my head to hers and whispered, "Oh, shit."

My entire body was trembling like it was in shock. Her pussy felt so fucking good, I knew there was no way I was letting her get away from me now. I didn't give a shit if I had to take performance enhancement drugs. I'd pop one of those blue pills and handle up. As I began stroking her, she moaned and said, "Vance, yes. This is everything I hoped for."

Picking her legs up, she wrapped them around my waist as I dug deeper inside of her, hoping to hit that oil vein to have her lube up my heavy artillery. After kissing her lips, it felt like I'd found my groove, but I could also feel my nut rising. I silently cursed my dick out, knowing I wouldn't be able to hold that nut off too much longer. Jennifer brought her hands to my face and said, "Give it to me, Vance. If you nut, you just nut. But don't play with me."

I closed my eyes for a moment, then grabbed her leg, hooking it with my arm and gave her pussy what she wanted as she screamed. It felt like every vein in my fucking body was about to explode as I gave her the savage beast I'd had caged up moments ago. "Oh, fuck! That's the shit I want... Vance! I'm cumming!"

"Me too... fuck!"

When I nutted, I almost screamed like a bitch. Her cave had pulled out everything I had in me and I practically wanted to go to sleep. The true test would be if I got hard again, though. I didn't have problems in that area before I got locked up, but I knew stress could affect everything. I had a ten-year relationship and we'd finally divorced, but the effects of the relationship could still be lingering. I lowered my head and kissed Jennifer, then slid out of her. When I looked at the condom, I said, "Shit!"

There was so much ejaculate in that shit, I could have impregnated three women off that one round. Jennifer chuckled and turned on her side. "Vance, that was amazing. But next time, stop worrying so much."

"I got'chu. I just wanted to please you the first time, just in case... you know."

"Well, I don't think we'll have that problem, Mr. Etienne," she said while staring at my dick.

He was once again, rising to the occasion. I couldn't help but smile. When I looked back at her, I said, "You're in for a world of trouble, now."

"Mmm. I can't wait."

$\mathcal{J}$ennifer

"You muthafucka! Shit!"

Vance and I were in our third damn round and I knew, without a doubt, that my pussy was gon' be sore as hell tomorrow. For round two, he had my feet touching the damn headboard behind me. His second round had gone quickly, too, but this third round was everything. I'd been in more positions than I could count and now he was indulging from the back. He popped my ass and yelled, "Fuck!"

His dick was so deep inside of me, I could taste the latex. The way he gripped my ass as he pounded my shit, told me that just that quickly, we were both attached to one another. I hoped he wasn't the jealous type. Good pussy could make a man lose his damn mind, and throughout the night, he'd said so. "I love this juicy shit! Fuck! This my pussy, Jenn? Tell me this my shit."

"It's yours, Vance," I panted. "As long as this dick is mine."

"Signed, sealed, delivered," he said as he thrust within my depths.

He had to have destroyed my cervix with that last thrust. I felt a slight cramp go through my stomach. Nothing crippling, but just a mild discomfort. He practically collapsed on top of me, then rolled to his side. Listening to him pant, I closed my eyes for a moment, thinking about how perfect today had been. Turning to my side, I stared at him. When he looked over at me, he kissed my forehead. "Jenn, you done fucked up. I'm gon' wanna stay buried in yo' shit. You're mine now."

"Well, I guess it's a good thing we're both retired, because I enjoyed sliding down that pole of yours just as much. I know I'll have to soak, but once I get used to your drive, it's really on."

He pulled me to him and kissed my forehead again. "I know we need another shower, but I'm tired as hell. I'm not the forty-three-year-old I was the last time I had sex. I'm gon' have to get back in shape."

"You can come work out with me at the gym if you want to."

"Yeah, sure. What gym do you go to?"

"Exygon."

"Okay. We can start Monday."

I kissed his lips, then turned my back to him so he could spoon me. Vance was a lot to handle, but I was well-equipped for the job. I just hoped that our relationship blossomed and became just as strong as the sex had been. I was a little worried during the first round at first. But when he hit me with that two-piece to my pussy, I almost wanted to throw in the damn towel. He was well-endowed and my girl needed to adjust to all that man. Oscar was probably a good five inches long but had the nerve to try to slang the shit every-where. I was never totally satisfied sexually, but in the beginning of our relationship, his personality was worth what he lacked in that department. As I gained weight, he gained confidence in his medi-ocre sex.

Vance kissed my back and said, "Goodnight, baby. I can't wait to introduce you to the kids as my woman tomorrow."

I smiled slightly. He wasn't playing around. I guess more than my pussy was his. But if things continued to be as great as they were now, my heart would be his, too.

***

VANCE DIDN'T HAVE a damn thing in this house. He was still asleep, so I'd gotten up, thinking I was gonna cook him breakfast. Wrong. All he had was water, cereal, and milk. Geeze. He said he'd forgotten to go to the store, so maybe we could do that today. Going back to his bedroom, I saw that he was still asleep. So, I went to the bathroom and turned on the shower. I was so damn sticky, it was ridiculous. When I stepped out of the bathroom, Vance was on his knees on side the bed, praying. If that wasn't sexy, I didn't know what was.

I went to him and got on my knees next to him. He grabbed my hand without opening his eyes and continued his prayer aloud. "And thank you, Lord, for this beautiful woman that You've placed in my life. I know she was sent to me by You and I promise to do right by the gift You blessed me with. Help her to know that my purpose and intent is to make sure she's satisfied and happy in all aspects of life. In Your name I pray, Amen."

"Amen," I repeated.

He smiled at me and said, "Good morning, baby."

"Good morning."

He stood to his feet and helped me to mine, then escorted me to the bathroom. We brushed our teeth and once he rinsed his mouth, he stood behind me and wrapped his arms around me. Gently kissing my shoulder, then neck, he said, "Last night was amazing, Jenn."

I smiled and agreed. "It was."

"We can have amazing days like that all the time."

"We can," I agreed again.

He smiled at me in the mirror, then lifted my shirt, exposing my nakedness beneath. After taking his boxers off, he led me to the shower. I'd never felt so precious and fragile. He treated me with care like I would break. Squirting my shower gel into my loofah, he washed my body. The gentle treatment damn near had me crying in that shower. I was somewhat embarrassed when he lifted my stomach to wash beneath it, but he made it his business to kiss every roll on my body... every stretch mark, showing me that even my imperfections were perfect to him.

I couldn't help but reciprocate the tenderness he was showing me. As I washed his body, I kissed him, massaged him beneath the hot spray, and admired the helluva man he'd shown me so far. Once he'd rinsed off and I was about to get out, he grabbed my hand and pulled me to him. "You know you're a queen... my queen. I plan to treat you as such. Promise me that you'll let me continue to do that."

I gently rubbed his face and said, "I promise. And I plan to treat you as my king. Promise me that you'll let me do that."

"I promise, baby."

He slid his hands to my ass and kissed my neck. "As much as I love kissing on you and caressing you, I'm gonna have to stop. I'm hungry as hell and ain't shit up in here to eat."

I giggled as he helped me out of the shower. "I know. I was gonna cook breakfast, and I was like, what the hell? So, we have plenty to get from the grocery store, right?"

"Yes, we do. And I'll cook for you today, if that's cool with you."

"That's cool, but I would prefer we cooked together, King."

"Well, damn. Wear your crown, Queen."

He popped my ass and I laughed at how much that shit hurt. He went to his knees and kissed the spot, then proceeded to get dressed. This was the start of something special and I'd be damned if I was gonna let anyone disrupt our vibe.

Once we got dressed, we headed to the store. We made small

talk about all the shit he had to do tomorrow with Meena. They were supposed to go get his driver's license renewed and buy him a car. He had plenty money that had been sitting up and Meena made sure to invest some of it, giving him a nice nest egg. Vance was so open with me... sharing things that most people didn't know after months of being together. He wanted to assure me that I wouldn't be taking care of him just because he'd been locked up.

I had no intentions of taking care of a grown-ass man. He was misreading that shit. Just because I was nice, didn't mean I was that damn nice. As we walked through the store, filling the basket with necessities, it seemed like we were going to be in the store forever. Every time we stopped to put something in the basket, we ended up staring at each other for a moment or offering one another a kiss. As we stood in front of the meat selection, a woman called out, "Vance?"

Shit, that might as well had been my name, too, because I turned around to see who was calling him out. He hadn't been out long enough to make any connections besides ours, so she had to be from his past. Turning around and grabbing my hand in the process, he said, "Milina?"

"Yeah... wow! It's been a long time since I've seen you. How have you been?"

"Good. And you?"

"Good."

Vance stood there with a frown on his face, staring at her awkwardly and not offering to introduce us. I cleared my throat and said, "Hi. I'm Jennifer."

"Hi, Jennifer. Nice to meet you."

I nodded. It wasn't nice to meet a bitch who was trying to hold a conversation with my man. "Well, we have shopping to do," Vance said.

I was uncomfortable as hell because he was being slightly rude. Knowing that it had to be for a reason, I didn't say anything. "Oh,

I'm sorry. My number is still the same. You ought to call me so we can catch up."

The frown that graced my face wasn't to be mistaken. I stared her down and just as I was about to say something, Vance said, "I only have dealings with queens, not disrespectful whores." Turning to me, he said, "Come on, Queen."

I was stunned into silence. *That's how a fucking man stands up for his woman! Shaat!* He was gripping the hell out of my hand. I briefly turned to glance back at the woman he called Milina and saw her staring at us, stunned. Her face was red as hell, and her mouth was partially opened. She looked like one of those bougie bitches from high school that thought they were all that. Sis didn't know that those hard wrinkles and bags under her eyes were saying something that she wasn't. She was probably a beautiful woman at some point, but that point definitely wasn't the here and now. Vance looked at me and said, "Is there anything else you can think of that we might need?"

I shook my head as he grabbed my chin. "I'll fill you in once we're in the car, okay? I'll never leave you in the dark."

"Okay."

This man... it was like he knew my thoughts. He wasn't the typical man that acted like things wouldn't have been weird after that moment. Before we could leave, I asked, "Can we go to the deli before we go?"

"Of course."

HEB had the best peppered turkey. After ordering that and roast beef, I grabbed some pepper jack cheese and sour dough bread from the bakery. Once we got to the register, I began separating our things, trying to pay for some shit that I'd gotten for my house. Vance looked at me and said, "I hope the only reason you separating that is so they can bag it separately."

I looked away for a moment, then back up at him. "I got'chu, Queen. Remember your promise."

"I'm sorry. I just didn't want it to seem like I was taking advantage."

"A queen doesn't take advantage of the king, baby. She allows him to be what his title suggests. You feel me?"

"Hell yeah..." I nearly moaned.

He kissed my cheek and I couldn't help but stare at him as he watched the screen while the cashier rang up our groceries. There had to be a fault. He was too perfect. It was still early in our quest to get to know one another, so I knew if I gave it enough time, he would eventually relax. Once he did, I just hoped it wasn't something that I wasn't willing to deal with, because I was feeling the hell out of his ass.

Loading the groceries into my trunk, I noticed Vance had been rather quiet. I wondered what the deal was with this woman. She must have hurt him in some way because he seemed bitter. She was a lot smaller than me, maybe half my size or smaller and she spoke using proper English with some sort of accent that I couldn't make out. Once we finished, he walked around and opened my car door, then walked around to get in as well.

Before I could put the car in gear, he grabbed my hand. "I talked to her a couple of times over the phone before I got in trouble. I met her right here in this store. When I told her about what had happened, she dropped me quick. I mean, I couldn't blame her at the time. She didn't know me that well. Which is why you are so special to me already. It's not about sex, but it's that I can tell you are genuinely feeling me as a person. What pissed me off in there was her speaking to me like we were cool. Yeah, it's been ten years and she knew where the fuck I'd been, but I still hadn't forgot how she treated me."

"I figured it had to be something. Your personality doesn't seem to fit with who you were in there."

"Well... I can be rude if I need to be. Just because I'm nice to you and friendly and expressive, doesn't mean I'm like that with everybody. Again, you're special, Jennifer."

Gliding his fingers down the side of my face caused me to heat up with a want... a need that only he could fulfill. The things his touch did to me were simply amazing and I couldn't wait to see what was in store for us. Leaving the parking lot, we headed to his house and got everything put away in its proper place. Once we did, we began seasoning some steaks we'd bought, and I began working on the sides of broccoli rice and cheese casserole and steamed carrots.

We occasionally stopped to kiss or for him to hold me throughout our team cooking. It was so romantic; I was dreading having to go home. It wasn't like I had something to go and do, but I for sure needed to be home to get Belan from Meena while they went out to handle his business. As the casserole baked in the oven, Vance pulled me close to him and I couldn't help but kiss his thick lips. Everything a woman should feel when she was with her man, was what I felt when I was with Vance.

Once our dinner was cooked, I poured us two glasses of wine and brought the steak sauce to the table. Vance looked over at me and said, "We're a great team. This food looks almost as amazing as you."

He chuckled and I couldn't help but chuckle, too. I tried to conjure up a shocked expression, then said, "It's that close in comparison? Damn."

"Hell naw. Nothing and nobody can dim your shine, baby. Always remember that."

"You damn right, King. Straighten my crown for me."

$\mathcal{V}$ance

IF I WERE the type to call a woman a bitch, Milina would have caught all that aggression in HEB yesterday. She was so disrespectful to Jennifer. I was hoping she didn't try to say anything else after I called her a whore, because I didn't want to have to free my temper that I was desperately trying to keep on a leash. Jennifer meant a lot to me already, and I'd be damned if I was going to stand by and let another woman disrespect her. Although Milina was slightly younger than us, we were too old for those type of games. She had her chance... albeit I'd gotten locked up. That just proved to me that it wasn't time and she wasn't the one.

I'd met my match in Jennifer's fine ass. After we'd eaten dinner yesterday, I stripped her down and fed her the dick like she liked it. I'd found my happy medium between aggressive and gentleness. She seemed to appreciate that. Although, she seemed to like that rough shit at times. I didn't mind fucking her world up. She was a queen in every sense of the word, especially since she controlled herself in that grocery store. I fully expected her to cuss Milina's ass out. When she left last night, I laid in bed for a couple of hours before I was able to go to sleep.

All I could think about was how just the night before, her soft body was against mine, offering me sweet dreams. It was the first night I'd slept as sound as I did in a long-ass time. My nerves had settled around her quick as hell. There was no paranoia or angst. Her aura was soothing and comforted my soul in ways I could have never imagined. A woman, whom I didn't know before two days ago, had provided me such solace, it seemed our spirits had met before. Grabbing my phone from my nightstand, I sent her a good morning text.

Meena would be here in an hour to pick me up, but I couldn't move a muscle without praying and texting my queen. Almost immediately, she responded, *Good morning, baby.* That had my soul feeling bright. I got out of bed and got cleaned up, then threw on some jeans. I was gonna have to go clothes shopping. Some of my shirts were a little tighter than I liked them. Thanks to Meena, I had more than three hundred grand saved up. She'd kept my debit cards active and everything. My baby girl made sure I had something to come home to and I appreciated her so much for that.

My house was paid for, so she didn't have to keep up with a mortgage, but everything else had to be tough on her. I planned to talk with her today and do something nice for her. I didn't know what she needed, if anything, but whatever her heart desired, I wanted to make it happen. When I killed Chad, I wasn't thinking about how she would have to function without me. She was only twenty-one years old, matriculating on the campus of Lamar University. At that age, I was married to Madelyn and was a new fire fighter, but things were different for her. I'd spoiled her. She'd never had a job. Sure, she'd volunteered at different places, but she never had a paying gig.

She'd paid more attention to me than I realized, though. What she didn't know, she would ask when I called her. I called her every day for a while, so I knew the phone bill was high as hell. Then I started emailing her after I'd been there for a while and we'd talk once a week. But... I owed her. I owed her my gratitude. In a fit of rage, I did something that I had to live with for the rest of my life. While I didn't regret it, it taught me a valuable lesson. Attending anger management classes while in prison helped me determine that my temper had a hair trigger. That trigger was Meena. Now, Belan and Jennifer were included. That was why walking away from Milina after she'd disrespected Jennifer was the best thing I could do.

After conditioning my goatee and the already growing stubble on my face, I grabbed my wallet and phone just as I heard, "Daddy! I'm here!"

A smile graced my lips as I walked out to the front room to see my baby girl standing there. It was still somewhat surreal that I was seeing her again... that I was free. "Hey, baby. How's your morning?" I asked, then kissed her cheek.

"It was good. I should be asking you that question."

I slightly rolled my eyes as she laughed. "Jennifer is amazing."

"I already know that, but for some strange reason, I feel like you may know more than I care to know."

"Man, let's go," I said as she laughed.

As she followed me out of the house, she said, "Daddy, I'm happy that you have somebody to be close to while you transition back into the swing of things. That's important. I won't always be available, but knowing you have her soothes my mental. I know what type of woman she is, and I trust her completely. To know that y'all are really feeling each other brings me joy unspeakable."

"Thank you, Meena."

Once we got in the car, I turned to her and said, "Tell me... How hard was it? While I was gone. Don't sugarcoat it. I want the real."

She'd started the car, but she couldn't back out of the driveway.

She put her head down and suddenly, she started crying. That shit tore my heart to pieces. I quickly got out of the car and went to her side and pulled her out. Hugging her tightly to me while she let it all out, I thought about how long she'd held all this inside to be strong for me. "Daddy, I couldn't tell you before. I didn't want you to worry about me. I was devastated when you left, and I didn't know how to cope with not having you here."

She continued to cry into my chest as I swallowed the lump in my throat. I should have let the police do their job, so I wouldn't have caused her so much heartache. "I dropped out of school that semester so I could get my life together. I stayed in your house, only coming out to go to the store for a couple of months. A couple of your former coworkers checked on me a couple of times, but that was it. I was on my own. It was a hard adjustment, but by the next semester, I was ready to make your sacrifice worth it. I'll never forget how you sacrificed yourself for me."

She lifted her head from my chest and kissed my cheek, then put her palm to it. "I'm sorry, Meena. There were other ways I could have handled that situation. My temper got the best of me. I was filled with rage, knowing and seeing that someone had the nerve... the audacity to hurt my innocent, delicate flower. I should have let the police handle it. So many of them would have been in my corner, since we worked hand in hand a lot. But I plan to make it up to you. I love you so much, Meena, and you know I'd give you the world. Just tell me what you need... or even want. I got'chu."

"What I want and need is you. I already have that. Now, let's go get your life back on track."

I smiled at her, then helped her in the car. My heart was on full and I used the time that I walked around the car to get myself together before getting in. After buckling up, I turned to her and smiled. "I love you, Daddy."

"I love you, too, baby."

After waiting to be seen at the department of public safety for a couple of hours, I learned that I had to retest because my license had been expired for six years. I should have known that. While we were there, they allowed me to take the written test and the vision test, but I had to schedule an appointment for the driving portion of the test. That put searching for a car on hold. As we walked to the car, I turned to Meena and asked, "Is Tia Juanita's still open?"

A slow smile appeared on her face. "They sure are."

I nodded and nothing more needed to be said about it. It was the last restaurant I'd taken her to before I got arrested for murder. We'd enjoyed the lunch bisque that day. I felt like going there would sort of offer closure or healing to my ten-year absence. As she drove, I sent a message to Jennifer. *Well, I won't have a car today. Do you mind being my means of transportation this week? I promise to be yours, too. Letting you ride whenever you want to.*

I could feel my lips generate a smirk as I hit send. As we sat at a red light, Meena asked, "So, you and Mama... I mean, Ms. Jennifer... are y'all a couple or just hanging out?"

"That's my queen, Meena. We're a couple. Things are moving quickly between us, but I think that's because we were both so ready for something special. We saw that in each other immediately. And I don't have a problem with you calling her Mama."

She smiled at me and continued on to our lunch spot as my phone vibrated. I smiled and opened the text message from Jennifer. *I don't mind taking you anywhere you wanna go... including ecstasy.* Okay, I had to stop playing with her. I couldn't be getting turned on in front of my daughter. I shifted in my seat and Meena looked over at me. "You okay?"

"Yep."

She continued on to Tia Juanita's, and when we got out of the car and walked inside the restaurant, I regretted my decision to come here today. There was a table of firefighters there. I was hoping they were all fairly new hires and people that had hired in after I was gone. Not so. When I saw the man in the white shirt, I turned my head, hoping he hadn't seen me. "Vance? Is that you?"

Fuck! I turned to him and feigned surprise. "What's up, Oscar? How are you?"

"Man, I'm great. How are you? When did they release you?"

"A couple of days ago. I'm good."

"Hey, Meena. How are you?"

"I'm okay," she said, then turned away.

I glanced at her as he continued to talk. She didn't look too excited to see him. Maybe because of Jennifer. That's all it better had been. "You still look the same. Ten years hasn't aged you one bit."

"Thanks. I see you a fire chief, now. Congratulations."

"Yeah, thanks. Well, it was good to see you, man. You ought to come to the firehouse sometimes."

"Naw, I probably won't. I'm retired."

He laughed and said, "I feel you, bruh." After shaking my hand, he said, "See you around."

I nodded, then turned my attention to Meena as she mumbled, "Jackass. He treated Mama so bad. I can't stand looking at his ass. You know it takes a lot for me to hate somebody, but I hate his ass."

"Whoa. Hate? What all did you see?"

"I didn't *see* a whole lot, but I saw the aftermath. Daddy, he cheated on her so much. I told her I was surprised he didn't bring shit home to her. She was like, he couldn't bring it home to me if he refused to have sex with me. And I know for sure he'd hit her at least once. He's a piece of shit. Sorry for cursing so much, but I really can't stand him."

"I see. Are you sure that's all that happened?"

"Positive. You know how close I am to Ms. Jennifer. She's the sweetest person I know and to watch her decline to the point of being suicidal was hard. Her self-esteem had sunk so low because of that bastard. Because of her size, she thought she was no longer beautiful. God, I hated seeing her that way. But to watch her overcome all that was rewarding. Her strength is so admirable."

"Damn."

That was all I could get out. I hadn't brought Oscar's name up since the first night we met. I could see how it made her uncomfortable. Now I knew why. *Fucking bitch-ass nigga.* Knowing the abuse she endured only made me want to love on her even more so. As Meena and I sat at a table, I said, "I need you to bring me to a store to get some things to have a romantic evening with Jennifer."

"Okaaay," she said in a high-pitched tone. "I see you, Daddy."

I rolled my eyes as she ordered her bisque. After getting a seafood plate, I texted Jennifer. *Can you meet me at my house at about six? Meena should be there by four to get Belan.*

"So, what are you getting from the store?"

"Flowers, wine, fruit... stuff like that."

She didn't need to know what all I was getting, that wasn't her business. "Well, if you're getting fruit, make sure you get whipped cream and chocolate syrup."

My lips parted as I stared at her. Had we not been in the restaurant, I knew she would have laughed louder than she did. "Daddy, I'm a thirty-one-year-old married mother. I think I know a lil something."

"Yeah, but I don't have to know what *all* you know."

That caused her to laugh more as Jennifer responded to my text. *Can't wait to see you, King.* I licked my lips, imagining her taste as the waitress returned with our drinks. "On a serious note, being here feels great." Closing her eyes, she took a deep breath. "I avoided this place while you were gone. So, this is my first time here since that day, too. I feel like we're picking up where we left off in a sense."

"That was what I hoped you felt. I wanted to feel the same thing by coming here and I do."

I grabbed her hands and smiled but could feel eyes on me. When I looked up, I noticed Oscar was staring at us. He smiled and waved as he and his crew left. I gave him a head nod while I hoped he wouldn't be the reason I ended up back in jail.

8

*J*ennifer

WHEN I GOT to Vance's house, I was excited to see him. After spending pretty much the last two days with him, I missed being around him. While Belan and I could have gone for the ride with him and Meena today, I knew he needed time alone with her. As I knocked on the door, he opened it shirtless with a glass of wine in his hand. *Well, damn.* "Hey, Queen. Come in."

I walked through the door and looked around the dimly lit house. When he walked up behind me, I barely got out, "Hey."

I was so overwhelmed by his efforts. Looking around at the candles flickering and seeing the flower petals everywhere made my heart even softer than it already was. Turning to him, I asked, "You did all this for me?"

He leaned in close to my ear and said, "Mmm hmm."

He kissed my cheek, then handed me the glass of wine. I

noticed a bowl of fruit sitting on the floor where he'd made a pallet, along with the bottle of wine, whip cream, and chocolate syrup. I smiled at his thoughtfulness. "This is amazing, Vance. Thank you so much."

"You're welcome, baby. Have a seat at the table. I cooked dinner."

Watching all his chocolate-ness walk away in those sexy-ass linen pants, I was stuck where I was. His sex appeal had me frozen in time, taking mental pictures of all that dick hanging loosely in his pants. That shit was swaying while he walked. Shit, I wasn't frozen in time, I was mesmerized and drooling. Without looking up at me, I could see the smirk that appeared on his face. "What's the matter, baby?" he asked.

"Huh?"

"You haven't sat down yet."

"Because your dick was waving at me. It would be rude to not acknowledge his presence."

He laughed so loudly, I couldn't help but join him. Walking over to me, he pulled me in his arms and kissed my lips. I grabbed his dick and said, "Hey, baby."

"You talking to him or me?"

"I already spoke to you. I'm talking to him."

He chuckled and said, "You tripping. But that's okay. He like that shit."

"I can tell. He's getting happy."

"A'ight, a'ight. Let me go finish getting our plates together before I just have you for dinner."

"Mmm. I wouldn't mind that at all, but since you took the time to cook, I guess we should eat."

He shook his head slowly as I sipped from the glass of wine he'd given me. "You need help in there?"

"Nope. Go sit'cho sexy ass down like I told you earlier."

I shrugged and walked over to the table. He'd set it beautifully. There was a bouquet of roses as the centerpiece and a couple of candles lit. As I sat, he brought salads, then returned to the kitchen to get the main course. He came back with plates of spaghetti and garlic toast. "This looks and smells delicious, baby."

"Thank you. Let me get us some water."

When he came back, he blessed our food and we began eating. It tasted just as delicious as it looked. "Mmm," I moaned.

"I take it that it's pretty good."

"Mmm hmm," I acknowledged, my mouth full of noodles.

"I just wanted to show you a romantic evening. I actually want to make it my business to do that whenever possible."

"Vance, you're so perfect. What flaws do you have so I'll know you're human?"

He chuckled, then said, "Well, I'm obviously an ex-convict. I have a temper when it comes to the people I love or really care deeply for... the reason I was locked up. I lost my cool. But I'm trying to keep that side of me under control. As long as there are no issues, I'm good."

I nodded. I could clearly see that temper threatening to make an appearance in HEB yesterday. "I still think you're perfect and definitely perfect for me. I wish..." I took a deep breath as I paused. Because I started the sentence, I had to finish it. What was I thinking even bringing this up? "I wish I would have met you before I met Oscar."

"We met exactly when we were supposed to meet. When you met Oscar, I was probably married to Meena's mother, Madelyn."

"True. You're such an amazing man. It feels like I've known you forever and I can't wait to know you even better than I do now."

"And you're an amazing woman. A woman who I can tell has been through a lot of heartache. I could see the pain in your eyes when you mentioned his name. I'm here to make you forget all that. I wanna be so good to you, until it feels like all you've ever known was me."

A soft moan left my lips as I continued to eat my food. The rest of our dinner was somewhat quiet. It seemed like he knew more about me than I'd told him. I was sure Meena had filled him in on a lot about me and my past issues. Thankfully, he didn't press me for more information because that was a moment I didn't want to have with him this soon. Revealing my vulnerabilities and struggles was hard. I wasn't worried about how he would handle it, but how I would handle releasing all of that to him. For him to know how weak I had become would seem like I was giving him power over me. That was a moment I no longer wanted to afford. "Hey."

I looked up at Vance as he stared at me. He continued, "I don't know what happened, but I need you to come back, baby."

Standing from his seat, he walked over to me and knelt beside me, causing me to turn in my seat. "I don't know everything that happened in the past and I don't want you thinking about it, either. Now is the time to dwell on what's happening between us, beautiful."

He slid his hand over my cheek, and I leaned into it, closing my eyes. When he took it away, I opened my eyes and took a deep breath. "You're right. I'm sorry."

"No need to apologize. I get it. Let's get done eating so I can worship your body, baby."

My face heated up. I wasn't embarrassed, but this man had me all in my feels. *How is that possible after only three days?* After the hurt I'd been through being married to Oscar, one would think that I wouldn't be as quick to attach myself to someone else, but like Vance had said, he was making me forget about everything else. My body and heart were completely focused on him and everything he was bringing to the table that I'd always longed for... the things money couldn't buy. I relished in it... and just that quickly, I was falling for him.

"So where will Belan and I be chauffeuring you to this week?"

"Well, tomorrow, I have to get blood work done and I have to take my driving test. Then maybe I can take you lovely ladies to lunch."

"Okay. Sounds like a plan. What are you doing today?"

"Absolutely nothing. I just ate breakfast."

"Can Belan and I come pick you up?"

"Of course."

"Okay. Let me change her and then we'll head your way."

"Okay."

I ended the call with Vance. We'd had an amazing time yesterday evening after dinner. He'd done exactly what he said he would. He worshipped every inch of my body and I wasn't the least bit upset about it. Taking his time, he gave me all the attention he said I deserved. Appreciating every moment of it, I was sure to give his body attention as well... every chocolate inch of it, with the exception of his dick. Ugh. I couldn't wait until his bloodwork was done and he got clear test results. I wanted to lick and suck on his erection so bad. I'd never yearned to suck dick like that. But everything in me wanted to please him the way he'd pleased me. And Lord have mercy was I pleased... several times.

While thoughts of Oscar had sought to take me down, Vance was the type of man that wouldn't allow me to be overcome with the past. He deserved my full attention and Oscar had no place in my thoughts, especially not while I was with Vance. But Oscar was all I had known for years. It was like natural instinct for me to compare how great Vance was to how much of an ass he was. Thankfully, I'd managed to avoid him for the past three years. Whenever I saw him, I went the opposite direction. But now that I had regained my confidence, I'd strut right in his face if I saw him. He was no longer allowed to be that much of a distraction to my life. My only worry was how he would react to seeing me with Vance. It wasn't my fault I didn't know his co-workers.

After getting Belan changed, we headed to Vance's and I was beyond excited to see him. The only thing that had been on my mind was how he would make me forget about the twenty-five years of my life that involved Oscar's cheating ass. I met Oscar when I was twenty-three years old and we got married when I was twenty-five, the biggest mistake of my damn life. He'd just started working for the fire department. We didn't have a big wedding because my parents refused to pay for it. My daddy had said that Oscar was no good. But I loved him, and Daddy didn't know what he was talking about, especially since he was an ass to my mother. But I was wrong as two left shoes.

If Vance could make me forget all the pain, hurt, disrespect, and abuse, then I was all for that. Oscar didn't become a monster until almost ten years into our marriage. It took me another ten years to divorce his ass. Now that I was embarking on something special with Vance, it was like all those thoughts of how horrible he was to me were coming back to haunt me. Maybe I wasn't as ready for a relationship as I thought I was.

When we got to Vance's house, I sat for a moment and took deep breaths, trying to remember why I was here and the connection I felt with him. He'd been everything to me and I could *not* and *would* not make him suffer for the sins of my ex-husband. That wouldn't be fair to him. Getting out of the car with a renewed mind, I got Belan from the back seat, along with her bag and headed to the door. Before I could knock, he opened the door with a huge smile on his face. Belan's face brightened and her smile was bright as the sun. "Hey, PaPa's baby!"

She reached for him, nearly jumping out of my arms. He laughed as he took her from me, then leaned in to kiss me. "Hey, baby."

"Hey, PaPa."

He grinned as he stepped aside to let me inside. Belan had already attached herself to his goatee, running her fingers through it. There was something about that white hair that she loved. Once he'd closed the door, he said, "Follow me."

I did as he asked, following him down the hallway. In one of the rooms, he had a blanket laid out with stuffed animals and little toys for Belan to enjoy. He sat her on the floor and helped me to the floor as well. Belan looked amazed and didn't know what to play with first. "I found all of this in a closet. These are all Meena's old things. I sprayed everything with Lysol and made sure it was clean. Can't have my baby getting sick."

I smiled as he got on his knees and pretended he was dog. Belan was laughing loudly and it was contagious. She crawled to him, then used his head to bring herself to her feet. Vance pressed his face into her belly as he held her back and pretended to eat her. She was screaming with laughter so loudly, I had to take my phone out to record their interaction. It was beyond heartwarming. Sending the video to Meena, I scooted to the wall to rest my back as Vance glanced at me. He and Belan scooted closer to me and he sat next to me while Belan played a little piano. "How has your morning been, Queen?"

As he grabbed my hand and kissed the back of it, I said, "It's been good, but now it's great."

"Mmm. That's what I like to hear," he said as my phone chimed.

It was a text from Meena, saying how cute the video was and how she wishes she was here with us. Gently bringing my hand to Vance's cheek, then sliding it to his neck, I pulled him to me. I needed to feel his lips against mine. As I softly kissed him, I could feel the presence of a certain little girl staring at us. She pulled herself up and rested her hand on Vance's face as his smile broke our kiss. "I don't think she likes us kissing."

"I think she's trying to figure out what's going on."

"Listen, BeBe, NaNa is my woman. She's gonna be my wife one day. I need you to be cool with that."

I smiled softly at him. He was speaking what he wanted into existence and I couldn't help but be excited to take the journey with him. Belan smiled at him, then started gibbering. She did that when she was excited. The only thing we could make out was da-

da. We both laughed at her excitement as Vance's phone rang. He frowned deeply, I assumed wondering who could be calling him. He left us in the room and went to get it as Belan stared at the door, wondering where he was going. I could hear him talking, so he obviously knew who it was.

When he walked back in the room, he slid a hand down his face. "Everything okay?"

"That was umm... Oscar. Meena and I saw him yesterday when we'd gone to lunch. He took a chance dialing my number to see if it still worked."

I swallowed hard and turned away from him, pretending to be occupied with Belan. "What did he want?"

"He wanted me to go to lunch with him tomorrow, so we could catch up."

"Oh. What did you say?"

"No. Oscar and I were never really friends. We only ate together when we were at the firehouse. So, I don't know why he thinks we should be cool like that now."

I nodded as Vance sat next to me. He gently turned my face to him. "You have nothing to worry about. I'm going to talk to him about me and you, then I'm gonna block his number."

"I'm okay, Vance. I feel like you wouldn't do anything to intentionally hurt me and it's obvious that you being friendly with my ex-husband would be no good."

"Even if he wasn't your ex-husband, I have no desire to be in Oscar's company. I never really liked him all that much."

"Why?"

He looked down at Belan and then said, "Because I knew he was married, as did everyone else, but he didn't hesitate to hide his philandering ways. As a married man at the time, that bothered me."

"He was that bold about it... to bring random women around the firehouse?"

"Yeah. I felt for his wife without even knowing who she was," he said as he gently stroked my cheek.

I rolled my eyes. That only made me even more embarrassed. Vance felt sorry for me. My eyes narrowed slightly. "That isn't why you wanted to proceed with me, is it?"

"What?"

"Because you felt sorry for me?"

"Hell naw. I felt sorry for you back then. Back then, I was a married man, not looking for a side-piece. I'm not happy about how he treated you, but I am happy that he fucked up. I wouldn't have a chance at your heart."

He slowly slid his hand down my chest as I stared in his eyes. I was mesmerized by their intensity until Belan started whining. I looked over at her to see she was wiping her eyes. It was just about her naptime. Pulling her bag to me, I grabbed the bottle I'd packed from it as she crawled to her PaPa and sat in his lap. I smiled at him as I gave him the bottle. When he gave it to her, he looked back at me and said, "Jennifer, please don't doubt my promise to you, baby. I know this is starting to seem messy, but I'm gonna handle it, just like a man should. Okay?"

I nodded as he shook his head. "Naw, Queen. I need to hear you say that you feel me."

Scooting closer to him, he put his arm around me as I kissed his lips. "I feel you, King."

9

V ance

"MAN, to say you just got out, you shol' busy a lot."

"Listen, we need to talk."

I was having the dreaded conversation with Oscar. Yesterday, I'd gone to have blood work done and I took my driving test, passing with flying colors. Today, Jennifer would be taking me to look for a car. This depending on her, Meena, and Tyrone just to go to the store was wearing my nerves thin. I was getting ready because Jennifer would be here in a little bit to pick me up when Oscar called to ask me if I could hang today. "What's up, Vance?"

"I met this woman the same day I got out of prison. The most beautiful woman I'd ever seen, and I promised myself that I would get to know her. Our connection was so intense, that I've already made her mine."

"Well, damn, nigga. Say no more. That's why you ain't got time. I feel that."

"Naw, but I need you to know that this woman's name is Jennifer."

The line went completely quiet. I was waiting for him to lash out, so I remained quiet as well. Suddenly, he said, "I don't believe this bullshit. You went after my ex-wife?"

"I had no idea she was your ex-wife. Had you not been hoe-ing around with so many women, I would have known. She never attended any functions. I didn't find out until after the fact when I asked her if she knew any Monroes that worked at the firehouse."

"Man, whatever. That's still fucked up. Jennifer has issues she need to get a handle on before she kills herself with food. Madelyn was a fine woman. How you lower yourself to fuck with a big bitch like her?"

"What's fucked up is how you abused and disrespected her. Just so you know, that shit ain't gon' fly with me. By my record, you should know I'll fuck anybody up when it comes to my family. Jennifer is family and was family long before she met me, but I'm sure you know that. I wanted to show respect and come to you like a man. It wasn't like we were friends. I'm not even sure why you so hell bent on us kicking it. But I do know this... I did that time like a G and if I ever need to, I'll do that shit again, no hesitation. Let that be a warning for the next time you try to come at me like you did today."

I ended the call and literally wanted to tear shit up. That was how angry I was. I stood from my bed and put my shirt on, then paced back and forth in my room. I really needed to hit the gym soon. I'd be able to work off this aggression. My phone rang, so I picked it up to see Jennifer's beautiful face on it, almost instantly calming my spirit. "Hello?"

"Hey, King. Two of your favorite people are outside waiting on you."

"Okay, Queen. I'll be out in a little bit."

I ended the call and tried to get myself together, because the last thing I wanted to do was go into detail about the conversation I had with Oscar to Jennifer. All she needed to know was that he knew about us. Actually, she didn't need to know that, because she would want to know what his response was. After grabbing my BeBe's teething ring she forgot here day before yesterday, I headed out to meet them. The minute Belan saw me, she started kicking and screaming. That lil girl was my baby. The smile on Jennifer's face was just as bright. When I opened the door, I said, "Hey, two of my favorite people."

Belan screamed again, so I went to the backseat to kiss her, but lil mama wasn't having it. After kissing Jennifer's luscious lips, I had to sit in the back with her. "Look, BeBe. PaPa love you, baby, but I can't be riding in the backseat. I need to be in the front with my queen."

The killing thing was that she actually tried to talk back to me, like she was running something. Jennifer laughed as she drove to Classic. "So, do you know what type of vehicle you want?"

"I've been looking at the new Blazers, preferably a black one."

"Oh, those are nice."

"Yeah, they are. If not that, then a Traverse. They almost look the same anyway."

She nodded as Belan started screaming to get my attention. "Oh, I see you gon' be demanding, aren't you?" I looked up at Jennifer's face in the rearview mirror. "I feel like I've created a monster somehow."

She laughed as she shook her head. "I mean, she couldn't help but get possessive with you. I feel the same way. You looked in the mirror this morning? You're a gorgeous man, baby. And if you think she's a monster... humph. Bet' not let the beast get activated in me. The lady in HEB could have gotten it, had you not handled it."

I chuckled and said, "I had that feeling. But since the situation involved me, I had to shut that shit down. Can't have my queen scrapping in these streets."

She laughed and said, "Oh, baby, I don't scrap. It's never a fight. Just call me Laila Ali."

"Well, damn. I hope I never have to see that side of you."

"Me either. I haven't seen her in a long time, but I know she's still there."

As she drove in Classic's parking lot, I shook my head. Sounded like we were two peas in a pod, tempers and all. "Well, I hope both of our alter egos can stay lying dormant before we both end up locked up somewhere."

She laughed as I unstrapped Belan. Baby girl grabbed ahold of my goatee as soon as I picked her up. Jennifer had her diaper bag. Walking around the lot, I held her hand, occasionally lifting it to my lips to kiss it. "Oh, shit, that's it right here."

Releasing her hand, I walked up to the black on black ride and peeped through the window. The leather seats had red stitching and there was a sunroof and a panoramic roof, too. By the time I walked around the back of it, a salesman had joined us. It was time to take a test drive and talk numbers.

"DADDY, this is nice! I love it!" Meena said as she walked around my new Blazer.

"Yeah, Eti, this is nice."

I frowned. *Who in the hell was Tyrone talking to?* Then it dawned on me, that might be the name he was trying to test out on me. Since my last name was Etienne, I supposed it was cool, but I had to give him a hard time first. "I thought I told you to run names by me before you called me anything else."

"Umm... I'm sorry. You did. I just thought... never mind. My bad, Mr. Etienne."

"Man, calm down. It's cool. I like it."

He took a deep breath, then laughed. "You had me all nervous."

I laughed, too, as I realized he was just as soft as Jennifer said he was. No grown man should get *that* damn nervous in front of anybody. Shaking my head, I said, "So, to celebrate my new independence, I was thinking we could have a fish fry at my house this weekend. Tyrone, you can invite your parents, and we can chill outside and have a good time... play cards, dominoes, or whatever."

"That sounds good. I'll buy some shrimp to go with that," Jennifer said.

I winked at her as I gave Belan to her daddy. When I walked over to her, I pulled her in my arms and kissed her lips. "So, your man got wheels now. I'm gonna go home and pack a bag, then come back to you and stay with you tonight if that's cool."

"Mmm. It's beyond cool. I'm gonna go get cleaned up and cook something quick for us to eat."

"Sounds like a plan, baby."

Meena cleared her throat and said, "Uh, love birds!"

I gave her my attention as she laughed. "You two are too cute. I was asking if we need to bring anything."

"Just paper plates and water. Or soda if y'all want that."

"I was gonna try my hand at a peach cobbler, though."

I glanced at Jennifer and did my best not to laugh at her facial expression. "Naw, baby girl. That's not necessary. It's hot outside. Get some popsicles or something."

"You sure?"

"Uh huh. Save that for another occasion."

"A'ight. I'm gon' practice in between time and try it out on Tyrone."

I almost chuckled. Jennifer's face had started to turn red from holding in her laughter. I kissed Meena and Belan and shook Tyrone's hand as they headed inside, then looked at Jennifer and said, "You better not laugh."

That was all it took. She fell out laughing and I couldn't help but join her. "Lord knows I love that girl, but I'd starve first."

"She can't be that bad."

"Okay. Whenever she decides to make it, I'm gon' make sure she saves some for you, since she can't be that bad."

"That ain't necessary, baby."

"Oh, it's indeed necessary. Go home and get what you need so you can hurry back to me."

I kissed her lips and watched her walk to her house next door, then got in my ride and headed home.

As I FRIED THE FISH, I had the blues playing. I knew Mr. George loved the blues since he was hollering about some damn Marvin Sease at the barbeque. B.B. King was on when they drove up. I chuckled to myself as I watched him get out the car with his cooler. Tyrone was outside with me, but when his parents arrived, he walked to their car. I kept my eyes on Mr. George and the minute his ears picked up on "The Thrill Is Gone" he threw his hand in the air. I laughed so much at the barbeque and I knew today would be the same. He was funny as hell.

Ms. Donna didn't seem to find humor in it at all and I could see her talking to Jennifer at the barbeque. I wondered if she mentioned anything to her about it. As I watched them, Jennifer stepped outside, carrying the hush puppies and French fries. Meena was behind her with the salad. BeBe was in her playpen, screaming her face off. She was so upset about being caged in. I could sympathize with my baby. But we'd all been busy doing things to where we couldn't constantly watch her.

Once Jennifer sat the food on the table, she walked over to me. The past couple of days had been filled with love and we'd been working out together now that all my business was handled. But the weekends were really our time to relax into one another and make love at every turn. It was hard to do that when we had BeBe. It was getting harder and harder to resist letting her suck me off, 'cause I'd been craving it so bad. My results should be in Monday, though. The minute they said I was good, I'd lose the condoms and all inhibitions.

I kissed her lips, then said, "The fish is just about ready. By the time y'all get the rest of the condiments and stuff outside, I should be taking it out the grease."

"Okay, baby."

"Heeeeeyyy!" Mr. George yelled and swayed side to side with his beer in his hand.

I chuckled and said, "What's happening, George?"

Donna went inside with Jennifer as he said, "Not too much, Vance. How you doing? You playing some music today! I don't know what the hell Meena had us listening to last time."

I laughed as he started to sway a bit, then he went over to speak to Belan. As I took the fish from the grease and laid it in a pan lined with paper towels, the women and Tyrone joined us outside. Tyrone had a noticeable frown on his face. I didn't know what had gone down inside the house, but Meena sat next to where he'd flopped and put her arms around his shoulders and talked softly in his ear. When Jennifer walked over to me, I asked, "What's going on?"

"Donna told Tyrone that she'd filed for a divorce yesterday and that she would be moving out Monday. Mr. George has been extremely drunk ever since. Drunker than his normal self."

"Why she had to tell him that shit now?"

"I don't know, baby. Now the whole fish fry is gonna be awkward as hell."

"Well, we're gonna do our best to get everybody out of their funk."

As I finished getting the fish out of the grease, Belan started screaming, getting all of our attention. George was on top of her, passed the hell out. Me and Tyrone ran over to him, lifting him from the playpen as Jennifer scooped Belan out. She seemed to be okay, but George's breathing was shallow. "Meena, call an ambulance."

Maybe he'd been drinking too much the past couple of days. He was probably severely dehydrated. I felt sorry for him for a moment. He obviously used alcohol to cope with life's disappointments. We sat him in a chair as Donna brought a bottle of water. I poured the water in his face and his eyes opened for a moment, then they closed again. "Pops! Wake up!" Tyrone yelled.

I turned off the music, then went back to Tyrone and George. I had to make sure he was still breathing. Again, it was shallow, but he was breathing. It couldn't be enough, though. Meena cradled Belan to her as she continued to cry. "Baby, you may need to take her to get checked out, too. Check her head and make sure there aren't any knots."

Jennifer and Donna helped her check out Belan from head to toe as I heard the ambulance in the distance. When they drove in the driveway, they rushed to where George was, then another went back for a gurney. They began checking him out and Tyrone and I moved out of the way. Another began asking questions about what happened and when we told her that he fell on Belan, she went over to Meena. Belan was still screaming and that had me nervous. I wasn't angry that he'd fallen on her, but I was upset that they brought their problems here instead of declining the invitation.

Once they got George stabilized, they brought him to the ambulance and Tyrone and Donna walked to the ambulance with them. It looked like they were arguing for a moment, then Tyrone got in with his dad and Donna went to their car. Walking over to Meena and Jennifer, I noticed Belan had stopped crying. She seemed to be okay. That probably just scared her half to death. My poor baby. When she saw me, she reached for her PaPa. I grabbed her from Meena, and she immediately grabbed my goatee. It was like it comforted her to have it in her hands. "Daddy, I'm gonna follow them to the hospital. Can y'all keep Belan?"

"Of course, baby."

She took off for her car and sped out to catch up with the ambulance. Looking over at Jennifer, I said, "Well, I guess it's just us."

She shrugged and said, "I'll get the food inside."

"Naw, Queen. Take BeBe. I'll get that."

She smiled softly at me, then took Belan from my arms.

10

*J*ennifer

IT HAD BEEN A HELLUVA WEEKEND. Mr. George was doing much better and they said he was severely dehydrated and had alcohol poisoning. All the binge drinking he'd been doing, it was a miracle that it wasn't worse. Today, Meena had decided to give me a break. I could use one. I was tired as hell. But I knew I couldn't go an entire day without seeing Belan and Vance. I slept in late, then decided to go to the grocery store for some of her favorite Gerber snacks.

As I drove, I couldn't help but think about everything Donna had said Saturday when we'd gone in the house. She said she was tired of feeling like she was in bondage. Their marriage had taken all it could take. From George's drunkenness and infidelities, she felt alone, so she might as well be alone. I understood that totally.

She said he refused to talk to her about what was going on with him and he also refused counseling. After not being able to convince him of either, she gave up. At that point, she had to look out for herself.

Getting out of the car, I headed inside the store with a pep in my step. I felt rested and I was ready to see my man. I was sure he had some great news for me as well. He should be getting the results from his blood work today. Grabbing a basket, I hummed a tune to myself as I pushed it from aisle to aisle. However, it felt like my blood curdled when I heard, "Well, damn. You had to divorce me to do something about your appearance?"

Turning around, Oscar stood there all smiles as I frowned at him. "I see why Vance digging in that now. You look good, Jennifer."

"Get the fuck outta my face."

His eyebrows shot up in surprise. I would have never spoken to him like that while we were married. But he just didn't know that he'd run up on a different Jennifer and could get done up at any moment. I wasn't the same timid woman he'd married. But over the past three years, I'd empowered my-damn-self. While I still had thoughts of inadequacy, I didn't dwell on them. I chose to focus on the positive things I knew about myself. That was how I became so strong.

I supposed Vance had spoken to him about us, since he knew. "No need to get defensive. I just hope you ain't fucking him in that house I left you. Just in case, I think we probably ought to sell it and split the money like the judge suggested."

I rolled my eyes, while on the inside, I was crumbling. My heart was filled with pride when I purchased that house. Pushing my basket forward, I rammed it right into his middle. He stepped aside, holding his dick. "It never worked worth a shit anyway. And had the nerve to cheat with a rusty-ass tool. I'm working with Craftsman now, bitch."

"You gon' regret today."

"Fuck you, Oscar, and go find you someone else to control."

I rolled past him and felt good about myself, but I was angry as hell. They never missed their water until their well ran dry. When I got to the next aisle, someone touched my back and I spun around, expecting to pop the shit out of Oscar and it was a beautiful, black lady that asked, "I'm sorry. Are you okay?"

"Yes, ma'am. Thank you."

She reached in her bag and handed me a business card. I looked at it to see she was an attorney. "I heard him harassing you. It's the nosiness in me. If he tries to make good on any of those threats, please contact me. Although I'm a criminal defense attorney, I'm very knowledgeable about all types of law and there are other lawyers in my firm that can help. I can't stand bullies. My website is on my card and you can read up about me and my success rate. He's a jackass," she said as she cut her eyes in his direction.

I liked her. She was professional but she was real as well. "If I need to, I will definitely contact you. Thank you. God was really looking out for me."

"He works in mysterious ways, that's for sure."

"I'm Jennifer Rubin Monroe; hopefully, I'll be able to drop that Monroe soon."

"I can help you with that, too."

Before I could say another word, I saw Oscar watching me with a smirk on his face. Noticing that my attention had shifted, the attorney whose name was Sidney Taylor, turned her head and mean mugged his ass. I already knew that she would be my attorney if I needed one. When she turned back to me, she said, "He looks familiar to me."

"He's the damn fire chief."

"Oh, shit. He don't want this. I will nail his ass to the wall." She covered her mouth and I laughed. "I'm so sorry. I try to remain professional."

"No, I love you already."

She smiled brightly, then said, "Thank you. Well, I have to get going. My husband is waiting for me outside."

"Okay. Hopefully, I won't have to call you, but if I do, I will."

We shook hands and she left. I fingered her card in my hand, then slid it in my wallet. Walking through the store, I gathered my baby's snacks and grabbed a bottle of wine for myself. I grabbed a six-pack of Heineken for Vance, then got some snacks for us as well. I didn't know what we would be doing today, but whatever we did would be fine with me. I hadn't made a bow, t-shirt, or shit else since I met Vance. His personality was so magnetic, I couldn't help but want to be around him.

As I made my way to the register, there was Oscar's ass with that same smug look on his face. We'd been divorced for right at three years. The only reason he was trying to fuck with me was because he knew about me and Vance. He could kiss my entire ass. If a judge ordered me to sell my house because he changed his mind about wanting it, then they needed their bench brought into questioning. There should be an expiration date in place on a judgement. I didn't ask Oscar for a fucking thing. He told me that I could have the house, because the shit smelled like me... his exact words.

"By the time I get yo' fucked up scent outta here, I could just buy another house. Yo' big ass stank. If I wanted a sloppy bitch for a wife, I would have married one. I'll be out by Sunday. I should have never married you. Being tied to you for the past twenty years has been hell. Well, maybe not the whole twenty, but at least the past ten for sure."

"Oscar, how could you say those things to me? Yeah, I've gained weight... I know that. But you can honestly stand there and pretend like you don't love me... like you never loved me?"

"I don't love you anymore. I fell outta love wit' yo' ass a long time ago. Why you think I'm rarely here? You're a pitiful excuse for a woman."

"For twenty years, I did whatever you wanted. I kept a clean house, cooked your meals, and held down a full-time job, working overtime hours like you requested. I even let you convince me to allow another woman in our bed. So, doing everything you wanted me to do made me pitiful?"

"No. You letting yourself sink to the state you're in made you pitiful. Over the years, I'm willing to bet you gained over a hundred pounds. You can barely walk without breathing all hard and shit. You know how embarrassing that shit is? I just wanna pop you in yo' fat ass mouth. That's why I never brought you anywhere."

"That's not true, Os—"

He hit me across the face, and I fell to the floor in tears, hating the person I'd become. I would be better off dead than the shell of a woman I was. "See, you always make me hit you. I'm glad you filed for divorce. I don't know why I was letting you hang on to me. I feel so much lighter now."

He'd succeeded in tearing me down for the past ten years, fucking other women, giving me chlamydia in the process. I obviously wasn't good enough if he sought attention from other women, and if I wasn't good enough for him, I wasn't good enough for anybody, including myself. Trying to get up from the floor was a task and I was completely out of breath when I finally did. "That's the shit I'm talking about. Listen at your breathing just getting your fat ass off the floor!"

He walked away, leaving me sitting in the chair, breathing hard as hell, tears and mucus excreting from my eyes and nose. Standing, I made my way to the bathroom and got cleaned up, then accepted that he was right.

My face was twitching in anger. All the hate I had for myself back then had been redirected to his ass. Any man that can make a woman sink as low as I was, wasn't a man at all. He was a fucking monster, and the only way for him to feel good about himself was to make me feel horrible. He was the problem and once I realized that, with the help of Meena, I started counseling and focused on becoming a mentally, emotionally, spiritually and physically healthier version of myself. As I stared at him, I could sense he was becoming uncomfortable. I was no longer the weak individual he was used to. I was strong and had become a fighter again. And I'd fight his ass until the bitter end. He wanted to poke the bear, so I was gonna bite his fucking head off.

After leaving the grocery store, I went straight to Vance's house. When I got there, he was backing out of the driveway. Once he saw me, he smiled and drove back into his garage. He got out and said, "I suppose we were thinking the same thing. BeBe and I were heading to your house."

"I guess so. When I woke up, all I could think about was the two of you."

"Is that right? Well, let's see what the three of us gon' get into," he said as he took Belan from her car seat.

I grabbed the bags from the car and walked toward the two of them. Belan had the biggest smile on her face. But I nearly lost my sense when she said, "Na-Na!"

Vance's eyebrows went up as I yelled, "Belan! Yes! NaNa's here!"

She laughed excitedly and kicked her legs as she reached for me. Vance laughed as he took the bags from my arms and handed Belan to me. I swung her around and laughed along with her while Vance unlocked the door. I followed him inside and said, "So, I had an interesting discussion with two people at the grocery store."

"Who?"

"First, Oscar. So, I take it that you spoke to him about me."

The look that graced Vance's face caused me to cower some, but then I caught myself. What was I cowering for? "I did. He kept calling, wanting to go to lunch or out for drinks like we were friends. So, I pretty much told him that I was seeing you and that you were my queen."

"Mmm. I'm sure there was more to that conversation, but I'll leave that alone. He was pretty much threatening to take me to court again for the house if I didn't sell. Fortunately for me, this lady overheard our exchange and approached me after I rammed him with my basket. She's an attorney."

His facial expression eased some, then he said, "Well, that's good."

"Yeah. She said she can't stand a bully and I could tell she wanted to get at his ass right there in the grocery store."

"She sounds like somebody to have on your team," he said, walking closer to me.

Once he was close, he leaned in and kissed my lips, letting me taste the fruit on his tongue. I slowly pulled away because I felt eyes on us. Belan was staring hard. "Okay, she looks too interested in what we were doing. We can't engage in kisses like this in front of her."

"I see that. BeBe, you got a long time before you can do anything like that." He chuckled and pecked my lips again as Belan reached for him. "You know it's taking everything inside of me to let that shit ride, right?"

"I figured as much."

"But, for now, I'm gon' chill. He come at you crazy again, I'm gon' be at that firehouse to strangle his ass with one of those hoses."

WE'D SAT AROUND and watched cartoons with Belan. She loved *Sesame Street*. After an hour or so of that, we went to the park and walked as we pushed her in her walker. She seemed to enjoy the outdoors as well as the breeze. We pushed her in the swing for a while, then went back to Vance's house to get her cleaned up and feed her. I made sandwiches for us and slid ribs in the oven for later. After Belan ate, she'd gone down for a nap. However, as we laid in the bed to put her to sleep, we'd both gone to sleep, too. The sun had whipped us today.

The doorbell had woken me, but Vance and his BeBe were still knocked out. It was too early for Meena to be here, so it had to be Tyrone. He must've gotten off early. Sure enough, when I opened the door, it was him. "Hey, baby. Come on in. How's your dad?"

"Hey, Ms. Jennifer. I'm pretty tired today. I had a lot of patients. Dad is doing okay, I guess. He's missing Mama, but what can I do about that?"

"Nothing. Just pray for him, baby. I know what it's like to grieve a love lost."

"I have been, but if he doesn't want to do better, prayer ain't gon' change that."

Hearing the sadness in his tone caused my heart to hurt for Mr. George. I hoped he got it together soon, because I'd definitely heard of people dying from a broken heart. "Is he still drinking?"

"Does a fish need water?" he asked in a serious tone.

I shook my head slowly. "I'm sorry, baby. Why don't you go home? We'll keep Belan until Meena gets off. She's asleep anyway."

"Thank you so much, Ms. Jennifer. I'm so tired. I just wanna shower and go to bed."

"Don't worry, baby. I'll text Meena and let her know."

"Okay."

He hugged me, then left. I was actually glad he'd come because I'd forgotten all about the ribs in the oven. They'd only been in there thirty minutes, so they weren't burnt. Thank God. After taking them out, I sat on the couch with my sketch pad and sketched out the next bow designs I wanted to do for my baby girl. I was too excited that she could say NaNa now. Grabbing my phone, I sent Meena a message before I forgot. *Hey, baby. Tyrone was extremely tired, so I told him to go home. Can you get Belan when you get off?*

I went back to sketching, knowing that she would respond

when she had time. By the time I finished sketching my fourth bow, which was about an hour later, a shirtless Vance and his half-naked BeBe had joined me. As usual, she was holding on to his goatee. "How did the two of you sleep?"

"Na-Na."

"Hi, my cutie pie. How did you sleep?"

She smiled, then reached for me. "I slept well, probably a little longer than I should have. Now I feel sluggish."

"Well, you better go work the sluggishness out, because I need you as soon as Meena gets Belan."

"She told me Tyrone was picking her up."

"He came while the two of you were asleep. He didn't look good. I asked questions about his dad and I can tell he's worried about him. He kept saying that he was so tired, so I told him to go home and I would text Meena to get Belan."

"Oh. Well, did she respond?"

"Not yet. Maybe I should call her desk phone."

"Well, she told me she had a meeting at two, So, she may be still unavailable."

"Oh, well that's probably why I haven't heard back from her then."

Looking at the clock, I noticed it was only three-thirty. When I worked for the state, our meetings never lasted longer than an hour. They knew we were like kids and they wouldn't be able to keep our attention long, especially not at two o'clock. That was the worst time of day. We were all sleepy as hell at that time, trying to do as little work as possible. I smiled at the thought. Some days, I missed my job, and other days, I was happy I retired when I did.

Putting my sketchpad to the side, I checked my phone to see that Meena had texted back. I wasn't sure how I didn't hear it. She'd said, *okay*. "She responded. Somehow, I missed the chime of my phone."

"Okay," Vance said as he played with Belan.

He hadn't said a word about his test results. I didn't want to ask, but I did at the same time. Something told me that if he'd gotten his results back, he would have been excited to tell me. So, I kept my mouth shut. If he didn't say anything by the time I was about to go home, I would definitely ask. Everything about his dick was screaming for me to put my lips to it, which was why I needed those results ASAP.

$\mathcal{V}$ance

"So, he came here, then just left, because you said to? He was already here. He could have taken Belan with him."

"Baby girl, that man was tired. He obviously has a lot on his plate," Jennifer said.

I hadn't seen this side of Meena... ever. She seemed extremely irritated and she was taking it out on us for not making Tyrone take Belan. "And I don't? Everyone has a lot on their plate at times. I always have a lot on my plate. I'm a social worker! But I can't get lax on my responsibilities just because I'm having a bad day."

"So, if he's as tired as he looked and he got in a wreck on the way home, would you rather lose just him or both him and Belan? Be real, Meena. Jennifer saw him. If he looked as tired as she described, I would have preferred *he* even stayed here to take a nap. Since he didn't, I'm glad he left Belan here. Think about that," I said as she fell silent for a moment.

Without saying another word, she picked up Belan's baby bag, then grabbed Belan from my arms. When she got to the door, she said, "Thank y'all for watching her."

I didn't know what was going on with her and Tyrone, but hopefully, they got to the bottom of it and me and Jennifer could stay out of it. Before either of us could respond, she'd walked out. Jennifer looked up at me and sighed. "What do you think is going on?" I asked her.

"I think they're both stressed out and overwhelmed with life. Meena has always been stronger than Tyrone when it comes to handling pressure, but it seems she's at a breaking point. Maybe we should have kept Belan tonight."

"Not tonight. Maybe tomorrow. I wanna spend tonight with you." I slid my arms around her waist and asked, "Can I do that?"

"You never have to ask permission for what belongs to you."

She said that so seductively, I wanted to say to hell with dinner. Grabbing her hair, I pulled her head back and kissed her neck. Her moan intoxicated me, causing me to lower my hands to her ass. As I squeezed it, I said in her ear, "I'm gonna go take a shower... you coming?"

"I'm coming and cumming, but first, let's eat. I have a feeling this shit gon' last a while."

"You damn right. Especially since I didn't get any last night. You know I'm addicted to that shit between yo' legs," I said as I kissed her neck again.

Releasing my grasp, she stepped away from me and went to the kitchen. I followed her and got our plates down, although, all I could think about was feeding her all this dick in the shower. When she put the ribs, greens, yams, rice and gravy on my plate, I forgot all about eating pussy. Setting our plates on the table, I got us bottles of water and said grace. "Damn, Jenn. This looks amazing. I didn't realize how hungry I was until I saw this food."

"Well, eat up and get your strength, baby, 'cause I'm ready for all the freaky shit we gon' engage in when we're done."

"You think you ready, but I'm gon' suck and fuck that pussy so good, you gon' have an out-of-body experience," I said as I sucked the meat right off the bone of the rib.

The ribs were so tender... just like her over ripe pussy was the first time I dove in it... meat falling off the bone. She watched me as I sucked the tips of my fingers, savoring the taste. "The food is good, baby."

"Mmm hmm," she moaned as she ate some of her yams.

I couldn't fucking concentrate, watching the way she was pulling that food off her fork. She was so damn nasty, and I loved every bit of it. She was making me resort to jailhouse formalities and eat my food fast as hell. I needed to be within her walls like yesterday. Forcing myself to slow down, I drank some water, watching Jennifer as she kept her gaze on her food. *Lord Jesus, she's beautiful.* "So, what time did you wake up?" I asked her, trying to change the subject.

"Instead of the usual sex... I mean, six, I woke up at eight."

The smirk on her lips let me know she did that on purpose. My eyes narrowed as I stared at her. "See, I'm trying to spare you and change the subject, so I don't tear your ass apart in a lil bit, but you ain't cooperating."

I'd eaten most of my food and I couldn't take no more of her teasing. Standing from my seat, I walked over to her and jerked her up from the chair and walked her to the nearest wall, kissing and nipping at the skin on her neck. She brought her hands to the back of my head, holding me close to her as I pulled at her shirt. She did the same to me, then I led her to the bedroom. Pushing her to the bed, I slid on top of her and kissed her like it would be my last time. Jennifer was gonna be my forever. There wasn't a doubt in my mind about that shit.

She slid her hands in the waistband of my jeans, pressing my pelvis into hers. Slowly sliding off her, I took my clothes off as she went up on her elbows, then walked away to start the shower.

When I returned, she was standing, about to take off her bra. "Naw. That's my job, Queen."

She stood there watching me approach her, looking like she was barely breathing. When I got to her, I rested my hands on her breasts, then slowly slid them around her to unfasten her bra. I loved her pretty-ass titties. Bringing my hands back in front of her, I slid my palms over her erect nipples, then went to the waistline of her pants. As I unbuttoned her jeans, she reached down and grabbed my dick, stroking it slowly.

My shit had to be leaking in her hand. Since I'd been out, it was like the nigga had been trying to make up for lost time. Throughout the day, when Jennifer was nowhere near, I'd find myself hardening at every thought of her... wanting to stroke her pussy at any given moment. I definitely needed to find a hobby before I crippled her. Pulling her pants down her hips, I kissed her stomach, then the top of her thigh and the back of her knee. She stepped out of her pants as she rested her hand on my shoulder. "I need to wash my hair while we're in there."

"I got'chu, baby."

I grabbed her hand and led her to the walk-in shower. Allowing her to step inside first, I grabbed a handful of her ass to squeeze, then I popped it. Following her inside, she went to the shower head and let it soak her from head to toe. If that wasn't the sexiest shit I'd ever seen. When she opened her eyes, water all over her face, I nearly bust. *Fuck.*

What I loved about her the most was how free she was sexually. It didn't seem like she'd been through any of the shit Meena had described. While I still thought about and loved my deceased wife, Madelyn, she wasn't nearly as sexual as Jennifer. She was easily embarrassed and soft-spoken. The savage beast inside of me was tame whenever I was near her, causing people to think I was one of those privileged niggas that all the White people loved.

Jennifer didn't suppress him; she coaxed him out and let him run free. The first time I spoke to her roughly sexually and it turned her on, I knew I'd met my match. Of course, while I was locked up, no one took me as being the friendly type, but that was how I had been on the outside as a firefighter. Despite hating being locked up for all that time, I liked the man I had become... one that wasn't looking for acceptance from no one and that was free to be exactly who he was.

Jennifer grabbed me by my dick and pulled me to her and I gladly obliged, letting my lips roam wherever they desired. I grabbed ahold of her wet hair and pulled her to me. Our passion was so explosive, it was dangerous. It threatened to consume us both, but neither of us minded. She grabbed the shower gel and lathered her loofah. Grabbing it from her, I washed her body and was grateful for every curve it took... every roll I lifted... every crease I washed. She was fearfully and wonderfully made, and I thanked God for sending her to my daughter, preparing her just for me.

She lathered the towel and washed me, too. These intimate moments were what I loved. While I loved destroying her pussy, I loved being soft with her, too. Although it made me feel sensitive, I didn't mind feeling that way towards her. When we'd rinsed off all the soap, I began washing her hair. But what she didn't expect was what I said to her. "Jennifer, get on your knees."

She frowned slightly, but she did as I asked without question. That was another thing I loved about her. She never questioned me. It spoke of just how much she trusted me already. A woman this perfect deserved the world and I planned to give her everything I could afford. I worked up a good lather in her hair as she stared at my dick. She'd been begging to suck him, but I wouldn't let her. Placing the tip on her lips, she looked up at me, her eyebrows raised.

I licked my lips as I continued washing her hair, not saying a word. She still wasn't sure if I was teasing her or what, so she continued to stare at it. When her lips parted, I guided my dick between them. She hummed immediately and her eyes closed as she held the head of it in her mouth, swirling her tongue around it. "Mmm. Yeah, Jenn. Suck your dick, baby."

When the words left my lips, she deep throated my shit, making my entire body tremble. It was hard to continue washing her hair with the shit she was doing to me. She wrapped her hands around the base of my dick and stroked it something fierce as she applied killer suction to what was in her mouth. I had never had a woman to give me head this damn superb. That shit made me wanna find Oscar and thank him for fucking up. I couldn't even be mad at that nigga for letting her go.

It felt like my dick was trying to burst through the fucking skin. I'd never been this hard. Stroking her mouth as I washed her hair proved to be the most sensual shit ever. "Baby... ahh fuck! Queen... I'm 'bout to bust."

She hummed on my shit and didn't stop humming until I nutted down her throat. I didn't wanna pull my dick from her mouth. "Ain't no fucking way... I ain't gon' ever be able to go without that, baby. Shit!"

My dick was so damn sensitive, but she wouldn't let up. She sucked him slowly, never taking him from her mouth. "Jenn... baby."

I tried to pull out of her mouth, but she shook her head, causing the head of my dick to graze the walls of her throat. She had me feeling all kinds of crazy because I'd lost all train of thought as I watched my own nut coating my dick. She clearly loved my flavor since she hadn't swallowed it. Increasing her pace, she literally began slamming her mouth on my dick, gagging herself, her throat tightening around the head of my dick. Before I even realized it was happening, I was nutting again. "Fuck!"

When she sucked me dry, she stood to her feet and washed the shampoo out her hair like ain't shit happened. I felt like I was about to collapse, and she just went on about her business like she hadn't just sucked the fucking soul out of me. She stared at me with a smirk on her lips as she put more shampoo in her hair. "See what you've been missing out on?"

"Fuck! I see. I bet a nigga ain't gon' miss out no more, though. My dick gon' stay between both sets of your lips. Shit, Jennifer!"

My heart was beating fast as hell. She was gon' give my ass a damn heart attack. I wasn't expecting all that shit. As I calmed down some, my dick started to harden again. As she conditioned her hair, I spun her around, bent her over, and slid right into that hot-ass pussy. I shivered as I felt her for the first time without a condom. "Oh, fuck!" she said.

"Yeah, I came to get my manhood back," I grunted.

I could have sworn she giggled. She wouldn't be laughing for long. I long stroked her pussy a couple of times, watching it coat my dick, then I went deep hole drilling. She put her hand against the shower wall while I plunged the fuck out of her shit. She was screaming but taking every centimeter of what I gave her. Her pussy was addicting with a condom on, but now, I was strung out. I pulled out and went to my knees to suck perfection. When her excellence graced my tongue, I hummed in satisfaction.

Since her legs were already trembling, I knew this wouldn't take long. After a few strokes to her clit with my tongue from the back, she fulfilled my desires... what I was in search of. "Vance! I'm cumming! Shit!"

While she was still riding the wave, I stood to my feet and pushed back inside of her as I felt her juices traveling through my goatee. "Jennifer... damn, baby."

This was by far the best sex we'd had. Knowing that my test results were clear, opened the door for so much more. I had no idea Jennifer was this type of freak. Her wanting to suck my dick had me excited about tonight, but shit! I had no idea what I was in for. Wiping my chin, I plunged deeper inside of her as she screamed obscenities, only making me that much closer to nutting. Grabbing her hair, I pulled her more upright, then wrapped my hand around her throat, feeding her the dick... raw. I hadn't been with a woman without a condom since Madelyn. It felt better than I remembered.

Jennifer stood up, causing my dick to slide out of her, and washed the conditioner out of her hair. "I'm sorry, baby. I can't let this sit too long," she said breathlessly.

I stood there, watching her as she watched me stroke my dick. Within a couple of minutes, she went to her knees and began sucking her juices off it. Closing my eyes, I allowed my head to drop back. This woman was everything. Pulling her to her feet, I turned the water off, then led her to the granite countertop. I sat her at the edge of it and she leaned back on her elbows. Lifting her legs in the air, I entered her swiftly, missing the way her walls felt wrapped around me already. "Baby, this shit feels so good."

"Yes, King. Oh, fuck!"

Her legs began trembling, so I was sure to spread them wide to watch her cream and it was the most beautiful sight. "Jenn, I'm about to cum with you, Queen."

"Fill me up, baby."

I began pumping harder and faster, feeling like I was on a crash course about to have a head-on collision with ecstasy. The way her walls contracted around me threatened to pull my nut right from me. Leaning over, I pulled her nipple into my mouth as she wrapped her legs around my waist. "Kiiiinnng! Oh, shit!"

Grabbing a handful of her wet hair, I gave her about four more strokes before I thrust deeply into her, letting my seed free to roam in the pasture. "Ahh, shiiit!" I yelled.

I literally felt my age at that moment. That nut had zapped my damn energy. After I'd help Jenn by cleaning the kitchen while she detangled her hair, I was only gonna be good for one thing... sleep. Putting her hands to my face, she pulled me to her and kissed me passionately. When I separated from her, I said, "You nasty, but I like it."

"I knew you would. It's amazing the things you can learn from a cucumber."

taste the fountain of love, and the man was profoundly enamored. Besides, her acting had been impeccable.

Lotzano couldn't live like that. When he closed his eyes, all he saw was Viviana's beautiful ass. When he opened them, all he saw were numbers.

He was crazy for her. He remembered with delight how he had possessed her. How she had placed his penis in her beautiful mouth. He remembered her scent. Her pink nipples.

Wednesday morning he decided to write the check for a hundred and ninety thousand pesos. Since it was such a large amount, the check needed two signatures. His own and that of the president of the union.

Lotzano pulled from his desk a document that carried the president's signature and began to practice signing the other man's name. After more than an hour, he typed the check and signed his name in blue ink. To give it more veracity, he forged the president's name in black ink. He looked at his work for a few seconds and then left the office.

He went straight to the car dealership.

The salesman didn't recognize him.

"I'm sorry, señor, but we can't sell you this car. It's being held for someone."

"I know. It's a surprise gift for her. You see, she's my—"

"Daughter?"

Lotzano felt ridiculous.

"No, my . . . niece."

"Very well, when do you want to pick it up?"

"Tomorrow at noon."

"Fine." The salesman took the check and a few minutes later handed Lotzano a receipt.

Lotzano stood looking at the car and decided that it had been designed especially for Viviana.

Since that fateful day when she had discovered her husband with his lover—in her own house!—Señora Lotzano had been in a daze. It seemed as if everything going on around her was a terrible dream. A movie.

That afternoon she had tried to talk with her husband, but he hadn't paid her any attention. Finally, she had grabbed him angrily by the lapels of his jacket and shouted at him. "You bastard! How could you do this to me? In my own bedroom! In the sanctuary of our house!"

He stood there looking at her without knowing what she was talking about. She kept on yelling. "Not only have you been unfaithful to me, but you did it in my own home! With that damned whore!"

That time, Lotzano understood what she was saying. He didn't know how his wife had found out about it, but before his brain could sort things out, he gave Lucila Lotzano a hard slap, and she fell backward on the floor.

Nobody was going to call Viviana a whore! Nobody!

Señora Lotzano shook her head a couple times, trying to clear her thoughts. Lotzano had never laid a hand on her before.

She stood up with difficulty and left the room. Tears of rage burned her cheeks.

* * *

Thursday at noon Lotzano appeared at the Casquivans' door. Viviana herself answered. She looked at him for a few seconds disdainfully before speaking.

"Who are you?"

"Viviana, I want you to come with me. I have to show you something."

"No. I don't want to have anything to do with you. I don't like to be made fun of."

"Please, my darling! Come with me!"

"I'm not your darling."

"I beg you."

Viviana guessed that he had come to explain why he hadn't bought the car or to tell her that he would buy it soon. Anyway, since she didn't have anything better to do, she went with him.

When they left the building, Señora Lotzano was near the front door, but they didn't see her.

They walked to the automobile showroom.

"I don't want to go in there. You made me look ridiculous the other day."

"Just let me ask them something."

"I'll wait here for you."

Lotzano came back a few minutes later.

"Do you really like the car?"

"What do you think?"

"Well then, why don't you go and get it?" he said and held out the keys to her.

Viviana opened her eyes wide and flashed an enormous smile. "You're joking!"

"No, I'm not. It's yours."

Viviana hugged Lotzano and gave him a noisy kiss on the lips. For the first time she didn't feel disgusted.

Lucila Lotzano had followed close behind the couple. She didn't understand anything that was going on, but when she saw Viviana kiss Lotzano and then watched them leave in the new car, what little had remained standing in her world came crashing to the ground.

She returned to the apartment and was overcome by an attack of hysteria when she entered her bedroom. She feverishly tore the sheets from the bed. Then, panting, she sat on the bare mattress for a few minutes, staring off into space.

Finally, taking the shreds from one of the sheets in her hands, she went to the bathroom, tied one end of the sheet to the showerhead and the other around her neck, and hung herself.

Her last thought was that this was not really happening, and that in a minute she would wake up in her bed, next to her faithful husband.

As the coffin was lowered into the grave, Lotzano felt liberated. Lucila had gotten out of the way voluntarily. Now it would be easier to marry Viviana. And besides, his wife had a life insurance policy worth two hundred thousand pesos, so things would work out perfectly. He would replace the union's money and everything would be back to normal, except that Viviana would occupy the odious Lucila's place.

Virgen was already gaunt and weak when she received

the notice of her mother's death and went into a state of shock. She became delirious and had to be put in the hospital.

Purísima couldn't understand her mother's behavior and finally convinced herself that her mother had gone crazy. But she didn't think she would miss her much. Lately they had grown apart.

Fidel cried bitterly during the funeral and the burial. He looked like a young, defenseless boy. Even though she was present, Tita couldn't console him, because they had to keep up appearances.

Señor Casquivan attended the burial in his wheelchair with a blanket across his knees and from time to time took a sip from his flask.

Lotzano couldn't believe what he had just heard. "It can't be! There must be a mistake!"

"I'm afraid not, Señor Lotzano. The policy clearly stipulates that it does not pay in the case of suicide until two years and one day after the purchase of the policy. Your wife—may she rest in peace—purchased the policy a year and eleven months ago."

Son of a fucking bitch, thought Lotzano, she could have waited a few more days.

"Isn't there some way we can fix this?"

"I don't know what you mean, señor!"

"Well . . . you know . . . these things . . ."

"I'm afraid not, Señor Lotzano. Now, if you'll excuse me, I have other business to attend to."

Lotzano left the insurance company's office dragging his heart. Not only had his wife's death not produced a single cent but now he had to pay almost thirty thousand pesos for the funeral service and the burial.

He was screwed.

Casquivan could now leave his apartment, but he didn't give up the poker games there since they were producing a consistent income.

One afternoon as he arrived at the building, he found a pensive Lotzano. "My dear friend, why are you so down?"

Lotzano looked at him for an instant as if he didn't recognize him. "Problems, neighbor. Problems and more problems."

"Come on! Come on! Lift yourself up! You've suffered a great loss, but life must go on."

"What?"

"You have to start over."

"I wasn't talking about my wife. My problems are about money. And they are very serious."

"You don't say!"

"Yes."

Casquivan took exactly five minutes to convince Lotzano that poker was the solution to his problems. And he, himself, would teach his neighbor how to play.

Viviana's sport car brought other expenses. If she was driving a car of that class, she couldn't dress like a servant, could she? So one night, after feigning pleasure as she was penetrated by Lotzano's minipenis, she got out of bed and began to brush her hair at Lucila Lotzano's dresser.

"I'm going to need some money. I look like a mess."

Viviana had chosen the perfect moment to make the statement. Lotzano could admire her beautiful breasts reflected in the mirror and gaze directly at her heavenly buttocks, bouncing as she brushed her hair, completely naked.

"Of course, Viviana. How much do you want?"

"I don't want to take advantage of you, you're so good to me. How about twenty thousand pesos?"

Lotzano's testicles contracted painfully. He was on the verge of telling Viviana that it would be impossible to get the amount of money, but just looking at her finely sculpted body, the macho man inside him spoke. "Monday afternoon you'll have the money, my darling."

Viviana looked at him in the mirror and blew him a tender kiss with her sensual lips.

Virgen's condition worsened considerably. She was suffering from anorexia. The girl looked like a walking cadaver. During her scarce moments of lucidity, she begged for them to call Deseo.

Deseo, meanwhile, had met a forty-year-old Chicana widow in San Antonio and had decided to spend some time there. The woman wasn't bad looking, and she owned three Mexican restaurants and a Mercedes-Benz.

★ ★ ★

Lotzano's debut as a poker player was a complete success. The first night he left with more than five thousand pesos. The next night, fortune smiled on him again and he won two thousand.

At that rate, he thought, he would very soon be able to replace the money he had taken from the union very soon.

The first week he won fifteen thousand pesos. But fortune is fickle. By Wednesday of the following week, he owed Casquivan twenty-seven thousand pesos.

That same Wednesday, Fidel took off with Tita and got married in Taxco. They had their honeymoon in Acapulco.

Bad luck finally struck Lotzano.

Because of the economic crisis that had hit the country, there was a considerable cutback of personnel at the foundry where he worked. The workers who were laid off confronted their union treasurer and demanded the funds from their savings accounts and their pensions. If there had been only a few of them, it wouldn't have been a problem, but more than fifty men had been laid off. And if that weren't enough, they were the oldest workers and, therefore, had the most money saved.

When Lotzano found out, he was overcome by panic and spent the whole morning either vomiting or sitting on the toilet, victim of a terrible case of diarrhea.

Far from solving his problems, poker only made them worse. Thanks to the cards, Lotzano had had to steal another forty-nine thousand pesos.

When he found out there was no money in the account,

the president of the union ordered an audit and everything was revealed. The union president and the general manager of the foundry made an agreement with Lotzano. If he replaced the money, they wouldn't initiate legal proceedings against him and he would avoid going to jail. But they couldn't have a thief working for them, so he was fired, of course, without severance or pension.

After giving the matter a great deal of thought, Lotzano came to the only logical conclusion. He had to sell his apartment.

However, since he was under pressure to make a quick sale, he had to sell it at thirty percent of what he had paid for it.

Naturally, when he no longer had money for Viviana's whims, she dumped him.

"But, Viviana, you love me. You need me. You told me so many times."

She laughed rudely. "Me, in love with you? Why? Because of the ridiculous size of your penis? Please! You're just a boring old man."

Lotzano was furious, and he said the first thing that came into his mind. "Oh, yeah? Then give me back the car."

"The car is mine. The registration is in my name."

She was right. In the heat of the moment, he had decided to show off and had made sure the papers were in her name. He was completely ruined.

Viviana opened the door of her apartment. "Get out of here. You disgust me."

He never saw her again.

* * *

Virgen died a few days later. The medical report said she died from anorexia, but the truth is that she died from love.

Deseo had long ago forgotten about her.

Purísima had been picked up by the narcotics police one day as she left El Pollo's apartment with a large quantity of cocaine and marijuana in her bag. She was charged with possession with intent to sell and possession of stolen goods.

A federal judge sentenced her to eleven years in prison.

Things didn't go very well for Fidel and Tita economically, and she had to go back to prostitution. One night Fidel went to pick her up at the bar where she worked and found a man molesting his wife. In a fit of rage, he gave the man a karate kick in the face, killing him instantly.

Fidel fled to Guatemala and was never heard from again.

With the little money Lotzano was able to salvage, he bought a tiny government-subsidized apartment and never made friends with any of his neighbors. He had bought a hot-dog cart and worked it on the streets to survive.

Casquivan found another mistress in the bordello he frequented. Her name was Ani, and she was thirty-five.

The new inhabitants on the fourth floor were a young couple with two children, ages four and six.

They moved in on a Saturday.

The next Thursday, Adonis offered the wife two tickets for a raffle of two crystal goblets. As a gesture of goodwill to the new neighbor, he gave the attractive woman one of the tickets for free.

CORNELIA

T HE SUN had been up for over half an hour. Cornelia slipped out of bed and made her way into the bathroom. After relieving herself, she stepped into the steaming shower. Little by little, she replaced the hot water with cold, until finally only frigid water coursed over her body. This was one of her techniques for keeping her body taut.

Trembling with cold, she finished showering and dried herself by vigorously rubbing her whole body, which stimulated her circulation and helped to firm her white skin. She hadn't washed her hair—that was part of another, more elaborate ritual, which she began every evening at seven.

Cornelia looked at her reflection in the full-length mirror on the wall of the dressing room. At twenty-eight, she was a very attractive woman. However, her beauty was not merely a gift from nature, it was the result of a fierce discipline consisting of physical exercise and a beauty regimen that at times exhausted her. But everything pays off in life. Her body didn't have an ounce of cellulite, her breasts were round and firm, and there was not a wrinkle on her face.

In the bedroom, Federico was still sleeping. She watched

him for a few moments. His breathing was even, his face tranquil. He was a good man and an excellent client. She had met him four years ago, at a bachelor party. Since that night he had always treated her like a lady. Sometimes he would call her and they'd go out to dinner. He always respected her professionalism, and even when they didn't end up in bed, he invariably paid her for her time.

Once he had invited her to spend a few days with him in New York. They stayed at the Plaza, enveloped in luxury, and she felt like Cinderella with her prince. Even then, he had insisted on paying her fee. Over time Cornelia had come to care for him and they had become good friends.

She left the apartment, and the concierge greeted her casually.

"Good morning, ma'am."

"Good morning, Isidro."

"Your car has been washed," he said as he handed her the keys.

Cornelia said good-bye and drove to her own home, in a much less luxurious neighborhood.

She didn't like to drive. When she drove, her mind always turned to other things: her life, her profession, and the realization that—despite all the exercise and shaving—sooner or later she would become an old woman. An old whore, which saddened her immensely.

When she finally reached her apartment, she was very depressed. She halfheartedly ate a slice of ham, swallowed two Valiums, and went to bed. Fifteen minutes later she was fast asleep.

Meanwhile, Federico had been awakened by the sound

of the telephone. It was his mother calling to tell him that
Nestor, his younger brother, had been in a car accident, and
although nothing serious had happened to him, he was being
held at the police station.

Federico was the eldest son, and everyone turned to him
when problems arose. He showered and dressed quickly, then
hurried out to rescue Nestor from the clutches of the law. As
opposed to Cornelia, he liked driving because it gave him time
to think. Nestor had become a total and frequent headache.
He was not yet thirty and he was already a consummate alcoholic. The previous night's accident had surely been caused by
his unquenchable thirst.

It all began when Dolores, Nestor's wife, ran off with a
saxophonist in a rock band nearly a year ago. Since then,
Nestor found his only solace in the bottle. At first, Federico
considered his brother's reaction normal, but as time passed he
realized the dangerous habit was here to stay. But this was too
much. As he entered the parking garage at the police station,
Federico resolved to end his brother's problem, one way or
another.

Nestor's accident had not caused any major consequences.
The insurance would cover the cost of repairing both vehicles,
but Federico wanted to speak seriously with his brother—just
as he had several times before over the past year. He took
Nestor to breakfast, and as they drank coffee he said, "Nestor,
last night was just a warning. Next time the consequences may
be fatal. For you and for some innocent person who gets in
your way."

Nestor avoided looking his brother in the eye.

Federico continued, "You know I love you. We all love

you. That's why we want to help you." He took a few sips of coffee and continued, "Nestor, your finances are in the toilet. You're accumulating debt. Your body has deteriorated considerably. In short, you are killing yourself."

Nestor's hands trembled as he drank his coffee. With sadness, Federico noticed his brother needed both hands to hold the cup.

"Nestor, you need professional help, and I am willing to pay for it. You need to see a psychiatrist."

Nestor glared sharply at his brother and replied hoarsely, emanating a repugnant odor of alcohol. "I'm not crazy."

Federico was fed up. He'd already had this conversation. "Don't worry. If you continue like this you will be very soon."

"Don't you worry. Maybe that's the best thing that could happen to me, to lose my mind."

"Because of a third-rate whore who took off with a second-rate musician?"

Nestor fixed his reddened eyes on his brother for a few seconds and, without saying another word, stood up and walked away.

Federico didn't try to stop him. He was sure there was a solution for this problem, and he was determined to find it.

Cornelia opened her eyes at seven that evening. She didn't need an alarm clock, since her body possessed a perfectly synchronized clock. She started her regular exercises: abdominals, weights, sit-ups.

At eight-fifteen she entered the sauna with a bottle of mineral water in her hand. At eight-thirty, into the shower.

Always starting with very hot water. Then gradually lowering the temperature until it was freezing, withstanding everything that a human being can bear. In that North Pole, shampooing, rinsing, and meticulously cleansing those parts of her body that sustained her livelihood. After the usual vigorous drying, the makeup routine, but nothing exaggerated. She didn't like to ruin her skin with an excess of paint.

At ten-fifteen she drank a large glass of milk and swallowed a vitamin and protein complex with an amphetamine chaser.

At ten-thirty the telephone rang. It was one of her clients. "We're having a little party with some friends. Can you come?"

"Sure. What's the address?"

She quickly wrote down the details. It was a part of the city she knew intimately. Luxurious. Only men with a lot of money could allow themselves the pleasure of hiring her.

Cornelia had gone independent two years earlier, but she had been working for more than eight. At first, she was convinced by a friend to enroll in a modeling school. With her slender figure and beautiful face, she quickly began receiving offers of all kinds, from modeling underwear to going to bed with some manufacturer or a wealthy buyer.

She did well as a model, but the big bucks were made on assignments from a so-called promoter, who convinced her to model seminude at a few parties, as a hostess, the guy said, and finally she ended up going to bed for money. Later, when her client book was full, she decided to stop paying a commission to her agent and struck out on her own.

With so many years in the field, she had become a real professional. The rules of the game were absolutely clear, and the men who hired her knew them. When a client was referred to her, the first thing Cornelia did was recite these rules. She would undress in front of any group of men, no matter how many there were, but if they wanted to go to bed with her, she would charge each one her fee. If the guests at a party wanted to be with her two or more at a time, the same rule applied, each one had to pay his way. She did not allow anyone to hit her or to perform anal sex with her or to insert any foreign object into her. However, despite the rules, there was one inevitable risk—because of her high fees, she couldn't allow herself the luxury of requiring the use of condoms, which meant she exposed herself daily to the possibility of contracting a disease, including the most dreaded, AIDS.

When she arrived at the address she had written down, she found herself in front of a mansion. Luckily, she wasn't the only woman. That was always better, because with more hired girls around, there was less likelihood of being raped or hit.

The man who had called approached her and, before introducing her to the guests, offered her a little cocaine. Cornelia inhaled the drug with great pleasure and almost immediately began to feel good.

The party was like all the others—drugs, alcohol, and sex. At eight in the morning, she climbed back into her car and drove home with a tidy sum of money in her purse.

Federico had spent the day thinking about how to solve Nestor's problem. He had become incredibly depressed and was filled with a tremendous feeling of loneliness. At eleven he decided to call Cornelia. He needed to be with her. He needed to be with *someone*.

The phone rang a dozen times, but the girl didn't answer. So Federico took an Ativan and went to bed.

And dreamed.

He dreamed about Cornelia and Nestor. In his dream, the girl was having sex not with him but with his brother. And, surprisingly, Nestor was happy and satisfied—and sober—like never before.

The next day when he woke up, he knew he had the solution to his brother's problem. Cornelia.

Cornelia took her morning shower and breakfasted on a couple of slices of ham and some yogurt. Thanks to the amphetamine and all the coke the night before, she was wide awake, so she turned on the TV and swallowed three Valiums before getting into bed.

At six that evening the telephone brought her back to the world of the living. She was still drowsy, and her whole body ached. It took her a few seconds to realize what was causing the damned ringing. Finally, she picked up the phone.

"Yes?"

"Cornelia?"

"What's left of her. Who is this?"

"Federico. I need to see you."

"Well, you're going to have to wait at least four hours. The way I'm feeling now it's going to take me a long time to make myself presentable."

"I'll see you at my apartment at eight. I want to talk to you about something important."

"What time is it?"

"Six."

"I'll be there at nine."

"Perfect. Nine sharp."

"See you then."

Cornelia headed for the kitchen and washed down an amphetamine and two aspirins with an icy Coca-Cola. Ten minutes later she felt well enough to begin her routine of exercise and shower. She applied only minimal makeup because she knew Federico preferred a natural look.

At exactly nine she was ringing the bell at her friend's apartment.

As usual, Federico greeted her with a kiss on the cheek and offered her something to drink. Cornelia requested a Coca-Cola and an espresso. Once the drinks were served, Federico got right to the point.

"Do you consider me your friend?"

The question took the beautiful woman by surprise, and she just raised her eyebrows.

"Tell me, honey, it's important."

"Yes, I consider you one of my few friends. Why do you ask?"

"Because I need to ask a very special favor."

She looked at him with surprise. The man sitting across from her was a millionaire and quite sure of himself. What favor could he possibly want from a call girl?

"What is it?"

"I have a brother who is an alcoholic. Have I ever mentioned him to you?"

Cornelia shook her head.

"Well, it doesn't matter. The thing is, he's all messed up. He doesn't work very much, he owes money, he doesn't care about anything, and, what's worse, a couple of days ago he had an accident while driving under the influence. I'm afraid if he continues like this he's going to do something really stupid."

Cornelia nodded, comprehending the situation. She had never enjoyed drinking alcohol, but she knew several professional girls who had drowned their lives in the toxic liquid. They were truly pathetic cases.

Federico lit a cigarette and continued. "Here's the favor. I want to ask you to stop working for a while and dedicate yourself to making my brother fall in love with you, and, most important, I want you to get him to stop drinking."

Cornelia lit her own cigarette as she observed Federico, trying to figure out if the whole thing was just an absurd joke.

He remained serious and continued. "Of course, you will not be adversely affected economically. I—"

Cornelia interrupted him with a wave of her hand. The noble woman really considered him a friend, and, in terms of values, friendship was worth more than money.

"It's not about the money," she replied, "but what you're asking of me is a little strange. I need to think about it."

"You don't have to give me an answer today, Cornelia. I only ask that you really think about it, because this is a very serious problem for me. He's my only brother, and I don't want to lose him. Much less in this way."

She got up and went to the window, from which she could see nearly the whole city. It was a magnificent view. After a few minutes she spoke. "Let me think about it. I'll call you tomorrow, okay?"

"Of course," replied Federico, thankful for the woman's

compassion. Any other prostitute would have immediately accepted the offer, just for the money. But Cornelia wasn't just any prostitute. She was a lady. He walked her to the door and said good-bye with a kiss on the cheek.

Cornelia returned to her apartment. At ten-thirty one of her admirers called to invite her to his home. She declined, claiming to have a prior commitment, and spent the better part of the night thinking about Federico's proposition. At four in the morning she fell asleep without needing her usual Valium.

Federico knew the woman well, and that was why he had dared to propose the arrangement with Nestor. And besides, Cornelia was much more of a woman than the one who had abandoned his brother, plunging him into misery and alcohol.

The expense would be enormous, but he was not going to scrimp in the least on his only brother's well-being.

It was just an idea, an experiment, but all of his previous attempts to rescue his brother had failed. Nestor didn't want to consult a specialist or check into a clinic or even join an Alcoholics Anonymous group. So this could be the solution, and Federico had to try it.

He didn't want to pressure Cornelia, but he needed to know what she had decided, so he called and invited her to dinner.

As soon as they were settled in one of the restaurant's comfortable banquettes, he turned to her. "So . . . ?"

Cornelia took a few sips of her icy Coca-Cola and took her time lighting a cigarette. Finally, she spoke.

"You can count on me, but I want to establish certain conditions."

"Just name them."

"If the 'job' turns out to be unbearable, I will have to end it. Besides, I don't have the faintest idea how to deal with an alcoholic. Of course, my clients regularly get drunk or high on drugs, or both, but that's not the same as a relationship that could last several days or weeks—it's just a few hours, and it's all part of the business. I don't know how I am going to handle the situation."

"Of course," agreed Federico, gazing admiringly at the beautiful woman.

"There's something else. Suppose I succeed and he falls in love with me, won't he just go back to where he is now when I end the relationship? Wouldn't that be even worse?"

"Leave that to me," said Federico, with confidence. "If you get him to stop drinking long enough to consult a psychiatrist, we'll have the game half won. I understand your concern, and I appreciate it, but if we don't try anything now, Nestor could end up in terrible shape. He's capable of just about anything."

"All right then, I'm in. What's the plan?"

"Nestor can't know that we know each other, and, of course, he can't find out about your profession."

Those words might have sounded a little offensive coming from someone else, but Federico spoke them with complete respect.

"Certainly. How do you want me to meet him?"

"Just make an appointment. Nestor is a gynecologist."

* * *

Cornelia scheduled an appointment for the next day. She was even able to choose the time. It was clear the doctor did not have many clients.

Who had recommended her? A friend from the club. She didn't remember her last name. Maria something.

At six o'clock the next afternoon, Cornelia appeared at the doctor's office. At five past six, she met Nestor.

She had imagined that he would be chubby, with a prominent belly and a nose full of broken blood vessels from the excessive alcohol, but that wasn't the case. Nestor was a tall man, slender, with a straight nose, not broken. And there was something else about him, something that was extremely pleasing to Cornelia. The guy was exceedingly handsome. His gaze was like that of a surprised child, and he seemed very intelligent.

If she hadn't known what she did about his personal history, she would have assumed that this was all a joke in poor taste by Federico.

Yet, while the gynecologist asked questions about Cornelia's medical history, she noticed the unmistakable smell of alcohol in the air. Although the doctor did not appear to be drunk and he spoke clearly, his words came out enveloped in the odor of booze.

Cornelia told the doctor the reason for her appointment was that a few days ago she had felt a lump in her left breast.

After a series of brief questions, Nestor led the beautiful woman to an examining room, where the nurse gave her a gown and asked her to disrobe from the waist up.

When she was ready, Nestor appeared and began to examine her.

Cornelia noticed two things. The doctor's pulse was not completely stable, and the odor that he gave off now was of fresh alcohol, as if he had just had a drink while she was disrobing.

However, he examined her carefully and professionally.

Finally, he asked her to get dressed. Back in the doctor's office, he asked her, "Do you take contraceptives?"

"No."

"Any hormones?"

"No."

"Good. I didn't find anything. But, to be sure, I'm going to order a mammogram. There's nothing to lose by that. Don't you agree?"

"Of course!"

The doctor's attentions seemed quite agreeable and sweet to Cornelia. It was as if he had known her for some time. If it weren't for his alcohol-laced breath, she thought, Federico's brother would have more than enough patients.

Nestor scribbled a few words on a small sheet of paper printed with his name and handed it to her. "Call me when you get the results."

"Very well, Doctor."

Cornelia rose to leave, and as she reached the door she turned, flashing a timid smile and said, "Excuse me, Doctor . . ."

"Yes?"

"You'll think I'm a fool, but . . . Do you mind if we use our first names?"

He answered immediately. "Of course not!"

"Good. I'll see you soon, Nestor."

"I'll see you soon, Cornelia."

* * *

Nestor wasn't accustomed to having relationships with his patients. In fact, since that ugly day his wife, Dolores, had left him, he hadn't had a relationship with any woman. But Cornelia's perfume lingered in his nose, and the image of her beautiful face had become embedded in the deepest part of his alcohol-soaked brain.

Obviously the results of the mammogram were negative, but Cornelia insisted on having Nestor examine her again, just to be sure. "I'm a little paranoid, you know?" she said. "Especially since a friend of mine had her breast removed because of cancer."

He agreed to examine her again, just to please her. He really liked this woman.

"Nothing, absolutely, nothing," he declared. "You don't have to worry anymore. Besides, the mammogram is one hundred percent reliable."

That afternoon there was nothing further between the two of them.

Cornelia let a couple of days pass, then called him.

"Nestor?"

"Yes."

"You're going to think I'm very bold, but now that you've calmed me down completely, I feel I owe you something. Would you like to have a drink with me? Or maybe go out to dinner?"

The gynecologist couldn't believe his ears. Some women

had flirted with him in the past, but certainly never a beauty like Cornelia. He accepted immediately. "I would feel very honored."

"I'll wait for you at my apartment at nine then, all right?"

It was certainly all right with him, and at nine sharp he was at Cornelia's door. Of course, beforehand he had ingested half a bottle of scotch, just to give him the courage.

Cornelia was an expert with men. She knew their nature, their pleasures, their instincts. She knew that there are two ways of conquering them: by playing hard to get, or by giving them a little taste of the fountain of love and then withholding it until they were practically out of their minds.

With Nestor, she decided that he had to be the one to lead the way. If at a certain moment she noticed a lack of interest, she would apply her feminine wiles and her vast experience to winning him over.

Nestor arrived with his breath smelling of alcohol and breath mints. To Cornelia's surprise, the combination was not completely disagreeable. Besides, the man was impeccably dressed and groomed, and his aftershave smelled delicious.

Cornelia, by contrast, had taken an amphetamine ten minutes earlier, wanting to be sure she could handle the encounter with alertness and the greatest mental clarity possible.

For a woman like her, there were two worlds. Just as a doctor wears a uniform to work and wears civilian clothing away from work, Cornelia wore provocative clothing, very short and tight, to go out to a party or meeting for "work," but she also had a wardrobe for her personal life.

She greeted Nestor in a white dress, one piece, above the knee, which showed off her well-defined body perfectly but without exaggeration. She had also chosen flesh-colored stock-ings and white high heels. Her chestnut hair was straight and loose, and she wore very little makeup. She looked like a twenty- or twenty-one-year-old girl.

Nestor couldn't help gazing appreciatively at the beautiful woman. She offered him something to drink, but he politely refused. He knew that if he kept drinking at his usual rate, the night would end too quickly for him and, in all likelihood, embarrassingly. With a woman like this, he couldn't allow him-self that luxury. He suggested instead that they leave for the restaurant.

Cornelia chose a small, cozy Italian restaurant. She ordered her usual Coca-Cola, and Nestor had a Chivas and water, which he tried to make last as long as possible.

Cornelia monopolized the gazes of all present with her radiance, and the gynecologist felt proud for being able to show off such a beautiful woman.

She told him she was a model and sometimes designed clothing. But her real strength was modeling.

He told her he practiced just about any type of medicine, now that his clientele had dwindled so much, perhaps because of the crisis. Of course, he refrained from mentioning that it was not the economic crisis, but his own.

"How is it that a woman like you is still single?"

"My work takes up all of my time. Besides, I haven't found the man of my dreams yet. Are you single?"

"Divorced." Nestor omitted saying the divorce had been due to abandonment, because of a saxophonist.

Inspired by Cornelia's beauty, Nestor controlled his drink-ing and engaged her in an extremely interesting and agreeable conversation. It had been a long time since he had talked to anyone, and his words flowed intelligently and captivatingly.

As for Cornelia, accustomed to conversations with her clients—generally vulgar—in the doctor's words she found an oasis of ideas she had never heard before.

When they left the restaurant at one in the morning, she realized how the time had flown.

Cornelia invited him up to her apartment.

He accepted.

They listened to a little music in near silence and drank Coca-Cola, both of them.

Nestor didn't want to push his luck, so after a short while he said good night.

Cornelia accompanied him to the door and, taking his hand gently, asked, "Would you like to get together again?"

"Of course!"

"Then call me!"

"Your phone number?"

"It must be in my patient record," she said and tenderly kissed him on the lips. Barely brushing them. A caress.

As he left the building, Nestor felt as if he were walking several inches above the ground.

Cornelia took a Valium, and a few minutes later she was asleep. She dreamed about the gynecologist that night.

The next evening at Federico's apartment Cornelia told him about her date with Nestor. At first, Federico feared she wouldn't like Nestor. After all, the beautiful seductress must have been fed up with having to deal with drunks, and having one foisted on her nearly full time might have seemed a bit much. But what she was saying left him completely surprised.

"We had dinner at an Italian restaurant. He had only five scotches, which seems like a normal amount, doesn't it? Then we went to my apartment. You know what he drank there?"

"What?"

"Coca-Cola."

Federico had thought of the plan with fragile hope. Now, Cornelia was telling him Nestor had controlled his drinking during dinner, which he had not been able to do for quite some time.

Federico was pleased, but at the same time he was briefly struck by small stab of jealousy.

"Excellent." He continued, "Can you stay with me tonight?"

"I'm afraid not. Nestor wants to watch a movie on TV together, so I told him I would meet him at my apartment at ten-thirty."

"Fine."

Before the woman left, Federico said, "You don't know how much I appreciate what you are doing for my brother and . . . for me."

In reply, she brushed his cheek softly with the back of her hand.

When he closed the door behind Cornelia, Federico felt a wave of loneliness wash over him.

Cornelia and Nestor continued seeing each other. Both had completely changed their lives. They went to the theater together, attended concerts, went shopping, and, most of all, they talked.

Cornelia quickly realized the doctor was an extremely refined and interesting man. When he was at her side, she felt entertained and excited. She felt protected as she never had before. Nestor treated her with absolute respect, and at no time had he tried to overstep the boundaries. But he continued drinking. Any time he came for a visit or to pick her up to go somewhere, he arrived with alcohol on his breath, although she had never seen him drunk.

Nestor had forgotten about Dolores almost the moment he met Cornelia, but he still needed alcohol to relax and engage with the world.

A month after meeting Cornelia, he was head over heels in love with her, and one night, in her apartment, he tried to kiss her on the mouth.

She would gladly have responded; it wasn't at all unpleasant. But she was a professional and had been hired to get the gynecologist to give up alcohol, so gently but firmly she refused Nestor.

He felt lost. On the surface, the lady liked him a great deal, or so it seemed. He wanted to know why she was turning him down. "What's the matter, Cornelia, don't you like me?"

"I like you a lot, Nestor."

"Well?"

"Don't take this the wrong way, but I want to tell you a little story."

He settled into the couch, ready to hear what the beautiful woman had to say.

"My father was an alcoholic," she lied. "Not necessarily

one of those guys who falls down drunk or disappears for days at a time. He never came home drunk or anything like that, but he drank a lot and almost every day. He adored me and always treated me well. He kissed me a lot, you know? And one of the things I have never been able to forget is his breath. It always smelled of alcohol. Forgive me, Nestor, but I can't stand kissing a man whose breath smells like alcohol."

Cornelia told the little lie so naturally that Nestor believed her. A stab of guilt seized the gynecologist's heart. He felt like a fool. How was it possible that he would be denied the pleasures this beautiful woman harbored because of an absurd habit?

"I'm sorry," he said. "I shouldn't have tried to kiss you."

"No, it's not that. I already told you I like you very much. More than you can imagine. I wouldn't mind kissing you at all if it weren't for the memories that your breath brings to my mind."

He nodded gently a few times. He felt like a student being reprimanded by the teacher. Then he rose and picked up his jacket, saying, "I'll see you, Cornelia."

She didn't know if those words were a dismissal or a simple good-bye, so she was reluctant to release her prey and quickly said, "Nestor, I like you more than any man I've ever met."

He nodded, responding with a smile that showed a mixture of doubt and incredulity. He opened the door and left without another word.

Inexplicably, Cornelia felt a completely new sensation. When Nestor left, she felt as if a part of her soul had been torn out. For two days she was tempted to call Federico to tell him the plan had failed. But, deep down, she knew the problem wasn't Federico's, it was hers.

She had felt happier with Nestor than she had with any other man. Except for his being always somewhat inebriated, he was a total gentleman, and he had been extremely sweet with her. His innocent child's gaze completely captivated her.

Cornelia was accustomed to men looking at her with desire—even with open lasciviousness—but Nestor was different. He looked at her as if she were a helpless virgin princess who had to be protected from the evil of this filthy world.

That night, around nine, the telephone rang. The enchantress thought about not answering, imagining that it was one of her regulars calling to invite her to a party. But she picked it up. "Hello?"

"Cornelia?" It was Nestor's voice.

Her heartbeat accelerated, as if she were a schoolgirl being asked on her first date. "Yes?"

"It's Nestor. Do you think we could see each other tonight? I don't know if it matters to you, but I've spent two days drinking nothing but Coca-Cola. I think I've gained seven or eight pounds."

The beautiful woman couldn't hide her emotion and in an almost girlish voice replied, "Of course! Give me an hour. I'll see you here."

Cornelia showered and dressed quickly. She was so happy! She had done it. After so long, Nestor had stopped drinking for two days straight.

But her happiness went beyond that. She had a true desire to see him, to be with him . . . to kiss him and caress him. What was happening?

When she met him at the door, Cornelia could not contain her impulses, and she fell upon him, hugging him tightly and covering his face with kisses. She was like a wife welcoming her husband home after months of not seeing him.

He took her in his arms and kissed her on the mouth. She noticed the lack of the smell of alcohol, and they met in a prolonged and burning kiss, followed by another and another as she blindly led him to her bedroom.

Once there, her womanly nature overcame her professionalism and she let herself be carried away. Nestor caressed her awkwardly and undressed her timidly as he covered her body with kisses.

When Cornelia was completely naked, he became lost for a while, admiring the absolute beauty of the woman he loved. Finally, he undressed in a fraction of a second and got into bed with her.

Cornelia had never counted the number of times she had had sex over the course of her life, but that night she discovered something very important. For the first time ever she felt a stirring inside, a great, boiling cascade of love. For the first time, she had an orgasm. For the first time in her life she felt like a Woman.

It was Federico who called her to ask how the plan was going. By then, Nestor had gone without a drink for over a week. Cornelia and Federico met that night at his apartment.

She omitted the fact that she was completely in love with Nestor as she announced to Federico that his brother wasn't drinking anymore.

"It's just incredible."

"Why, you didn't think I could do it?"

"Of course I did! But I thought it would take longer."

"Your brother spent over a year beating himself up because of Dolores. Suddenly another woman came into his life. A woman of flesh and blood, not a fantasy, and she made him feel like a man again. So, he doesn't need alcohol anymore, because he doesn't have anything to forget."

"Good. I'll talk to him and ask him to see a psychiatrist. I'm sure he will now."

Cornelia shot Federico a look of surprise. "A psychiatrist, why?"

"Look, Cornelia, this is not a simple thing. It's as though Nestor nearly drowned himself. You took care of giving him first aid; now some real therapy is needed to revive him."

"But he's fine!"

"Don't worry, leave him to me. For the time being, just keep up the game. Wait until he's in treatment, and then we'll figure out a way for you to leave him."

Cornelia looked at Federico as if he were someone she had just met. He wasn't the same man he had been a few weeks ago.

"Sleep here tonight," he said suddenly. "You don't know how much I've missed you lately."

Cornelia had been a prostitute for several years. The new Cornelia had been a woman for a only few days, but that new woman would not tolerate being treated as an object, she would not permit herself to be used. "No!" she replied drily.

Federico was shocked. In all the time that he had known her, she had never refused to stay with him when he'd asked. In fact, she had once canceled another commitment to spend the night with him. Suddenly he felt very irritated with her, and he shouted, "No? Why not?"

"Because I don't want to spend the night with you."

"No? And since when does it have to do with what *you* want?"

Federico had turned into a madman. For the first time he treated her not like a lady but like a whore.

Cornelia stood up and walked toward the door. He put himself between her and the wooden door. Then, more calmly, he said, "Forgive me, honey, I didn't mean to insult you. It's just that I've realized you are much more than a date to me. You can't imagine how you fill my life! Now that I haven't seen you, I'm aware of how much I've missed you. And more every day."

Cornelia was surprised. She knew—or thought she knew—that they were friends, but a friend doesn't miss another friend in this way.

"I'm sorry," she said. "I should go."

"Cornelia . . . please stay! Cornelia . . . I think I love you."

The man sounded sincere; those words came not from a man desiring sex but from the soul of a man who wanted a particular woman.

"I'm sorry, Federico. I can't sleep with you. I'm in love, too."

"You? With whom?" His face burned with jealousy.

"With Nestor."

"With Nestor? A woman like you in love with an alcoholic? You don't know what you're saying. My brother is nothing more than a wretch. He's barely holding himself together. Where do you think you're going to go at the side of an irresponsible drunk?"

Cornelia felt an icy shiver along her spine, and the hair on her neck stood up. Then, filled with ire, she replied, "Federico, we're talking about your brother! Your only brother! And the man I love. The only man I have ever loved. What is wrong with you?"

Federico reacted as if someone had thrown a cold bucket of water in his face.

Then he opened his eyes wide, as if he realized what he had just said, and he moved aside to let Cornelia open the door.

She left without saying another word.

Federico went to the bar and drank half a glass of scotch in one swallow.

Nestor and Cornelia's wedding took place three months later. With the notable absence of Federico, who was too drunk to get himself together to attend.

One day, during their honeymoon, Nestor said to Cornelia, "My poor brother has become a drunk. Only when you have lived like that yourself can you know what a hell it is. But you rescued me with your love. Do you think the same thing could happen for him? Do you think some woman would be willing—let's say for money—to make him fall in love with her and get him out of this mess?"

Cornelia hesitated a few seconds before replying. "Maybe. There are all kinds of women in this world."

"It's just an idea, but it could work, don't you think?"

BEAT ME TO DEATH

Beat me to death
spit out the pieces
finish me with bullets
pick up the pieces
beat me . . . to death!
Grind me into powder
don't leave any traces
destroy me inside
start with the center
tear up my guts
use all your tricks
but beat me . . . to death!
Don't leave me hungry
take all my blood
finish me with bashes
take me in your arms
and beat me . . . to death!
just beat me . . .
. . . please beat me . . .
to death!

—KARLAH KARGHILL,
Poems of Violent Love

143

MATEO hadn't always been a misanthrope. In fact, a large portion of his life had been dedicated to goodwill. He had even been a good Christian, loving his neighbor as himself.

But life is full of changes.

Every day he heard more stories of violence, and not just on television but the real thing. He lived in the largest, most polluted city on the planet.

The pollution was not limited to atmospheric conditions. As with the air and water, the citizens' minds had become completely clouded, paranoid and aggressive, and now the condition was considered normal. It was like the experiment where a group of laboratory rats are put together in a cage and, from the beginning, are given a constant amount of food, which is not increased as they multiply. Gradually the rodents begin to kill one another, even their own children, and end up becoming cannibals. The largest city in the world was even worse, since it wasn't a laboratory experiment with rats but rather a daily reality featuring much more sophisticated animals: human beings.

Mateo had grown up along with the city. When he was born, it was a more or less agreeable place to live. He remembered playing soccer as a child in the middle of the street. When an automobile approached, someone would yell "car," and everybody would move aside. After the vehicle passed, the game would continue.

There were empty lots where he and his friends carried out all sorts of childish investigations, and they caught small, bright-colored snakes, which they sold at school.

However, as the human population grew, so did the number of automobiles, and everything that had existed before disappeared. A few traces of nature remained for a while. Some of the major avenues had wide medians in the center with grass and palm trees where one could lie in the sun and watch the afternoon unfold. Later, however, those median strips were reduced and finally covered with striped pavement. As the number of vehicles increased, so did the noise level, gas emissions, and a collective hysteria.

The city had become hell on earth.

And in hell there are no good angels, so one day Mateo decided not to fight the current any longer but just let himself be carried along by it.

The decision was forced by a guy in one of those tiny multiplex theaters that had cropped up like mushrooms in the seventies.

The movie was based on a book by Truman Capote and was about the insufferable life in an American prison. Mateo had gone to the theater with his current girlfriend, a nice, short woman with large breasts and narrow hips, who knew a lot about film.

Everything went well until the middle of the movie, when an obnoxious man—he must have been on drugs or drunk or both—entered the theater and decided to sit right behind Mateo and his girlfriend, even though there were a lot of unoccupied seats in other parts of the small room.

During a scene about a homosexual attack on a young boy who had just arrived at the prison, the recently arrived patron called out in a loud voice, "Faggots . . . faggots."

Mateo didn't do anything, but he felt his blood chill. To

express himself in that manner when there was a lady only a
few feet away and with the tone of voice he used could only
be interpreted as open aggression, but he decided to let it pass.
He didn't have an aggressive nature and prided himself on his
intelligence. He always thought about the consequences of his
actions.

A few minutes later, during another violent scene, pounding his seat, the idiot in the row behind yelled, again in a loud
voice, "Fuck him up. . . . Fuck him up."

Mateo had been studying karate—for the discipline and
exercise rather than for personal defense. He became tense and
was tempted to stand up and kick the guy out of the theater,
but again he contained himself.

The couple had grown uncomfortable and were no longer
enjoying the film.

Mateo made a decision. He took his girlfriend by the hand
and stood up to move to other seats.

As they stepped away the man behind them said, "The faggot and the whore are already leaving."

Mateo acted instinctively and, lifting his right leg over his
chair, smashed the heel of his boot against his provoker's nose
and teeth.

The blow sounded like a couple of nuts being cracked
against each other, followed by asphyxiated gasps.

Mateo and his date didn't wait to see what would happen
next, on the screen or in the theater. They left in a hurry. On
the way to his car, Mateo thought, The idiot. The stupid idiot.

That was the first time he had felt seriously violent, and, as
much as he tried to fight his feelings, the experience had been
exhilarating.

For a long time he excitedly remembered the exquisite sensation and sound of the guy's breaking bones. It was like stepping on an ugly insect, the crushing feeling as it's smashed into the ground. That's what the guy had been anyway, an ugly insect.

The city was plagued with insects of all types, and Mateo soon had a chance to crush another specimen.

This time it was a rude guy looking for a shortcut who made the mistake of crossing his path. Mateo had been circling the block, trying to find a place to park, when a space was finally vacated. He put his car in reverse and began backing into the space when a smaller car zipped right into the spot.

He got out of his car and approached the window of the other driver, who by now was almost finished parking. He intended, as always, to handle the situation intelligently. "Excuse me," he said politely to the interloper, "but I was here first and had my turn signal on, clearly indicating my intention to park in this space."

The guy in the tiny car was fat, and his hair was shiny with grease. He had finished parking and didn't even turn to look at Mateo. "Well, you got screwed," he said. "Next time forget about signaling and just park faster."

It wasn't fair. Especially after he had tried to deal with the troglodyte in a socially acceptable manner. He tried again. "Please. Would you be so kind as to move your car? This is my space."

Still sitting in his car, the ugly hoodlum had his feet on the ground about to get out and merely looked at Mateo as if he were a piece of bird shit splattered on the windshield. Then he grunted. "Think you're pretty tough, huh? You wanna make me move it?"

That was too much. Instinctively, Mateo stepped back a bit and gave a sharp kick to the door of the diminutive car, taking into consideration—of course—that the aggressive thug's shins lay between the car and the open door.

This time it sounded like a dry tree branch breaking. The cretin's tibias and fibulas broke in several places.

Mateo got in his car to find another parking space, leaving the driver of the other automobile unconscious from the pain. The last thing he saw of the insect was his ugly black shoes and socks hanging like rags from the side of the car. They looked like doll's feet.

Despite the unpleasantness of the scene, Mateo felt rejuvenated. Especially when he remembered the guy's face when his legs were crushed.

To Mateo's pleasure, opportunities for squashing insects began to multiply.

One day, he went into a video arcade. He was waiting for a friend, and since he was early, he decided to kill some time playing the machines.

A young man was expertly playing next to him. But he lost the game and, visibly angered, struck the machine with the palm of his hand. The machines were mounted on a hollow wooden base, and the sound echoed like a drumbeat. The kid moved on to another machine.

Mateo continued playing. Then a little insect with a bitter, twisted face, a man in his fifties, stood close beside him and interrupted his game by delicately saying, "Are you the bastard who goes around hitting the machines?"

More than a question, it was a declaration, but Mateo wanted—once again—to use reason. "Excuse me?"

"Don't play ignorant with me. Why are you hitting the damned machines? If you don't know how to play, don't. And if I see you around here again, I'll break your face."

The manager was at least ten inches shorter than Mateo, but he backed up his threat by opening his jacket to reveal the handle of a large pistol tucked into his belt.

"Excuse me, but I haven't hit any ma—"

"Shut up, you lying son of a bitch! And get out of here before I kick you out."

Mateo made a gesture of impotence, extending his arms out from the sides of his body, with his palms up, as if imploring clemency and comprehension from heaven.

A millisecond later, the tip of his boot struck the dwarf's testicles with such force that the man was lifted several inches off the ground.

The abusive midget's face was locked somewhere between complete surprise and overwhelming pain. He bent over double, and Mateo, not sure whether the dwarf was looking for a weapon or simply holding his aching scrotum, completed the job by giving another kick, this one aimed at the man's chin.

Crack! His mandible broke cleanly in two, and the tiny armed pest shot backward spectacularly.

The place was full of drifters and people from the neighborhood, who, nearly in unison, broke into enthusiastic applause at Mateo's actions.

It was obvious this was not the first time the insect had tried to intimidate a patron by displaying his gun.

Without knowing why, Mateo moved closer to the fallen man and took his pistol.

It was an automatic Colt .45 Commander. He opened the chamber to check the bullets. It was empty!

He left the place amid shouts and applause, taking the pistol with him.

Mateo knew these three incidents could have been avoided if he had not acted violently. Until then he wouldn't have used violence but would have remained calm and left with his tail between his legs, letting his aggressors laugh at him instead of appreciating his good judgment. But they had gone too far, and besides, he found that violence produced a certain type of pleasure. It excited him.

When he got home and examined the Colt, he grew more excited and felt like taking a couple of shots. Not at anyone in particular. He just wanted to feel the weapon's deadly power and its sharp recoil.

But he'd do that later. There were other instruments that he wanted to try first.

He quit karate classes one day when he accidentally broke the arm of one of his classmates.

He was a high school boy, a brown belt, very eager, one of those guys who studies karate so he can attack anyone who confronts him. Mateo was a green belt, and had been for two years. He was tired of it.

The sneaky kid had tried a combination flying kick and punch. His barefoot heel whistled a fraction of an inch from Mateo's nose, and the punch had been well aimed, but—again acting on instinct—Mateo stepped back catlike and caught the aggressor's fist with lightning speed, twisting his arm in the socket until it couldn't turn any further and broke. The young enthusiast emitted a loud yelp of pain more appropriate for a pregnant woman than for a youthful killer.

Oh well, that's how it goes sometimes.

At the same time, his fellow karate students had begun to notice a difference in the otherwise peaceful Mateo, and that wouldn't help his plans, especially now that he was thinking about exploring more sophisticated techniques.

He wished to study a new method of pest control. He wanted to see blood. Lots of blood.

So he decided to learn how to throw knives. He started with ordinary kitchen knives. He took a wooden door and drew the outline of a man's body. He covered the area inside the line with several layers of cork, until the "victim" was about three inches thick. He bought a set of twelve tempered steel knives, of all shapes and sizes.

Mateo had always been very diligent in all his activities, and this would be no exception. He dedicated himself to throwing knives for three or four hours a day. At first, the sharp instruments bounced off the cork, and if one stuck, it was merely by chance.

But practice makes perfect.

Mateo soon learned the feel of each knife. Before long he was able to sense the balance of each blade and the weight of the handle. He taught himself how to gauge the distance to the target, the force of the throw, the way to grasp the knife.

He surrounded himself with knives. He dreamed of them. They became his life.

He changed the cork on the door several times, and in less than two months he had perfected his technique. It no longer mattered which of the twelve knives he picked up. Each one had become an extension of his arm.

He became adept at sharpening and polishing the knives, and was able to balance them with exquisite precision by placing small drops of solder on key parts of the blades or handles.

But he wanted more. It was no good if, when an opportunity presented itself, he had to use an unfamiliar knife, so he purchased two good switchblades and in a few days was highly skilled in their use.

Mateo inspected and admired any knife he came across.

Soon he was an expert. Just by taking a knife in his hand, he knew how to hold it and could throw it accurately. There were no secrets for Mateo in the world of knives.

He needed to learn only one more thing: how to stick them in some cursed insect.

He carried his switchblades wherever he went, and, when he found himself alone somewhere, he would play with one or both, enjoying the metallic click of the blade sliding out of its casing.

He burned with desire to have an opportunity to try them out—to prove himself with some kind of deadly final exam.

As luck would have it—his, not the insect's—an opportunity soon presented itself.

One night he went to dinner with Vivanco, one of his last few friends, and during dessert they decided to go hire a couple of girls. They liked this type of relationship because it didn't imply any type of commitment. No love, tenderness, or guilt. Just sex.

When they were finished, the prostitutes went their way and the men headed for the garage of the sleazy hotel, where they had left their car. Vivanco—who besides being a good friend was pretty simpleminded—discovered that he had locked his keys in the car.

They found a wire hanger, and Vivanco began the struggle to unlock the door through a tiny crack in the window.

Meanwhile, Mateo leaned against the car, chain-smoking.

They'd been there awhile when another car entered the garage and parked a few yards away.

Mateo noticed two couples were getting out of the car. One of the girls was pretty drunk, and, when she was about two yards from Vivanco's car, she stopped and refused to go into the hotel. She tried to return to the car, complaining that she felt sick.

But the gentleman accompanying her didn't want to let go and tried to force her into the hotel. The girl broke away and returned to the car, settling into the backseat.

The other couple also returned to the car. Maybe, thought Mateo, I ought to check on the sick woman. The gentleman accompanying her got into the backseat, not to help the girl but to grope her.

The other woman, who Mateo assumed was a good friend of the drunk woman, refused to go into the hotel with her date, saying that her friend needed her and begging him to take them home—they'd had enough fun for one night. Mateo could tell she had a beautiful body, since she was bent over the car door, unknowingly displaying her rear end.

Meanwhile, Vivanco was swearing about his damned keys and kept trying to unlock his car door.

The guy accompanying the girl with the shapely behind tried twice to get her to go into the hotel, and both times she politely refused.

Finally, the guy who had been fondling the drunk girl got out of the car and, after exchanging a few words with his buddy, took the other woman, the one with the nice rear end, and tried to force her into the hotel. She fought him, but he whispered something in her ear and she stopped struggling.

When they passed in front of Mateo, who by now was smoking his fifth cigarette, the attractive young woman looked at him pleadingly. She was definitely being forced into the hotel against her will.

Then, to Vivanco's surprise, and the woman's, and, above all, that of the man accompanying her, Mateo said tranquilly, "If you don't want to go in, precious, don't. This insect can't make you."

The guy, who was already visibly upset by the negative attitude of the two young women about satisfying his sexual needs, turned to Mateo, making a threatening face, and said, "Who the fuck do you think you're talking to?"

Mateo didn't move, but every muscle in his body tensed with emotion. Finally, he thought, the long awaited chance for his test! Then he reiterated to the young woman, whose face displayed a look somewhere between surprise and astonishment, "If you don't want to do anything with this piece of shit, don't do it."

Vivanco's mouth was hanging open, and he stood there with the coat hanger in his hands. The other insect, who had taken his partner's place in the back of the car and had been busy groping the drunk woman, got out and joined his friend.

The first guy let go of the girl and made a karate gesture, putting one foot behind him and raising his fists. He forgot to yell "Ha!" but he still looked ridiculous. The other one had his hand at his waist as if he were about to withdraw a gun.

Vivanco was paralyzed.

Mateo's long hours of practice with his adored knives had not been in vain. Pulling his hand from his jacket pocket, and without waiting for an explanation, he held his knife, then threw it like a bolt of lightning at the presumed pistol bearer.

The knife flashed through the air in the semideserted garage and landed cleanly in the aggressor's eye.

The guy who had made the poor attempt at karate tried to follow the trajectory of the shiny item with his eyes, and he surely would have made some gesture of surprise or fear when he saw it embed itself in his buddy's face, but Mateo didn't allow time for surprises. He already had the other knife in his hand and gracefully threw it a distance of less than four feet. With surgical precision, the blade entered the trachea of the man. With a look of incredulity, he put his hand to his throat to feel the wound. He looked at his bloody hand for a moment before he fell to the ground shaking like an old man with Parkinson's disease.

The girl with the nice rear was aghast. She tried to scream, but nothing came out.

Mateo went to collect his knives with cool, decisive steps. His sense of satisfaction was plainly evident on his face. He had passed the exam with flying colors.

The guy with the knife in his eye was bleeding profusely

and had lost consciousness, but he was still alive. Mateo extracted
the blade and wiped it on his victim's jacket, then put it back
in his pocket.

The evil buddy was taking his last gasps of life when
Mateo pulled out the second knife and, as he had with the
other man, cleaned it on the trembling man's clothing.

Vivanco was paler than milk, but he hadn't let go of the
wire hanger. The girl with the cute behind had closed her
mouth, only to open it again a little later to vomit.

Mateo knew he had to act quickly. With a rapid kick he
broke a window in Vivanco's beloved car, got inside, started the
engine, and opened the passenger door. "Let's go, stupid!" he
shouted at his friend.

Vivanco dropped the hanger and quickly climbed into
the car.

He couldn't speak for more than five minutes. Mateo
didn't know if it was because of the violent scene in the garage
or the broken car window.

Vivanco decided to remain silent about what had happened for three reasons. First, he thought Mateo had gone
crazy and was very dangerous. He didn't want to end up with a
glass eye or a new mouth in the middle of his throat. The second reason was that he had been there too, and they had fled in
his car. He was an accomplice, and he didn't want any problems with the police. And, last, Mateo had paid for the installa-
tion of a new car window.

One thing was clear, in the future Vivanco would think
twice about going out with Mateo.

★ ★ ★

Over time Mateo became *really* violent. He no longer waited for opportunities to squash insects but rather provoked incidents so he could act upon his aggressive feelings.

But he still used his intelligence. Even though he loved using his knives, he didn't let his vice dominate him. He didn't want to get tangled up with the police, much less go to prison. He liked violence, but not if it was used against him.

In his new violent life, Mateo discovered a world of infinite possibilities. He no longer merely believed that the city should have fewer rats so the others could live better. That was a romantic way of looking at things. He had learned that by means of violence he could get practically anything he wanted. The more he applied this principle, the more experienced and self-confident he became. His look was tranquil but strikingly cold and hard. Still, it wasn't the look of a crazy man.

Once he had mastered knives and switchblades, he grew anxious to move on to another type of weapon. He took out the Colt he had "confiscated" from the dwarf in the video arcade, who by now probably had a soprano voice along with a cleft chin.

Mateo obtained bullets from a friend who knew a bank guard. He bought several boxes since he wanted to learn to handle the weapon expertly.

Practicing with a firearm was much more difficult—and noisier—than throwing knives against a cork-covered door. He registered the weapon with the army and joined a shooting club. That provided him with a permit for the pistol and a pass to the shooting range at a nearby military base.

Except for Mondays and Tuesdays, when the shooting range was closed, Mateo spent at least a couple of hours a day shooting the .45, which turned out to be an excellent weapon.

He began by focusing on loading and unloading his pistol quickly. Then he practiced pulling the trigger. This he did very slowly at first, so as not to move the barrel and redirect his aim. At the same time, he was becoming accustomed to the recoil, and, unlike the others around him, he didn't wear earplugs and safety goggles. He wanted to get used to the blast. He didn't want to jump like an idiot if somebody shot at him.

Next, he practiced drawing the pistol from a holster and shooting. First, one shot at a time, then two. Eventually he increased the number of perfect shots to three, four, and even five in a series. When he had mastered this, he bought twenty cardboard silhouettes and more bullets from a soldier and said good-bye to the military range. He never returned.

He purchased a book on firearms and began a detailed study of their function.

Next, he decided to buy a silencer for the Colt, but everyone he asked refused to help. They told him that if the police found a man with a silencer-equipped weapon in the most polluted city in the world, he'd probably be accused of half the city's unsolved gun-related crimes, regardless of the caliber of the weapon or whether he had been born when the crime occurred.

Mateo would have to fabricate a silencer. It couldn't be that difficult. With his book on weapons and a little imagination, anything was possible. Besides, didn't the exhaust system of a car use a similar apparatus to reduce engine noise?

He ordered an extra-long Colt .45 barrel from the United States. It was the one they use for the Gold Cup model. He used a hacksaw to cut off the pieces that projected from the barrel, leaving it smooth like a tube. Then he took both barrels to an Italian engineer friend of his who had vises and precision machinery. He asked his friend to make a half inch of threading on the outside of Gold Cup barrel and another half inch on the inside of the Commander barrel. That way they could be screwed together. He told his friend he wanted a longer barrel for more precise shooting.

When he got home, he reassembled the Colt to create a pistol with a barrel that was six inches longer.

He unscrewed the extra barrel and made several perforations with a small drill. Then he wrapped it with a roll of compressed gauze until it measured an inch in diameter. Over the gauze he forced a length of copper tubing of the same diameter. Finally, to keep the gauze in place, he soldered a piece of metal at each end of the copper tube.

It wasn't perfect, but maybe it would work.

The next day he located an isolated spot off the old highway to Cuernavaca. He stuck one of his cardboard targets on a tree and stepped back about fifteen yards to try out his weapon.

The silencer worked, but not like in the movies, where you hear just a soft *puff!* With the new pistol you could hear the metallic click of the trigger and a light explosion, but it was nothing compared with the gun's original sound.

Overall Mateo was pleased with the result and spent the morning shooting a box of fifty bullets. He had devised and mounted a small canvas bag to one side of the pistol where the empty shells gathered so he wouldn't leave empty shells lying around.

★　★　★

Everything was going smoothly with his new life of violence for the sake of violence. Like a lover longing to be with his love once again, Mateo eagerly anticipated the chance to try out his weapon on a live target. Of course, he could have shot randomly through the window of his car as he was out driving some night, but he preferred staying to enjoy the results of his insecticidal excursions.

But until then he didn't just sit around. He went to his private shooting range on the Cuernavaca highway whenever he got a chance. With the silencer he could shoot as much as he wanted without drawing attention.

One night on his way to target practice, heaven—or hell, depending on one's point of view—gave him the perfect opportunity to test his modified Colt.

He was driving along the highway when he saw a large black car approaching at high speed in his rearview mirror. He didn't pay much attention until the car pulled alongside his and the man in the passenger seat began signaling for Mateo to pull over.

At first he didn't understand what was going on, but when the ugly cretin motioned again for him to pull off the road, this time displaying a machine gun, he understood perfectly. They planned to rob him.

Mateo had heard a lot of hair-raising stories about what happened during these solitary robberies. The assailants were usually ex-policemen doing the only things they knew how to do: assault, kidnap, torture, and kill.

The black car pulled in front of Mateo's car, then braked suddenly, forcing him to stop.

Mateo wasn't afraid, although he hadn't anticipated encountering poisonous insects. He grew very tense. But he would soon fix them.

The black car stopped at the side of the road, and Mateo pulled his car over behind it. Then he jumped out of the car just as it came to a complete stop and started to run, zigzagging through the woods.

The aggressors hadn't expected this behavior from their victim, and they lost a few precious seconds deciding what to do. When they finally got out of their car, Mateo was already fifty yards away, hiding among the trees. The thugs immediately commenced the human hunt. There were three of them. Two carried machine guns, and the third had a sawed-off shotgun.

"You'd better come out now, you son of a bitch, or we'll shoot you out like a turkey," one of them shouted.

Mateo was leaning against the trunk of a huge tree and was not about to be shot at like a turkey. He aimed his .45 at the head of the guy who had shouted and slowly pulled the trigger. He heard the now familiar *pfum*. But nothing else happened.

It had failed.

Thanks to the silencer, the shot wasn't heard by his pursuers, who were now only about thirty yards away. But Mateo had just five bullets left.

The guy who had shouted earlier called out again, with the same sweet voice. "Get ready to get fucked up, asshole!"

This time Mateo pulled the trigger more carefully.

Pfum!

The shouting insect took a couple of steps, then collapsed. What had been his head only seconds earlier was splattered over a sizable portion of the woods.

It took the other two ruffians a while to figure out that they were being shot at. Mateo didn't waste any time. He opened fire on the one with the sawed-off shotgun. He didn't want to take unnecessary risks, so he shot him twice in the chest.

The second victim fired his weapon as he was knocked backward. He was dead before his body hit the ground.

The third insect crouched behind a tree less than ten yards from Mateo and shot a spray of machine-gun fire at the tree he was leaning against.

Splinters flew, and the shots rang in his ears. But he remained calm. He had just two bullets left.

There was a new spray of bullets, immediately followed by shouting. "You're gonna be sorry, stupid faggot! You're gonna be real sorry!"

The situation couldn't go on much longer. If they were active policemen, it wouldn't be long before backup arrived. If not, the machine-gun fire would soon attract police from the highway, and Mateo had just committed two homicides with a pistol, fitted with a silencer, that was approved for use only on an army firing range.

Mateo crouched like the actors he'd seen in the movies, carefully took a dead branch from the ground, trying not to expose his arm, and threw the branch to his left. The gunman shot at the spot where the branch fell, exposing himself enough for Mateo to fire his last two bullets.

Mateo didn't hit his target, but—ironically—a piece of the tree trunk that had protected the aggressor splintered into his eyes, making him scream in agony. He shot blindly until his Uzi was completely empty.

Mateo moved quickly. Holding the Colt in his left hand and grabbing one of his switchblades with his right, he walked over to the wounded man, who had already replaced the empty cartridge with a new one. Mateo was less than three yards away when his opponent lifted the machine gun and started shooting. His eyes were closed and his face was bleeding.

Mateo threw the knife, which landed squarely in his adversary's chest, but the wound wasn't fatal. He fell to the ground as the air was sprayed again with 9mm bullets.

"You're gonna die, you son of a bitch!" groaned the wounded man.

Mateo took out his other knife and concentrated for a fraction of a second. Then he threw it with all his strength, aiming at the throat of the other man, who by now had totally abandoned the protection of the tree trunk.

This time the knife stuck mortally. But suddenly, the man fired the Uzi again. One of the bullets whistled past Mateo's right ear.

The wounded man removed the knife from his neck, causing intermittent spurts of blood to flow from the gaping wound and with his last ounce of strength approached Mateo. He was still holding the Uzi. About a yard away, he pulled the trigger again.

Click!

The gun was empty.

Mateo stood up and, with an almost feline movement, pulled the knife out of his attacker's chest and swiftly decapitated the pig.

He looked around for his other knife, cleaned them both,

and put them back in his jacket pocket. Mateo put the Colt away and walked toward his car.

But curiosity and the large amount of adrenaline circulating in his blood pulled him back. His temples were pounding painfully, and he felt huge waves crashing inside his head.

He approached the man with the sawed-off shotgun. He was sprawled in a grotesque position, face up and eyes wide open, as if death had caught him by surprise. Mateo bent over the cadaver and lifted the man's shirt. He wanted to see the effects of the .45 bullets.

There were two small holes, about six inches apart, near his heart, not very impressive. Then Mateo turned the body over to look at the man's back. He didn't even need to lift the shirt. It had been destroyed. The exit holes couldn't be distinguished. There was just a mass of blood, splinters of bone and flesh. The exit wound, only one for the two bullets, covered roughly twelve inches.

The next cadaver presented a more impressive picture. The bullet had entered through the right eye. Almost all of the back of the poor guy's head was missing. His face looked like a Halloween mask.

Mateo hurried to his car and returned to the city. He had had enough target practice for one day.

One thing leads to another. Life is like a long chain, each event, a link.

The experience with the Colt had not been very satisfactory after all. Yes, it had killed and destroyed, but for Mateo it was too impersonal. Too removed. It wasn't something he could feel.

Besides, he couldn't very well walk around carrying an illegal pistol all the time. So he ventured into an area completely different from karate, knives, and guns.

One day he entered a sporting goods store to look for a gift for a cousin of his who was turning fifteen. He saw something that made his face light up with joy and excitement.

It was a black baseball bat. It shone as if it were made of marble. He ran his fingers over it, weighed it in his hands, caressed it, and instantly felt a thrilling shiver run down his spine. His cheeks were flushed.

This was an instrument of violence, *pure* violence.

Without thinking twice he purchased the beautiful piece. In his excitement he completely forgot about the gift for his cousin.

When Mateo got home, he sat down to study his new instrument of pleasure. After inspecting it at length, he knew this was the next link. From that day on, while watching television or walking around the house, he always carried his beautiful bat.

He knew the bat so intimately that if anyone had exchanged it for another, he would have noticed the difference immediately. His arms became accustomed to its weight, the slight roughness of the handle, and the gleaming polished wood.

After a few days, Mateo began exercising. Fifteen minutes with his right arm, then another fifteen with the left. He would hold the bat in the middle and twist his wrist in one direction, then the other. The first days were painful. His muscles ached within minutes of beginning. However, in just a week his arms were like ropes of steel and he handled the heavy bat with the same ease that a child would a chopstick.

Soon he decided to make a slight adaptation to the bat. He drilled a hole in its end, about ten inches deep by an inch across, and he filled it with tiny lead balls, then sealed the opening with epoxy. To prevent this modification from damaging the weapon's integrity, he wrapped a fine wire around the ten inches he had filled with lead and covered it with duct tape.

Now the larger end of the bat was gray, not as attractive as before but much deadlier.

Mateo moved on to another type of exercise. He learned to swing the bat. Not to hit a ball but to swat a punching bag he bought at the sporting goods store.

He practiced all the time. Morning, afternoon, and night, he hit the heavy bag over and over.

One day the bag fell apart from wear, and Mateo knew it was time to move into action. The bat had become an extension of his arms.

In order to transport his weapon without attracting attention, he bought a plastic tube, like the ones that artists use for rolls of paper. It was discreet enough, and he could carry it wherever he wanted. Mateo practiced opening the tube and removing the bat quickly.

He went out for a walk with the plastic tube under his arm almost every day. His mouth practically watered when he thought about using the bat.

One afternoon, when he was sitting in a park casually watching people go by, his great opportunity materialized—it was made to measure.

A little old lady was walking slowly by, her purse hanging from her arm. Suddenly, a young man sped past on a motorcycle and grabbed the woman's bag with such force that she was knocked to the ground. She lay there groaning and calling for help.

The thief sped off with his prize. However, before escaping into the street, he had to pass near Mateo . . . and his bat!

Mateo unsheathed the weapon in less than two seconds.

The thief was just about to make a clean getaway when Mateo lifted his bat and struck the fugitive's head with all his strength.

A horrendous *crack!* mixed with the noise of the motorcycle's engine; the cycle zoomed by as if nothing had happened. A fraction of a second later, the driver's body fell off the back of the bike, followed by his head, which hit the ground with a dull thud.

This time there was no trembling or asphyxiated gasps. Not at all. Mateo approached the cadaver as he returned the bat to its sheath.

The thief's head—grotesquely crushed—had rolled several yards from the rest of the body, which looked like an old, mutilated rag doll. His eyes had come out of their sockets and were dangling from bundles of muscles and nerves. They looked like a pair of fresh mussels.

A crowd of curious onlookers had already gathered.

Mateo turned around and walked away innocently with the plastic tube under his arm.

Deep inside he felt full, satisfied . . . He was completely happy.

However, Mateo's beautiful insect-killing instrument had suffered a mortal wound, invisible at first glance. There was a fine crack along the ten inches that contained the lead filling.

★ ★ ★

It was three weeks after the incident in the park before Mateo could use his beloved club again.

Tired of walking around looking for adventure, he sat on the patio of a bar to have a drink. Two extremely attractive girls were sitting two tables away. Mateo respectfully admired their long legs and short miniskirts. Suddenly, a pair of trouble-makers passed in front of the girls. "What a great looking pair of whores!" one of them exclaimed.

The hair on Mateo's neck stood on end. This was his opportunity.

He stood up and left a couple bills on the table, then fol-lowed the crude young men.

"Why'd you say that, asshole? Poor girls," said the other cretin.

"Who the hell told them to dress themselves up like whores?" the first responded.

Mateo approached them, pulling his bat from the tube, and, without saying a word, took a powerful swing with it at the head of the louder of the two young men.

To Mateo's surprise, the bat broke in two, sending hun-dreds of tiny lead balls flying through the air.

His reflexes failed him for a couple seconds, which the second guy used to stick his hand in his jacket pocket and extract an enormous silver revolver. Mateo reached into the pocket of his jacket in a desperate search for his switchblades, but in the back of his mind he realized that he didn't have enough time, so he tried to run, still holding the handle of the bat.

But, as he tried to flee, he slipped on the rolling lead balls and fell to the ground.

All that was left of the bat was a sharp stick. It looked like the stakes they used in movies to kill vampires.

As Mateo fell, the stake punctured his neck, slicing his carotid artery.

Mateo was killed by his own weapon of destruction.

Now there was one fewer insect in the largest and most polluted city on the planet.

FLIDIA

Walls and doors created secrets.

—BAGUN

THE PARTY was held at Lipia and Ricardo's house, in a haze of cigarette smoke and alcohol vapors, as usual.

Off to one side, the women formed a small cluster, like a coven, and broke into giggles and quiet laughter every now and then. At the other end of the room, the men told dirty jokes and laughed raucously as they sipped cognac and scotch.

Tornillo stole intermittent glances at Flidia's well-shaped legs; she was one of only two single women in the group.

It seemed unbelievable that in only a few years she had been transformed from a skinny, insignificant woman into the appealing Venus that he saw before him. Though she was no great beauty, her fine body did much to compensate for her plain, dark face. She was wearing a black Lycra miniskirt that displayed nearly all of her thighs and no stockings. When she crossed her legs, Tornillo easily glimpsed the tiny triangle of the girl's panties.

But she hadn't made the movement intentionally.

She wasn't like that.

At twenty-nine, Flidia was the living image of purity.

Though she dressed provocatively, she had never even looked at any of her girlfriends' husbands, especially Tornillo, toward whom she had always shown a vague, but constant, antipathy.

All the men present, without exception, had made advances to her. Some brazenly, thinking that a woman like her, and at her age, would be hungry for the taste of sex, while others had offered themselves to her sincerely, drawn by the sweetness of her character, which enhanced her physical beauty.

The former she rejected firmly but delicately; the latter she thanked for their well-meant intentions with a light kiss on the cheek. Tornillo had been rejected with an amused, disdainful look.

But, in contrast to the others, Tornillo didn't continue to pressure her. His conduct toward Flidia from then on was that of a true gentleman, and his glances at the girl's gorgeous limbs were always most discreet.

The other single woman, Olga, was the complete opposite of Flidia. She had flirted with all of the men, and they had all rejected her, since, even though her face was pleasant, her body resembled a dry tree.

Flidia stood up to go into the kitchen for another drink, and Tornillo felt a stirring in his groin. Her red sweater outlined her perfect breasts, and, as she passed the group of men, her perfume flooded his brain.

Several bottles later, the evening drew to a close and everyone went home.

That night, Tornillo decided that somehow he was going to make that woman his. Coincidences determine life's path, and, in this instance, they certainly did much to facilitate Tornillo's plans.

The company where Ricardo worked sent him to Boston for a training course, so Lipia and he were moving there for four months. Since Tornillo was their best friend, they gave him the keys to their house and asked him to take care of it while they were away.

The couple had barely boarded the airplane before Tornillo headed for their home. It was a large ranch-style house, conveniently located on a golf course. The nearest neighbor was fifty yards away, and, as if that weren't enough, the house had a basement, which had been furnished with a pool table and a Ping-Pong table. It was even carpeted and had a full bath and central heat.

Tornillo went directly to the basement, and a wide smile lit up his face. It was ideal for his purpose.

The next day he set his plan in motion. In a pharmacy downtown he bought a bottle of chloroform and five dozen disposable adult diapers. He took his purchases to the house on the golf course and got to work in the basement. He folded the Ping-Pong table and placed it in a corner; then he carried a mattress from one of the beds upstairs and set it on top of the pool table, outfitting it with sheets, a heavy down comforter, and a fluffy pillow.

The next day, with the utmost discretion, he dedicated himself to studying Flidia's routine.

She had worked for several years in a computer consulting firm. Like any single girl, she was very methodical. She started work at ten in the morning and around two had an hour break for lunch. At three she returned to the office and left for the day at seven. After work she headed to a women's gym, where she did her exercises and left around nine; afterward she went straight home, where she lived with her mother and her mother's husband. Flidia's father had died in a traffic accident ten years earlier.

Tornillo observed the routine for several days, and it was always the same. Only one night, after leaving the gym, the woman had gone to a restaurant, where she met a man for dinner. At eleven-thirty she left alone in her car and went straight home.

The living image of purity.

At the gym, Flidia had to park in a space some distance from the entrance, since by the time she arrived, the place was full of women wanting to have bodies as beautiful as hers. When she finished, she was one of the last to leave, and the parking lot was practically deserted. And poorly lit.

Tornillo took mental notes of all these details and developed his plan of attack.

The next Tuesday evening, he taped cardboard license plates over the metal ones on a car he had rented.

With remarkable tranquillity, he waited for Flidia to leave the gym.

As the girl was putting her bag in the trunk, he surprised her from behind, tightly pressing a chloroform-soaked handkerchief over her mouth and nose.

Flidia fought for a few seconds but soon yielded to the effects of the anesthesia. Pleased with his luck, Tornillo opened the trunk of the rented car and put the unconscious girl inside.

He went over to close the trunk of Flidia's car, then got into his own vehicle and proceeded to distance himself from the scene at a moderate speed.

Everything had gone perfectly.

He drove to the house on the golf course and parked the car in the garage, closing the door behind him with the remote control.

He trembled with emotion, and an immense feeling of pleasure coursed through his body as he looked at his prey in the bottom of the trunk. But he had to hurry, because he didn't know how long the effects of the chloroform would last.

Laboriously he transported Flidia to the improvised bed in the basement and covered her eyes with firmly adhering patches, being careful so that the adhesive did not stick to her eyebrows and lashes. He put a piece of packing tape over the mouth of his goddess.

He completely undressed the girl and put a disposable diaper on her, then tied each of her extremities to the legs of the pool table. He immediately covered her with the down comforter and went to turn up the heat. Once finished, he simply waited for his victim to recover consciousness.

He didn't have to wait long. In a few minutes Flidia began to make muffled sounds, and a little later she started to struggle against her restraints.

Tornillo did not intervene; it would be easier to communicate with her after she had tired herself out.

Within ten minutes the woman had stopped fighting and was sobbing helplessly.

Tornillo slowly approached and, disguising his voice, spoke to her. Flidia jumped when she heard her captor's voice and immediately began struggling again, only to give up a few minutes later.

Tornillo decided it would be best to leave her alone. A

night by herself would soften her up a bit. Besides, it would give her time to test the strength of her restraints.

He adjusted the thermostat to a comfortable temperature, fluffed up the comforter, turned off the lights, and went home to sleep.

Of course Tornillo knew the risks he ran if Flidia freed herself. Not only his marriage but his entire life would be threatened, since this was kidnapping—so far. But that gorgeous body was well worth it. He had become obsessed with it.

The next day he removed the fake license plates from the rented car and took it back to the agency. Tornillo bought a variety of provisions at a supermarket, and that night he returned to his lair.

He descended the basement stairs without making a sound. The comforter was on the floor, an obvious sign that Flidia had attempted to escape. The girl was now breathing rhythmically and appeared to be sleeping.

Tornillo put the comforter over her body, and she immediately flinched, but not nearly with the same energy with which she had reacted the night before. It seemed more like a temper tantrum than real struggling. He disguised his voice again and moved close to her to speak. "If you don't settle down, I'm going to have to kill you," he said, almost whispering.

Flidia immediately froze and remained motionless.

"You are going to have to spend a few days here," Tornillo continued. "If you behave yourself, I'll give you food and water, and let you go to the bathroom. But if you don't, I will have to kill you. Is that clear?"

Flidia nodded weakly.

"We are in a house in the country. No one can hear you out here. I am going to remove the tape to give you some water. If you scream, I'll kill you. Is that clear?"

Flidia nodded again.

Tornillo removed the adhesive tape covering the girl's mouth.

Flidia didn't yell, but she spat out a hysterical stream of words in a low voice. "Where am I? Who are you? What do you want from me? Why—" Tornillo covered her mouth with his hand.

"Do you want me to kill you?" he asked.

She shook her head no.

"Say another word and I will. I don't want you to say anything else, not a single word, unless I order you to. I am not going to keep threatening you. The next time you speak I will stab you with a knife. Is that clear?"

Sobbing, the girl agreed.

Tornillo put a straw in a bottle of water and moved it close to her trembling lips. "Drink," he ordered, in his disguised voice.

Flidia took a drink of water and coughed. When she recovered, she drank the rest of the water in the bottle.

Tornillo replaced the tape over the girl's mouth, changed her diaper, and dressed her. He turned off the lights and left without saying a word.

The next morning he returned to the house on the golf course. He prepared a sandwich and went down to the basement. This time the comforter was still on the bed.

He approached Flidia and spoke to her.

She flinched in surprise but didn't struggle or try to say anything.

"Do you want to go to the bathroom?"

The girl nodded eagerly.

"Fine. I'll take you. If you do anything stupid, I'll kill you."

Tornillo sounded convincing, and she nodded again.

He untied her arms and helped her to sit up. He put her arms behind her back to tie them, and she grimaced in pain since her body had been in the same position for such a long time. Tornillo paid no attention and quickly tied her wrists.

Warily, he untied her legs, maintaining a sufficient distance in case she tried to kick him. But nothing happened.

He helped her stand up and guided her by the arm to the bathroom, helping her to sit.

The woman's position was unbecoming, but as soon as she was settled she defecated abundantly.

Tornillo began to feel sorry for her, but when he remembered the disdainful look she had given him, the feeling immediately disappeared.

He asked her if she had finished, and she nodded. Tornillo gently cleaned her and took her back to the improvised bed. He tied her to it again, beginning with her legs. Then he put another diaper on her and covered her with the comforter.

"Are you hungry?"

She nodded.

He removed the adhesive tape from her mouth and put

the sandwich to her lips. Flidia devoured it rapidly. Tornillo gave her more water, replaced the tape over her mouth, and left.

Flidia's disappearance was big news. Her photograph ran on television for three days. Her stepfather offered a reward to anyone who could give information on her whereabouts. But there were no clues. No one had seen her, and a police detective had even dared to suggest that she had left with someone of her own free will, since there were no signs of violence around her abandoned car.

Eventually, as generally happens with cases of missing persons, interest waned, and after two weeks there was no further mention of her in the news.

Meanwhile, Tornillo had won total control of the girl by establishing a uniform manner in which he fed her and took her to the bathroom. Now these functions were performed simply as a part of their daily routine.

In addition, Tornillo had bathed Flidia several times. With her hands tied behind her back, he had removed his own clothing and gotten into the shower with her, having to make a superhuman effort not to penetrate her right then and there. Tornillo was going to have her, of course, but not that way. He had a plan.

He tenderly soaped her body and washed her hair with shampoo that smelled of oranges.

At first Flidia made efforts to resist being touched, but he threatened to kill her, so she relented.

If Tornillo had delighted in contemplating her naked body, it was nothing compared with the pleasure of sliding his hands over her soapy skin.

When he finished bathing her, he dried her with a towel in each hand, rubbing hard to stimulate her circulation. He didn't want her body to deteriorate from lying still so long.

One night while he was bathing her, he noticed with satisfaction that her nipples were hard.

Tornillo brushed her teeth and exchanged a piece of gauze and a soft adhesive band for the packing tape covering her mouth, since removing the tape had begun to damage the girl's otherwise perfect skin.

Once a week, by candlelight and wearing a ski mask, he changed her eye patches and washed her eyes with a special solution. The light was too dim for Flidia to see any details of the room. Besides, Tornillo washed one eye at a time, always keeping the other one covered.

When he noticed that Flidia had grown accustomed to him, Tornillo permitted her to speak, but only to respond to his questions.

The first thing he asked was what her favorite foods were.

From then on Tornillo fed her the foods she liked to eat, along with a few other treats. In addition to water, he gave her wine, and he sat her up in bed to feed her so she would be more comfortable.

He questioned her about her preferences in music, and when he left at night he set the stereo to play a few hours of her favorites at a low volume.

At first she had been noticeably frightened, but as the days passed she seemed to accept her situation. Then Tornillo said, to reassure her, "I can't tell you why I brought you to this place, but you won't be here much longer. In less than a month you will be back in your house, safe and sound. I promise. I will not harm you, as long as you do as I say."

Flidia felt, somehow, that these words were truthful. The gentleness with which he had bathed her convinced her of that.

The woman had been held captive nearly twenty days when Tornillo moved on to the second part of his plan: intense physical contact.

Of course, he could have had her from the very first night. There was no one to prevent it. She belonged to him completely. But Tornillo wanted it to be different. He wanted to conquer her purity. He wanted her to love him in return.

Tornillo put her to bed alternately facedown and faceup so that her body wouldn't suffer unnecessarily. That night, he had tied her facedown. He gave her chilled champagne to drink. After a few minutes, he told her he was going to give her a massage. Her muscles needed it.

Flidia indicated dissent with her head, terrified by the idea, but he paid no attention.

He put baby oil on his hands and proceeded to massage her. Tenderly yet firmly, he began massaging from her neck down, occasionally reapplying liberal amounts of oil.

At first Flidia was very tense, but the hands were experienced, and soon she gave in to the sensations. A few minutes later, when Tornillo massaged her thighs, Flidia found herself enjoying it.

Tornillo used this technique for several days. Then he made more direct contact with her erogenous zones, always with great caution and calm. Upon feeling his soft fingers on her labia and clitoris, Flidia jumped, but he continued masturbating her, caressing her back and her well-formed buttocks with his other hand. After ten minutes, Flidia had fought all she could, and she had been beaten. Tornillo was rewarded for his efforts by a vast orgasm.

From there, he moved on to oral caresses. First he lovingly kissed her cheeks, nose, and chin, then licked her chest and nipples, kissed her navel, her pubic mound, her thighs and calves, until he ended up mercilessly licking her clitoris.

Tornillo always brushed his teeth and applied heavy amounts of cologne before visiting Flidia. He wanted to make sure he had clean breath and smelled of fresh cologne; that way, she wouldn't be quite so repelled at being touched by a stranger.

By the fourth day, Flidia didn't resist at all, and Tornillo excitedly observed how gooseflesh appeared on the young woman's buttocks with each orgasm.

He became even more tender when he bathed her and concentrated solely on performing the task at hand.

Caresses were reserved for the bed. Tornillo imagined—in a strange sort of way—that the woman would appreciate any show of respect for her.

When Flidia menstruated, he restricted himself to kissing her and lovingly caressing her hair.

Tornillo knew that Flidia would have only one clue for recognizing him in the future, and, obviously, he didn't want that to happen, so he bought a half dozen bottles of the cologne he had been wearing—all from different shops. He sent by messenger, with a false return address, a bottle to Flidia's stepfather and one to each of her friends' husbands with a brief photocopied letter in which, signing falsely as director of public relations for the company that manufactured the cologne, he invited the recipient to try the fragrance. On each bottle he attached a photocopied label reading: "Free Sample, not for resale."

A month had passed since Flidia's disappearance, and—aside from the closest members of her family and her best friends—the girl's whereabouts no longer mattered to anyone. The authorities closed the file on the case since they had other, more immediate matters to deal with. Flidia's stepfather, nevertheless, doubled the reward, and her photograph appeared every few days in the "Missing Persons" section of the newspaper.

But it was all in vain. It seemed as though Flidia had been swallowed by the earth.

The woman, meanwhile, in absolute darkness, had lost count of the days she had been held captive, and she had undergone severe personality changes. The discomfort of being constantly tied up had converted her into a spoiled child. She was fed her favorite dishes, bathed, meticulously cared for, and—most important during this recent period—had experienced more orgasms than she had in her entire life.

Her captor's scent was exquisitely manly, and she had imagined his face in a thousand different ways. At first she thought, because of his voice, he must be a troglodyte, but as time passed she realized that he was disguising it. When his body brushed against hers as he bathed her, she could feel the firmness of his muscles and the softness of his hands.

She had begun to develop feelings toward this man—

whom she had hated intensely at first—since he had been treating her with such sweetness and tenderness. One day she surprised herself by feeling eager for his arrival.

Tornillo's original plan had been to penetrate his Venus after two weeks, three at the most. In fact, his plan had been to rape Flidia as soon as she had her first orgasm. He wasn't much interested in her pleasure, but he knew that if she were well lubricated, everything would be easier for him and more humiliating for Flidia.

However, after all this time and so many caresses, he had come to truly like the woman and didn't want to hurt her. Besides, he wanted to prolong as much as possible the pleasure before the pleasure. So he didn't set a specific date, he just knew it had to be done before Ricardo and Lipia returned from Boston.

One night, as Flidia sighed in response to Tornillo's oral caresses, he stopped and, whispering into her ear, asked her if she wanted him to remove the gag. Flidia nodded eagerly, and he took the gauze off her mouth. Her lips were red and swollen. Her open mouth revealed her beautiful teeth. Tornillo returned to his labors, licking her between her thighs and kissing her already moist clitoris. Then, surprisingly, Flidia began to speak, emitting sighs of genuine pleasure. "Oh yes . . . there . . . yes . . . don't stop, please don't stop!"

Tornillo became incredibly excited when he heard her unconditional submission, and he knew that the moment had arrived. Nevertheless, before things went too far, he wanted to try something.

He continued feverishly licking her, and, when her orgasm had subsided, he moved closer to the woman's inviting mouth and kissed her softly on the lips. Flidia didn't reject him or turn away but rather reciprocated eagerly. He inserted his tongue into her mouth, conscious that the beautiful woman could rip it out with one bite. But she didn't. Flidia licked Tornillo's tongue with unbridled passion. Then he gratefully and lovingly massaged her clitoris, all the while exploring her warm mouth with his tongue.

Flidia knew that this was her opportunity to punish the criminal. One good bite would be enough to leave him mute for the rest of his damned life. But that would be crazy, not just because he could stab her to death but because she was out of her mind with pleasure.

He calmly and gently inserted his middle finger into the young woman's flooded vagina while she captured his tongue with her lips, caressing it with her own in a clear indication of the immense pleasure she was experiencing.

Although her vaginal tissues were very tight, Tornillo quickly realized that Flidia wasn't a virgin. Again he inserted his finger, this time accompanied by his index finger, and once they were well lubricated, he pulled them out and massaged her clitoris before reinserting them. Flidia was completely lost in a world of pleasure.

Several minutes later Tornillo untied her beautiful legs and undressed himself.

Still in the complete darkness in which she had lived for weeks, Flidia knew immediately what was next, and she opened her legs, preparing to receive her kidnapper into the most intimate part of her being.

* * *

From that night on their sexual games continued more or less in the same manner. Flidia now openly—*unabashedly,* she thought—enjoyed everything that Tornillo did to her.

Two weeks after the first penetration he began to walk her around the basement for exercise. He usually removed the gag from her mouth but always kept her hands tied behind her back. Tornillo did not want to risk her removing the blindfold and recognizing him.

During the walks, he would suddenly stop her and kiss her passionately on the mouth, feeling in return extreme tenderness from Flidia.

She didn't know what would become of her, but the man had promised that he would free her soon, and she trusted him. Her real fear was precisely that: being freed without knowing who her captor had been and, of course, with no hope of ever finding the man who had made her completely happy sexually.

Each day that passed would be one less in the diminishing count, and Flidia tried to enjoy each experience more than the one before.

The tenderness with which he had taken her was worthy of a fairy tale. At no time had the man shown any hint of violence, and he had never penetrated her without first having excited her completely, thereby making sure she was properly lubricated with her own juices.

Even more than that, after finishing each session, Tornillo washed her thoroughly with a warm, damp towel. He kissed her sweaty forehead and her ears, and, after putting on her favorite music—and the gag over her mouth—he said good night, promising to return the following day.

Nevertheless, each time the wait seemed longer to Flidia. She had been seized by a panic attack once when she slept most of the day and thought that two days had passed instead of one.

What if he never returned? What if something happened to him? She would die of hunger and thirst.

But her fears evaporated as soon as Tornillo arrived and helped her walk around the basement.

She told him what she had been thinking, and he said, disguising his voice, "I wouldn't abandon you for anything in the world," and, in a sudden burst of stupidity, added, "I love you, Flidia."

She knew he meant it. He must have. No one was capable of giving so much care and tenderness without being— *really*—in love. So she dared to ask, "Who are you?"

"You'll find out soon."

"Promise me."

"I promise you, my love, soon I will free you and you will know," he concluded, guiding her to the bed to begin their nightly ritual.

Of course, Tornillo had lied.

That night, while she enjoyed the longest and most satisfying orgasm of her life, Flidia exclaimed, sighing with pleasure, "I love you, too."

Nearly two months after the kidnapping, Tornillo decided he'd had enough. He felt his ego had been restored, and his libido had been satisfied to the point of physical exhaustion by his exuberant captive.

The time had come for her to return to her life.

On the designated night, Tornillo arrived at the house on the golf course in a rented car with false license plates.

They made love, the only exception on this occasion being that Tornillo, instead of leaving for his house afterward, dampened a cloth with chloroform and put Flidia to sleep. He untied her and dressed her in the clothes she had been wearing the night he kidnapped her.

He took the patches off her eyes and cleansed them thoroughly. Then he carried her to the trunk of the rented car.

Tornillo drove to the gym. It was almost two o'clock in the morning, and the place was deserted. He drove around the block to make sure no one was watching, then he parked the rented car near the entrance. He opened the trunk and gently removed the girl, sat her against the glass door of the gym, and left.

Several blocks away, he stopped at a telephone booth and called the police to tell them where to find her.

Flidia groggily opened her eyes, and immediately she noticed that the patches were gone. At first she thought she was dreaming. She closed her eyes and rubbed them. She had a sharp headache and put her hands to her temples, amazed that she could—she was no longer bound. Then she opened her eyes again, seized by panic. She tried to stand but couldn't.

She knew she was awake, but she was still dopey from the chloroform.

As she tried to stand for the second time, two city patrol cars and a federal police vehicle pulled up.

Flidia was hospitalized for several days, more to check her physical condition than for any real health problem. At first everything was blurry and light hurt her eyes, but after a few days things returned to normal.

The police began to question her about her mysterious

disappearance the night they found her, but her stepfather intervened and asked them to come back the following day.

The doctors discovered that Flidia suffered from conjunctivitis and was very weak, but apart from that she was in excellent health.

Flidia flatly refused a vaginal exam.

Finally she gave the police the details of her kidnapping. There had been at least three kidnappers. She had heard that she was in a house in the country, but she had no idea where.

No. They had not sexually abused her.

No. They had not mistreated her at any time.

No. She had no idea what their motive might have been.

The policeman who questioned her in the hospital was the same officer who had suggested that she had taken off on her own free will.

When the brief interrogation was over, the policeman left and, as he got into his car, said to his partner, "I'm sure that whore went off to screw her boyfriend and made us do all this to look like a bunch of idiots."

Tornillo, meanwhile, returned the rented car and restored Lipia and Ricardo's basement so that it looked exactly as it had before all the commotion.

As soon as he freed the girl, Tornillo changed colognes.

Flidia came back to her mother's house in a terrible state of depression. As absurd as it seemed, she had fallen in love with her mysterious captor.

The morning after she got home, the hair on the back of her neck stood on end when her stepfather gave her a kiss on the cheek as he was leaving for his office. He was wearing the cologne that she had recently come to know so well.

She began to think. Her stepfather was almost eight years younger than her mother and played tennis and squash and lifted weights. At forty-three, he was in excellent physical condition.

Could it have been him? No, it wasn't possible. Why not? She was a beautiful young woman, and she and her stepfather had lived in the same house for several years. He had seen her in a nightshirt and occasionally in her underwear. But he had never flirted or even looked at her with desire.

No, it simply wasn't possible.

But . . . why not?

In addition to the nagging questions about her stepfather, as night approached, almost like a sixth sense, Flidia experienced a rapidly growing sexual hunger. She missed her daily dose of intense sex and wasn't prepared to let it go easily. So one afternoon, while her mother was out of the house, she decided to find out whether her stepfather had been the man who had kidnapped and seduced her.

She asked herself what she would do if it had been him. She didn't know. She knew only that she needed his love—any way she could get it.

He was reading the sports section of the paper when Flidia sat on the arm of his chair. He was a little surprised by his step-daughter's behavior, but he understood that she needed affection after what had happened to her.

She put her arm over his shoulder, and he put his around her waist, distractedly, as he continued to read the paper.

Flidia misunderstood the gesture and whispered in his ear, "Why don't we go up to my room?"

The newspaper fell from her stepfather's right hand, and he immediately removed his arm from around her waist. "What did you say?"

She looked at him intensely and continued. "Don't worry about anything. You know what I want."

The man stood up and, without saying a word, left the house. The girl's mental faculties must have been affected by her recent ordeal. From now on she would have to be handled very carefully.

Flidia was totally confused by her stepfather's behavior. Had she been mistaken?

Although there were hundreds of fragrances, wasn't it more than a coincidence that he would use the same one her kidnapper had used? It had to be someone she knew. He knew her routine, and he had called her by her name. As if that weren't enough, he had said that after he freed her he would give her a clear signal by which to recognize him.

She let a few days pass and then decided to clear her doubts for once and all.

One morning, after Flidia's mother had gone to work and her stepfather was getting ready to leave, she intercepted him. "I have to ask you a question."

"Go ahead," he said cautiously.

"Do you desire me?"

"No. You are a very beautiful woman, but I have always thought of you as a daughter."

"Wasn't it you who kidnapped me?" she demanded, looking him straight in the eye.

"What are you saying?"

"You heard me."

"Flidia, I think you should see a doctor. I'm worried about your emotional condition."

His conviction made her see that she had made a grave error. He was definitely not the man she was looking for.

He left for work. That night he told his wife about the two episodes with his stepdaughter. Flidia's mother understood that her daughter would be upset after what she had suffered, but she couldn't allow it to ruin her marriage. If Flidia continued with this behavior, maybe one day her husband would not be able to resist and . . .

The next day she tried to speak with her daughter. But it was difficult. Flidia couldn't confess her motives to her mother, and she felt ashamed of the way she had acted. Her mother suggested that it might be best for everyone if Flidia moved out of the house.

So she did. Without explanation, Flidia asked Irene, one of her closest friends, if she could stay with her. Irene's husband, Roberto, had also received a free sample of cologne.

Irene welcomed her friend with open arms and told her she could stay in their house as long as she wanted.

Roberto was out of town and would return in five days. It wasn't until then, as he gave her a kiss on the cheek in greeting, that Flidia smelled him.

Of course!

Roberto was a gynecologist and had very soft hands. It must be him. Since they had met, more than ten years earlier, Roberto had always been very sweet and had flirted with her on several occasions.

Roberto had never lost hope that this gorgeous woman would become his partner in bed. And would there ever be a better opportunity than now that she was living in his own house? When Irene was away, he threw intense looks at Flidia. The girl was a little shy at first, but his insistence was such that she began to reciprocate.

One morning Flidia came out of her room with her hair still damp. She was wearing jeans and a T-shirt that clung provocatively to her beautiful chest. She looked fresh and inviting.

As she passed Roberto on the stairs, he stopped her, and said, "You look so beautiful after your shower."

"Only after my shower?"

He delicately caressed her damp hair and ventured a whisper. "I'd love to take a shower with you."

She blushed, but at the same time it gave her goose bumps. What better signal could her captor give her?

Nevertheless, she decided to wait a little longer.

Since she hadn't rejected the offer, a couple days later, Roberto pressed her again. "When are you going to let me bathe you?"

Then, to his surprise, Flidia answered, "Whenever you want."

He didn't know whether she thought it was a joke and was just humoring him.

The next day Irene went shopping and the two were left alone.

Roberto was burning with desire for Flidia and said to her in a trembling voice, "Shall we take a shower?"

She took his hands and caressed them. They were very soft. "Is it really you?" she asked.

"Of course it's me," he answered.

"I knew it," she said and kissed him passionately on the mouth.

A few minutes later they were in the shower. But Roberto didn't bathe her the way she had expected. Rather he immediately directed his caresses to the area between her legs.

Flidia thought maybe it was because of the built-up passion and didn't say anything. She was becoming very excited.

Roberto caressed her for a few minutes with his fingers, and when he felt she was sufficiently lubricated, he placed himself behind her and penetrated her savagely.

That was the last thing that Flidia had expected. This was definitely not her man. She had been mistaken again.

She fought to get away from him, but he was stronger and forced her to remain where she was. Things had gone too far to stop now.

Flidia started to shout, and that only further excited Roberto, who in a few seconds achieved his orgasm under the strong spray of hot water.

As soon as he released her, Flidia ran out of the shower.

She felt more humiliated than ever, and the worst part was that she had provoked the incident.

Completely ashamed of what had happened, Flidia decided to leave. That afternoon she thanked Irene for her kindness and, saying that she had already been too much bother, moved to another friend's house.

Roberto, winking, offered to drive her. She refused and called a taxi. By that evening she had installed herself in Aura's house. Her husband, too, had received a bottle of cologne marked "Free Sample."

Gabriel was what you would call a womanizer. As soon as he learned that Flidia was going to live with them, he set out to conquer her. He had flirted with her a couple of times in the past and on each occasion had been rejected with a gentle touch on his face, but now that he would have more extended contact with the shapely woman, he was determined to get her into bed.

But he didn't want to rush things. He had all the time in the world to win her over, so he began treating her like a prodigal daughter. Through Aura, Gabriel learned what Flidia's favorite dishes were and that was what they ate. If Flidia wanted to see a show or go to the movies, all she had to do was mention it and her desire was immediately fulfilled.

Aura wasn't upset by the attention Gabriel was giving her best friend, just the opposite. Her husband had always been very attentive with Flidia, and, taking into consideration the two horrible months she had just suffered, she deserved special treatment.

Gabriel's behavior and the smell of his cologne left little room for doubt in Flidia's mind. It had to be him. He was showing her, wasn't he? But she remembered the mistakes she had committed with her stepfather and Roberto, and decided to wait for a more obvious signal, even as she felt herself being consumed by desire for him.

Gabriel, by contrast, couldn't tolerate the situation much longer. Flidia dressed provocatively, and each day she looked more desirable. Finally, an opportunity presented itself.

Aura had gone to dinner at her parents' house, and Gabriel was preparing dinner for Flidia and himself. It was her favorite dish. Gabriel, wearing an apron, moved around the kitchen like an accomplished chef, and Flidia was happy just watching him.

While they waited for the fish to finish cooking, he poured a glass of port and, in a spontaneous gesture, held it to her lips. She drank enthusiastically, remembering the experience.

Gabriel expertly placed the fish on a plate and, standing there in the kitchen, put a morsel in Flidia's mouth. She looked intensely at him.

He was pleased. Everything indicated that he had her in his pocket.

When they finished eating, he delicately wiped her mouth with a napkin. She couldn't be mistaken. She was in the presence of her kidnapper. Flidia took Gabriel by the hand and led him to her bedroom.

They kissed passionately for several minutes while he ran his trembling hands over her body. Although Gabriel was caressing her tenderly, for some reason Flidia felt something was wrong.

He unbuttoned her blouse and her bra. He had wanted her so many times, for so long. He eagerly kissed and licked her hardened nipples. He unzipped her miniskirt, and it fell to the floor. With expert hands and great tenderness, he caressed the girl's buttocks and groin.

She forgot her fears and gave herself over to him and to the pleasure he was giving her.

Gabriel gently laid her on the bed and removed her tiny panties. Then he undressed and began licking Flidia's delicious body.

She was perfectly lubricated and he was about to enter her, when, dazzled, he commented, "Flidia, my darling . . . I always imagined that your body was beautiful, but I never thought it would be this incredible."

"What did you say?"

He was surprised by her tone and said, "I have dreamed about you a thousand times, my love, but the reality is much better than my fantasies."

Before Gabriel's astonished eyes, she stood up and, instinctively covering her groin and breasts, she asked, "Are you telling me that you've never seen me naked before?"

Stunned, he replied, "You know very well I haven't, darling."

Then Flidia quickly gathered her clothing and raced to the bathroom to dress, locking the door behind her.

Gabriel stood there naked like an imbecile, waiting as if it were all a silly joke. But after a few minutes she came out of the bathroom and asked him to leave her bedroom.

He demanded an explanation.

She said only "It's all been a misunderstanding, Gabriel. Please forgive me."

He looked at her as if she were crazy and, nodding slowly, picked up his clothes and left the room.

Later that afternoon Flidia said good-bye to Aura— Gabriel wasn't home—thanking her for her kindness, and went to her friend Olga's house. Olga was the other single girl in their group, so at her place, at least, Flidia didn't run the risk of getting involved with a man.

Flidia concluded that the fact that her stepfather and her friends' husbands used the same cologne couldn't be a coincidence.

She imagined it had been purposely arranged by her kidnapper to confuse her. But even if he had consciously deceived her, she couldn't help admiring the man's intelligence, and it only made her love him more.

She was able to confirm the love that she had experienced when, a month later, after her period was ten weeks late, her gynecologist confirmed that she was pregnant. Of course, she could have arranged a legal abortion, since her pregnancy had been the result of a rape, but she wanted the baby. If she was never going to find her man, she at least wanted to have something from him. What better than a child?

She moved to another city and got a job. She was very competent and didn't have any trouble in finding a good position. As time passed she accepted the fact that she would never again be caressed as she had during her captivity.

Months passed, and Flidia gave birth to a seven-and-a-half-pound baby boy. As the child grew, she thought he reminded her of someone, but she couldn't quite determine who.

Years went by, and one day she returned to her native city. She happened to run into Tornillo's wife in a shopping mall and was invited to dinner.

While Teresa, Tornillo, and Flidia were drinking an aperitif, Tornillo's son appeared. Flidia almost choked when she saw him. He was identical to her son.

The next day she invented a pretext for seeing Tornillo. He welcomed her into his office and closed the door as she had asked.

Without hesitating, Flidia said with complete certainty, "It was you who seduced me."

"I beg your pardon?" Tornillo said, feigning complete surprise.

"Last night, when I saw your son, I realized it. He's identical to my son . . . our son."

"I don't know what you're talking about."

"Please, Tornillo, don't pretend. You can't imagine what I have gone through trying to find you. You don't know how it has been to live without you."

"Excuse me, Flidia, but I really don't know what you're talking about."

The woman grew impatient and got up from her chair. Tornillo also stood, fearing that she might attack him.

But that didn't happen. She put her arms around his neck and, leaning close to his face, said, "I forgive you, my love. I forgive you, but just hold me. I beg you, my darling, make love to me!"

Tornillo removed the girl's arms and softly but firmly said, "Look, Flidia, years ago I would have done it with pleasure. I loved your innocence, but you have changed too much, and I don't like loose women."

Then he took her by the arm and led her to the door. "Good-bye, Flidia." Tornillo closed the door behind her.

Flidia thought she had been mistaken again and left feeling humiliated and ashamed. But at least, she consoled herself, Tornillo had acted like a gentleman and hadn't tried to take advantage of the misunderstanding.

ORQUÍDEA

I HAD BEEN invited to give a lecture on decorating to a Catholic women's group. I had always been a firm believer in sharing what little knowledge one might have. Especially when one can get a free meal and charge for the nonsense one shares. I had studied architecture, and a twist of fate had sent me on a scholarship to Paris to study interior design. I learned many things in the City of Light, the most important of which was how to lead a bohemian life.

The evening of the lecture, I had hardly begun speaking when a tall, thin girl, about eighteen or nineteen, entered the room. To my good fortune, she took a seat near the podium, where I could observe her as I recited from memory a lot of foolishness.

When the farce was over, the twenty or so women present applauded and the club's president took the microphone and invited the guests to an adjacent room for refreshments. I worked things so that I would be near the girl who had caught my attention, and, once I was beside her, I was even more taken with her beauty. She had enormous green eyes, like a pair of finely shaped emeralds but even more precious. Her nose wasn't perfect, but it fit her face as if purposefully molded slightly to the right. Her upper lip was impossibly sensual, and the lower one gave me an immediate urge to nibble it. All this was crowned with exquisite chestnut hair, which cascaded over her shoulders in waves.

She wore loose clothing, which, far from disguising her figure, made me concentrate on the hidden curves and voluptuous labyrinths that could easily have become an obsession and, if one weren't careful, could drive one crazy.

I quickly started up a conversation with her, ignoring the rest of the guests, who were just a bunch of noisy, disagreeable old ladies. I decided not to risk losing this opportunity or waste my time, so, as we said good-bye, I invited her to dinner, preferably later that week. To my surprise, she accepted without wavering. But there was one small condition: her parents were old-fashioned and would want me to appear at her house so they could meet me and see "the class of person" I was.

I didn't like that sort of thing, but as I contemplated Orquídea's beauty, I accepted without hesitation.

I had borrowed my friend Francisco's car for the occasion since mine was nearly worn out and borrowed a good amount of cash from my friend Fernando. That night, whatever happened, I wasn't going to scrimp on anything.

I wore my best suit, of the two I owned, and a freshly ironed shirt. My cologne was nearly gone, so I had to open a new bottle, which I had planned to give Fernando for his birthday.

When I looked at myself in the mirror before leaving the

house, I could hardly believe what I saw. For Orquídea, I had become the perfect bourgeois gentleman. I was eager to make sure that I made the right impression on the beautiful girl's parents.

I parked Francisco's red sports car right in front of her house and rang the bell.

After an eternity with no response, I grew nervous and rang the bell again. Meanwhile, an endless string of paranoid thoughts filled my head. What if all this had been a youthful prank and Orquídea didn't even live in this house? Or maybe she was nearby with a group of friends, watching me, and would die of laughter when they saw how I was dressed.

I took a pack of cigarettes from my jacket and, with a trembling hand, lit one.

Aeons, or so I thought, had passed since I had rung the bell, and still no one answered. I threw the newly lit cigarette into the street and immediately lit another. I was seriously thinking of honking the car horn repeatedly when a dog began to bark inside the house. I rang the bell again, and, not content with that, I began to pound on the door with my fist.

If any of my friends had seen me at that instant, they would not have recognized me. I was very nervous and desperate to see Orquídea.

As I walked toward the car with the firm intention of alerting the whole neighborhood, I heard a sour voice. "Who is it?" The voice was almost feminine.

At first I wasn't sure if my imagination was playing tricks on me or if the dog had gotten bored and started speaking.

Then the question was repeated in the same unhappy tone. "Who is it?"

The tone of voice made me feel like a kid who had been misbehaving.

"It's me, Javier," I answered.

My nerves were frayed from the waiting, and the words stuck in my throat, making me speak in a ridiculous voice that wasn't my own.

"Jaime who?" the voice on the other side of the door wanted to know, between barks from the dog—or maybe there were two dogs?

"Not Jaime," I answered indignantly. "It's Javier."

Still without opening the door to the street, the voice inside wanted to know more. "Which Javier?" it asked.

I didn't know if Orquídea had notified the people in her house that a guy named Javier was coming by to take her to dinner, but the situation was rapidly tiring me. However, as soon as I thought about those green eyes, which would be looking at me for a good part of the night, I calmed myself and politely answered the woman on the other side of the door.

"I've come for Orquídea. We're going out to dinner."

At that moment the dogs started barking louder. Now I was sure it was three or four animals—and large ones.

The voice was silent, allowing the animals to intimidate me with their barking. Finally there was a response. "I will go tell her."

The barking drifted off into the distance, and I stood there in complete silence for several minutes.

Just as I was about to ring the bell again, the dogs approached and another voice—this time masculine—began to interrogate me. "Who is it?" the voice asked softly but firmly.

I began to think that the whole thing had been a big joke and that I would stand there until five or six people asked me the same idiotic question. Then, suddenly, the door would probably open a little and a gang of boys about the age of my goddess would appear on the doorstep, closing the door behind them and laughing at me hysterically.

Even still, I answered, almost shouting to be heard over the barking.

"It's Javier. I have a date with Orquídea to go out to dinner. Would you be so kind as to tell her that I am here?"

Again silence, then finally, the firm voice. "I'm going to open the door. There's a dog inside. He doesn't bite, but don't get too close to him and don't pet him."

I heard the sound of a bolt being slid aside. The door opened inward.

On the other side, a man of about fifty wearing a plaid flannel shirt studied me from head to toe, with the door standing open and with his left hand hidden. Perhaps—I imagined—he was holding a weapon or maybe restraining the dog that had been barking so anxiously, demanding my bones for dinner.

Once I had passed the visual inspection, the man opened the door a little more and allowed me to enter, murmuring, as if in secret, "Go straight into the house. I'll take care of the dog."

I couldn't contain my curiosity, and I looked over my shoulder at the dog. It was a cocker spaniel, but with the personality of a Doberman. It was so small that if there had been a sign saying "Beware of Dog," it would have been more to protect the animal from being stepped on than for fear that anyone would be attacked by it.

I passed through a pleasant garden and arrived at the house. I tried to open the front door, but it was locked.

Since the man in charge of the wild beast had told me to go straight into the house—I certainly had no other intention—I tried once more to open the door, this time using more strength, but it still wouldn't budge.

I was puzzling over this when the dog handler arrived. "Not through there," he murmured. "We hardly ever open that door. I hope you don't mind going through the kitchen."

I wanted to shout that I did mind. Especially after all the trouble I had taken to dress respectably. But the man was already on his way to a door at the rear of the house.

I closed my eyes for an instant to think about the beauty waiting for me inside that house of crazy people and then followed him.

We went through a filthy kitchen that reeked of garlic. Then a large serving pantry, where a child of about three was making a mess with a glass of milk and some cookies. "My grandson," said my guide conspiratorially. "Violeta's son." I nodded as if I had known Violeta all my life and followed him into a large living room.

"Sit down," ordered the man who had opened the door and saved me from being devoured by the cocker spaniel. He headed for some badly worn wooden stairs, and I pulled out my cigarettes. I desperately needed one, but the man turned his head and gave me a look that made me put the tobacco back in my pocket.

After that look I decided it would be better to respect the rules of the house, so I sat down. The cushions were soft, but they had seen better days. A cloud of dust arose as I settled on the sofa.

Since Orquídea was taking a while, I had time to study the room. That living room was like the set from a fifties horror movie.

There was a fireplace that looked as if it had never been used. On the mantel several figurines that looked like Lladró and others that looked like Chinese porcelain were crowded together.

I didn't dare abandon the relative security of the sofa to examine them more closely, but I imagined that the figurines were covered in rancid dust. In fact, the entire house smelled old.

Two table lamps crowned a pair of mismatched tables at each end of the sofa where I sat. One was a poor imitation of the *Venus de Milo* in gold and white—the white parts were where the gold paint had been chipped off the plaster. The other looked like some kind of Atlas holding up a shade, which must once have been beige and was now heavily stained.

The room was horribly depressing and discomforting. I was ready to leave that place. With or without Orquídea. Without being able to smoke, I tried to calm myself, but it was impossible. The low mumbling of a television on the upper floor added a sense of foreboding and brought disagreeable images to mind.

When I looked at my watch, I was astonished to see that barely ten minutes had passed since I had parked Francisco's car at the front door of the house. The expression "bad vibration" perfectly described the feeling I had in this house.

After rearranging myself on the sofa several times and abandoning my fear of impregnating the suit with dust, I heard steps at the top of the stairs, accompanied by the sound of creaking wood, as if the floor, too, were complaining about the wait. As if in a military parade, the man who had opened the door preceded a tall woman, who must once have been very beautiful but who now had a bitter face. She was followed by a beautiful but fat young woman, and then finally came my dream, Orquídea.

I hurried to get up from my seat. I wanted above all to create a good impression. It seemed curious, but Orquídea's father and I hadn't yet introduced ourselves. Now very cordially—I noted that he had put a sport coat on over his flannel shirt—he introduced me to his wife, Lila, and his fat daughter, Violeta, who was the mother of the child in the serving pantry.

I anxiously searched Orquídea's eyes for something to make me feel more at ease, but she had diverted them in what I interpreted to be an act of great timidity.

We all five sat down.

"Would you like something to drink, engineer?" asked the father, who I thought logically should have been called Chrysanthemum or Carnation but who had been baptized with the name Miguel.

"No. Thank you very much. And, by the way, I'm an architect."

At that moment, the thought passed through my mind that if I had accepted a drink, they would surely have brought me lemonade. That was how things were going.

"Wouldn't you like a glass of lemonade? Or maybe some chamomile tea, architect?"

"No. That's very kind of you," I answered, trying to stifle a smile of self-satisfaction.

Until then, I could more or less manage. I was just getting to know the botanical menagerie that constituted Orquídea's family.

"Well," said Miguel, clearing his throat, "then if you don't mind, I'll get right to the point."

This was beginning to take the shape of a business meeting. Orquídea's mother and sister were the witnesses, and she was the merchandise. I had felt somewhat uncomfortable with the situation from the beginning, but now I was finding it unbearable. The only thing that kept me there—besides fate—was Orquídea's presence. She was wearing a white dress with matching socks, and her hair was gathered back, slightly stretching her forehead and giving her face an even more sensual appearance although, for her parents' benefit, still completely virginal.

Miguel was still getting to the point. "Our family is very close-knit, architect. We have always stayed together, in good times and bad. We are practicing Catholics and believe in good moral values and proper behavior."

Clearing his throat again, he got to the heart of the matter. "Are you Catholic, architect?"

In other circumstances the answer would have taken a while to leave my mouth, especially because—as best I could remember—my first communion had also been my last, and on the one occasion I went to confession, the penitence had been so extensive that I just let things stay as they were. But the ambience in that house was so similar to that of a medieval monastery that I answered immediately, and convincingly.

"Yes, sir. Everyone in my family is a practicing Catholic." I was tempted to add that we, too, had some good moral values and all that stuff, but I decided it was better to quit without saying any more.

"How wonderful!" proclaimed Orquídea's father. "Then we'll be better able to communicate in the future."

The guy must have been a total optimist, since I couldn't see any future whatsoever between this very Catholic family and me. But I let him continue. The charade had already gone too far to stop.

He continued with his sermon. "My daughter Violeta, here before you, was dating Juan, my son-in-law, who is not here before you, for a period of eight months. Then they got married."

Clearing his throat once again, he continued. "I am not so antiquated as to require you and my daughter Orquídea to be accompanied by a chaperone—like Violeta, for example—but I am going to ask you the favor of giving me a brief summary of your life. If you don't mind."

That was too much. Even for a beauty like Orquídea. But there I was in the middle of this mess, and departing then and there would have left me as bad off as or worse than just continuing. So, gathering my prudence and patience, I softly answered. "Well, as I have said, we are a family of practicing Catholics." Inexplicably, I, too, stopped to clear my throat. I was dying for a cigarette, but I knew that was entirely out of the question.

"My parents get along very well and are very similar to you and your wife."

That was far from the truth. My father had run off with his

secretary when I was twelve, and my mother had married again, divorced, then married a third time, a man fifteen years younger than she, who subsequently took off with the little she had left to her name.

"I went to Catholic schools."

I omitted that I had been expelled from them for speaking badly of the Virgin and the saints, in whom I most certainly did not believe.

"I am single." I cleared my throat, though this last bit was true. I'll never know why I ended by saying, "And I am looking for a girl like me, with the same background, to share my life with."

That said, Doña Lila—who had been staring at me the way a colonel from Hitler's SS would eye a rabbi—gave a great big, satisfied smile.

Meanwhile, Orquídea looked bored. Who knows how many times the poor girl had had to go through this routine?

Even when the lies had reached an almost unbelievable limit, I kept going.

"As I mentioned earlier, I am an architect. Right now I am working on a project with a tire company, whose name I cannot divulge. However, I can tell you that the project is a thirty-five-story building." Which was true. "And in all modesty, I have had a brilliant and successful career." Which wasn't true.

Everything I said could have been true, judging from my suit, Fernando's cologne, Francisco's car, and a Rolex I had won years ago playing poker with some friends. I was really pushing the limits and it had gotten late, so I decided to close my mouth and gauge the flowery family's reaction.

Then the kid with the milk and cookies made his appearance. "You creep, this is not your house. This is my grand-father's house," he said to me suddenly. To complete the warm greeting, he stuck out a tongue covered with traces of cookie and milk.

I couldn't do anything but smile, though my face felt like cardboard and I feared that at any moment it would begin to disintegrate.

Violeta raised her heavy rear from her chair as if a poison-ous insect had bitten her and headed threateningly toward the tiny monster. She dragged him from the room to another part of the house—a dungeon, perhaps—surely to teach him some good manners.

I still wasn't certain what was going on when I heard the little ruffian start to cry. Apparently, the delinquent was being taught the Catholic way!

"Excuse the interruption, architect," said Doña Lila breathily.

"Don't mention it. He's just a child."

"Well then, architect, we won't keep you any longer," said Don Miguel, leading me to believe that I had passed the exam and could go out with his beautiful daughter. "I just want to ask you a favor."

"Anything you say, Don Miguel," I replied with apprehen-sion. I imagined a myriad of crazy scenarios, like having to go to mass or take communion before dinner, or pray the rosary. That night anything was possible.

Clearing his throat, the gorgeous girl's father ordered rather than asked. "We want you to be back here no later than one o'clock. Our daughter is very precious to us, and we know that it is dangerous to be out in the streets after that, so please, architect, one o'clock at the latest if you would be so kind."

I felt as if I had been drugged by all the happenings in that ugly house, so I accepted immediately, adding that I was in complete agreement with the curfew and that it was, indeed, very dangerous in the city at night, even before one o'clock.

I cast a discreet glance at my watch. It was nine-thirty.

Usually with the women that I was used to going out with, at one or two in the morning the fun was just starting. Well, whatever.

Doña Lila blessed us both, making Orquídea kiss her fingers after she had made the sign of the cross with them. Then Don Miguel escorted us to the door, assuring us that he would handle the dog.

Before getting back to the normality of the outside world, I turned my head instinctively toward a lit window on the second floor. There was the lonely little boy with his face pressed against the glass sticking his tongue out at me again.

Don Miguel begged us to be careful and solemnly entrusted me with the security and physical integrity of his precious daughter.

Finally, we got into Francisco's car and drove away. I was quiet and pensive, and still had not completely taken in what had just happened.

Less than two blocks from the holy house, Orquídea dug in her bag and pulled out a couple of items. Curiously, it was the first time she had spoken that night, and, with a voice that hardly sounded appropriate for the daughter of a practicing Catholic family, she said simply, "Do you mind if I take a hit?"

I frowned and tilted my head slightly, trying to figure out what the hell she was talking about. "A cucumber?"

"Yeah. Once Oscar left and I got myself together, I started practicing my skill on a cucumber until I could buy a dildo. I knew that one day I would be blessed with a man that would take my body, mind, and soul places I had never been, so I started practicing. I'm glad that my intuition was right and that I listened to it. I would like to believe that you're extremely satisfied."

"Shit, that ain't even an accurate description of how I feel."

She chuckled as I helped her from the countertop and dried her off. Tonight couldn't have been any better. But I knew I would be thinking about this shit until I could experience it again. After putting on some sorts, I put the food away and put dishes in the dishwasher, feeling absolutely exhausted. If Jennifer could make me feel this way in less than an hour, I wouldn't need a hobby. I'd need a masseuse and sleep.

J ennifer

I WAS tired as hell after fucking with Vance's ass last night. Once I put those skills on him, he couldn't get enough. I had to come home just so I could get some rest. I wasn't complaining, though, because the last four, nearly five years without sex had been a struggle. It didn't take much to turn me on. Simply watching two people kiss passionately in a movie had me on one. I didn't know what had made me think I would be able to hold out with him. I barely made it a whole twenty-four hours.

When I left this morning, he had a hard time letting me go. I knew if I stayed there with him, my restraint would be non-existent. We would have been fucking until I completely passed out. After getting home, I collapsed in my bed and stayed there for about four hours, until Meena showed up with Belan. She looked as tired as I did. "Hey, Meena. You feel okay, baby?"

"I'm fine. Just tired. I should be asking if you're okay."

"I'm fine. Yo' daddy just a savage, that's all."

"Ugh!" she said, rolling her eyes.

I giggled as Belan excitedly reached for me. "I'm glad you two are getting along well. I was so tired, I didn't bathe Belan last night."

"I got her, don't worry. Can she stay a couple of nights with me?"

"Oh, God, thank you," she said as tears fell from her eyes.

"Meena, what's going on, baby?"

"I've just been having to do everything. It's like because of what Tyrone's parents are going through, he's checked out on us. Besides going to work, he stays with his dad almost all night. He comes here until dinner, then he leaves. When he comes home, we're asleep. I'm so worn out... physically and emotionally. Please don't tell Daddy."

"I won't. But your dad isn't the man you think he is. He likes Tyrone and I believe he would be there for encouragement and help. Y'all get yourselves together and don't worry about Belan for as long as you can stand to leave her. Okay? If you need to take time off to get things straight, do that."

"Mama... really?"

"Really. Pack her some things when you get off work and me and your daddy will take care of her."

She hugged me tightly as tears continued streaming down her cheeks. "I really appreciate that. I probably won't be able to go without seeing her but having your support in the evenings and at night means the world to me. I'm gonna be sure to try to talk to Tyrone this evening before he leaves. I love Mr. George, but Tyrone is going to have to find a way to support all of us. Mr. George and his job are getting all of his attention and Belan and I are left with nothing."

"Why don't you let Vance talk to him?"

"I don't want him to feel like I'm talking about him. He's somewhat on-guard with Daddy. I'll use that as a last resort."

"Okay, baby. I understand. Just know that you don't have to suffer in silence. Even if you don't want to talk to me, you know all the programs and support groups out there. I love the two of y'all so much. You're both sweet and amazing people and you deserve to be happy. Even if you have to go to Mr. George's house with him, do that."

"That's a good idea, Mama. Well, I have to go. I'll put in for the rest of the week off and try to spend as much time with Tyrone as I can."

"Okay, baby. Belan, tell Mommy bye."

She waved with a huge smile on her face as Meena waved at her. I felt so sorry for her and not being able to talk to Vance about what was going on was gonna be impossible. He would question why Belan was with me every night or why we couldn't do whatever. Bringing lil mama to the highchair in my kitchen, I sat her there as I fixed her oatmeal. She absolutely loved oatmeal and bananas.

As I prepared it, she played with her rattle, making all kinds of noise. I was tired as hell. As I poured the warm milk, my cell phone rang. Figuring it was Vance, I answered without paying attention. He was the only one who called me anyway. "Hey, baby."

"Hey. I haven't really been able to sleep since you left. You're spoiling me," he said huskily.

I chuckled and asked, "Why don't you come over and meet me and your BeBe?"

Her eyes widened as I spoke. She was entirely too smart. Only one person called her BeBe. She knew exactly who. "Na-Na-Na-Na," Belan said repeatedly as she banged her rattle on the highchair.

"I will."

"I will have you know that I'm tired as hell, too. It's all your fault."

"No the hell it ain't. You didn't tell me your mouth was a human vacuum. Because I had no warning, I can't be responsible for my response to that shit."

I laughed as he chuckled as well. "I'll be there shortly, Queen. We can take a nap around ten, then go to lunch at one or so."

"Okay. You want something to eat? I'm about to cook a little something for me."

"Can you do me some eggs and rice?"

"I got'chu, King."

I ended the call and smiled, then took the leftover rice from the fridge. After putting a little water in it and sliding it in the microwave, I grabbed a few eggs from the fridge, butter, and a couple of Zummo sausage links. Vance was gonna have me gaining weight if we didn't start exercising more. After getting everything prepped, I fed my baby her oatmeal. She'd started whining, so I knew she was hungry. Belan was a happy baby, so there was always a good reason for her to whine. She was hungry, sleepy, or had a dirty diaper. With as much as we catered to her, one would think she would be spoiled as well, but not so.

After I fed her, I let her play in her highchair while I cooked. I knew it wouldn't be long before she *really* needed a bath. After I separated our food into two bowls, the doorbell rang. I looked at Belan and said, "PaPa's here!"

She smiled big and started to kick her legs. Taking her from her highchair, we went to the door. I swung the door open and my smile dropped from my face, becoming a frown. Glancing at Belan, she was no longer smiling, either. "Why are you here, Oscar?"

"I just wanted to apologize for my attitude in the grocery store. You obviously have my number blocked on your phone because I've called a couple of times."

My frown was still present as I said, "Yeah. You're blocked. I have no reason to talk to you."

"Jennifer, please. I'm trying to make things right. I accept responsibility for our failed marriage. I messed up and blamed you for it. That was wrong and I sincerely apologize."

My frown lifted some because of his words, but I didn't trust his ass as far as I could throw him. Oscar wasn't a small man. So, that obviously meant I didn't trust his ass at all. He reminded me of the fire chief on the TV show, *Chicago Fire*. Glancing at Belan again, I looked back at him and said, "I accept your apology. Now, you should go."

"Well, before I do, I also wanted to see if I could take you to lunch, maybe tomorrow, since you are babysitting today."

"Oscar, you know I'm seeing Vance."

"It's just a friendly lunch, Jennifer. While I would love to have you back in my life, I know of your involvement with Vance."

"Then you should know that I'm not that kind of woman. You were married to me for twenty years. I would never disrespect the man I'm involved with. That man is now Vance Etienne, whether you like it or not. But I need you to respect that."

He lifted his hands in surrender just as Vance drove in the driveway. *Shit!* I was hoping he would have been gone before Vance got here. He turned to see Vance getting out of his car and smirked. "I guess I better leave you to your... man. Although I don't know what you would want with an ex-con."

"Leave, now, before that ex-con whoops yo' ass. I dare you to say all that shit to him."

Oscar gave me a cynical grin, then walked away as Vance approached with a serious frown on his face. I'd never seen a look so lethal. When they passed one another, no words were spoken, but they were giving each other looks that could kill. They were now enemies and I seemed to be right in the middle of the shit. Oscar needed to grow up and move the hell on. He wasn't worried about me until he knew Vance was seeing me. Belan began kicking her legs, fanning her funk as Vance approached. His frown disintegrated as he said, "Hey, PaPa's BeBe!"

He grabbed her from me and came in the house. "Oooh, BeBe,

you a lil rank, baby."

I smiled slightly as I took her from him and put her in her high-chair. Putting my hand to his face, I kissed his lips and said, "Good morning. Have a seat."

His excitement had faded, and I hoped he wasn't angry with me. It wasn't my fault Oscar showed up here. I put his food in the microwave for a moment, then poured him a glass of orange juice. I didn't bother warming mine because my stomach was nervous. As I brought it to him, he said, "You gonna tell me what's going on?"

That was the first words he'd spoken to me, so I knew he was upset. "Yeah. I just wanted to get your food ready."

After wrapping mine up, I walked around to him and sat next to him on a bar stool. The frown was back on his face and I could see his jaw clinching. "The doorbell rang, and I assumed it was you. I didn't bother looking out the peephole. He claims that he came to apologize for the grocery store incident and wanted to take me to lunch. I read him his rights and that was when you drove up."

"See... he's trying to provoke me. I know a setup when I see one. You okay?"

"Yeah," I said, then got up to get Belan from her highchair.

Since I wasn't eating, I might as well get her cleaned up. As I was walking away, he stood and pulled me to him. "I'm sorry, baby. Good morning, and thank you for the food."

He kissed my lips and I nodded, then continued to the back with Belan. I thought it was weird how he took his anger with Oscar being there out on me. He was so giddy with Belan, so I knew it was meant to be directed at me. Although he put his atti-tude in check *after* I explained, I was a little irritated by that. As I ran her bath water and got her little tub situated in the big tub, she kicked and screamed in excitement. She loved her baths. Taking her to the countertop, I laid her there and took her clothes and diaper off, then cleaned her bottom.

I briefly thought about removing her tub and getting in with her, but I knew I would fall asleep if I did. I checked the temperature of the water, then put her in. She immediately started splashing water everywhere. Shaking my head, I chuckled at her excitement. I didn't hear Vance enter the bathroom, but I could feel that he was standing there. Coming closer to me as I sat on the floor alongside the tub, he said, "Jennifer..."

When I looked up at him, he knelt down on the floor beside me. After taking a deep breath, he said, "The situation with Oscar bothers the hell out of me. It takes me a minute to separate you from his bullshit. I'm so sorry, Queen. That's not your fault. It's mine."

I nodded as Belan started screaming, "Na-Na-Na-Na!"

I couldn't help but smile at her, despite my hurt feelings. The situation was understandable, and at least he recognized his error. Looking back at him, I slid my hand over his cheek. "It's okay."

"No, it's not okay, but please say you forgive me. I'll do better next time."

"I forgive you, and hopefully, there won't be a next time."

He kissed my head and said, "I hope you're right."

I smiled at him, then began washing baby girl and her hair. Sliding his arm around my waist as I went to my knees to handle her better only made me even more sensitive to him. "Jenn, the food was good. Let me finish taking care of BeBe so you can eat."

"I'm not really hungry. Plus, I have to give the princess her massage."

"Massage?"

"Yeah. I rub her down with Baby Magic. She loves it."

He chuckled as I rinsed off Belan. She screamed and played in the water as it sprayed from the handheld spout. Her mood always lightened mine, no matter how I was feeling. When I picked her up, I wrapped her in a towel and brought her to the room, Vance right on my heels. When we got to my room where her bag and bottle were, I sat on the bed and dried her more thoroughly. Vance gently rubbed my cheek as he watched me take care of Belan. I couldn't believe he had me feeling so vulnerable and sensitive.

When I laid her down on the bed and had gotten her lotion from the bag, Vance had taken over her. He was tickling her, and she was screaming in laughter. I could only laugh in response to their interaction. Putting some lotion in my hands, I began rubbing her down as she tried to divide her attention between Vance and me. It was too cute watching her look from him to me. "Vance, can you get her a onesie from the drawer?"

"Of course. Which one?"

After pointing him in the direction of the drawer, I turned back to Belan to find her eyes on me. "You enjoyed your bath, baby girl? I have a bottle ready for you once I get your clothes on."

I could see that she was tired. Her belly was semi-full, and she was clean. That bottle would send her right on in, and I planned to go right on in with her. After rubbing her down, I put on her diaper and the onesie Vance had brought to me. "Are you still gonna nap with us?" I asked Vance.

"No. I'll go in the front room, so y'all can rest. I'm fully awake now."

I didn't know how I would sleep now, knowing that he was here. I was hoping he would have gotten in bed with us anyway. Sleeping in his arms was the best feeling in the world. He was probably still bothered by the things I said about Oscar. Hopefully, Oscar would leave well enough alone, so I could move on with Vance in peace, but for some reason, I didn't feel like he would. Getting in the bed with Belan, she did something I'd just recently acknowledged she didn't do... whine.

I held her close, then gave her a bottle and she calmed down. She shouldn't have been hungry, but she probably wanted her PaPa. I stroked her hair and whispered, "I want PaPa, too."

She looked up at me with her big, brown eyes as she sucked her bottle and I saw the tear trickle from her eye. I gently wiped her cheek as she laid her hand on my face and wiped mine. I didn't even realize I'd lost a tear. He had us both spoiled and it was ridiculous, being that he was here in the same house.

13

V ance

I COULDN'T LAY in bed with Jennifer and Belan. I felt so much rage, it was hard to contain. Seeing Oscar at the door when I arrived, gave me almost the same feeling as I had ten years ago. Knowing the trauma he caused her, it was extremely hard to keep my cool around him. I was thankful he left and didn't say a word to me. It wasn't my intent to take that out on Jennifer. What I was thinking when I walked in her house right past her without speaking was still a mystery to me. I didn't even realize what I'd done until I noticed her demeanor toward me. She was hurt that I seemed cold toward her for something she had no control over.

As I paced back and forth in her front room, I decided to just clean the kitchen while I was trying to exert this negative energy. After I finished, I was still on one. Going to the couch, I went to my knees and prayed that the Lord would soothe my soul... take away the rage I was feeling. I prayed that he would take the desire to mess around with Jennifer and me from Oscar's heart. Not having control can be a horrible feeling. I'd felt it before, and it took me a few years to get over what happened when I did. I lost control when I killed Chop. Losing control this time was not an option.

Thankfully, when I stood to my feet, I felt so much better. I needed God to answer my prayer instantly, because everything in me wanted to take a ride to that damn fire station and fuck him up while my ladies were sleeping. Standing to my feet, I walked to the back room to see that they were asleep. After closing the door on them, my cell phone began ringing. When I looked at the caller ID, I saw it was Tyrone calling. He never really called me. "Hello?"

"Hey, Eti. How's your day going?"

"It's good, son. How about yours?"

"It's been long already and it's only ten-thirty. Can you do me a favor?"

"Yeah, sure. What is it?"

"My dad isn't answering his phone and I'm scared as hell. You think you can go check on him for me?"

"Yeah. What's the address?"

After giving me the address on Bristol Drive, I went outside and programmed it in my car, then sent Jenn a text. *Hey, baby. I left to go check on Mr. George for Tyrone. I didn't want to wake you. I'll be back.*

Heading that direction, I was somewhat worried, too. Since Donna had left him, I knew he wasn't doing well. Addiction was real and it also made me nervous for Tyrone and Meena. Tyrone seemed to be following in his father's footsteps. I liked him a lot and he seemed to be good to my daughter, so I knew I needed to have a talk with him. I looked at him as a son and I wanted to see him and Meena's marriage be everything they dreamed of it being the day they said, 'I do.'

After about ten minutes, I'd gotten to Mr. George's house and there were two cars in the driveway. I didn't take that to mean anything. I'd only seen one of their cars. Who knew how many they had? I didn't. Getting out, I looked around, checking my surroundings as I often found myself doing, then walked to the front door. I rang the bell and waited. While I waited, I could hear some shuffling inside, then after a minute or so, the door opened.

Mr. George was standing there with a look of shock on his face. Damn. He looked sober. "Mr. Etienne, hello. What are you doing here?"

"Hey, Mr. Mills. You can call me Vance. Tyrone called me, slightly panicking because you weren't answering your phone. He asked me to come check on you."

He smiled, then opened the door further. When he did, I saw Donna sitting on the couch. "We're trying to work through things. I turned my phone off to make sure she had my undivided attention, something I'd neglected giving her for years. Can you tell him that I'm fine?"

"I sure will. I'm glad that y'all are talking."

"Thank you, Vance. I appreciate that. My son has an amazing father-in-law."

I shook his hand and said, "Thanks, George. I'm glad y'all are on the road to healing."

He nodded, so I walked away, and he closed the door. I breathed out a sigh of relief. Getting in the car, I called Tyrone and he answered on the first ring. "Eti, please tell me everything is okay."

"It is. He powered his phone off and he and your mom were talking, trying to work through their issues."

I could hear him release a nervous breath, then he said, "Thank you so much for going check on him."

"No problem. Now, I know you saw the path your father was on. I need you to get the drinking under control before it gets out of hand."

"I know. Can y'all keep Belan for a couple of days? I've really been neglecting my wife since all this went down with my dad.

She's tired and I'm afraid that if I don't do something soon, she might leave me."

"Meena ain't leaving until she's exhausted every avenue to try to make it work. And I will gladly keep my BeBe. Thank you for sharing your mistakes with me, son. Keep the lines of communication open with your wife at all times, okay? That will prevent y'all from sinking into depths that neither of you may be able to pull yourselves out of. She loves you and I can tell that you love her. Don't worry about Belan. Me and Jennifer got her."

"Thanks, Eti. I appreciate it so much."

"No problem."

I ended the call and headed back to Jennifer's house. Meena hadn't talked to me about having any problems. If Tyrone thought that she might leave him, it had to have gotten pretty serious. After driving for a couple of minutes, it dawned on me why she didn't tell me. *You killed her last boyfriend.* I slid my hand down my face. Meena was afraid of my temper... that I would hurt Tyrone. She didn't realize that there was a difference between Tyrone and what that nigga, Chop, did to her. They were having issues that every married couple had... communication issues.

Chop put his hands on my daughter. That was totally different than what she and Tyrone were going through. He was a good guy. He just didn't know how to handle the stress of looking after his dad without neglecting his family. Thankfully, his dad was fine, so they could work on their marriage sooner than later. Now, I needed to work on what Jennifer and I had. Before going back to her house, I stopped to the grocery store and bought some flowers and sliced pineapples. Jenn loved fruit, particularly pineapples and strawberries. Of course, I bought my BeBe something, too.

When I got to her house, she and Belan were outside and it looked as if they were about to go walking. She never responded to my text, so I wondered if she'd gotten it. When I got out the car, she said, "Hey."

"Hey. Did you get my text?"

"No," she said, then lowered her head.

I walked over to her to see her eyebrows scrunched together, not frowning, but like she was gonna cry at any moment. "Jenn, what's wrong?"

"When we woke up and you weren't here, I assumed you'd left because you were angry. I never even thought to check my phone. I'm so sorry."

I grabbed her hand and kissed it, then walked back to the car to get her flowers and fruit. When she saw the lilies, she smiled big. "I'd gone to go check on Mr. George for Tyrone. He was fine and Mrs. Donna was there. They are trying to work things out."

"I'm sorry, baby, for making an assumption. I'm glad Mr. George is okay. And the flowers are beautiful."

"Let's go back in the house for a minute."

"Okay."

When we got inside, I handed Jennifer the bag and took Belan from her stroller. "Ooohh, pineapples! I'm gonna save these for when they can be put to good use."

I laughed and shook my head as I covered my mouth with my fist. "You nasty. Tyrone asked if we could keep BeBe for a couple of days. He and Meena are having some issues and he wants to spend quality time with her."

"That's good. Meena and I talked this morning."

My eyebrows had risen. Well, at least she talked to someone. "Yeah, I need to talk to my daughter. I think she believes because of what I did, that anyone who hurts her, whether it's physically or emotionally, would cause me to lose it."

"Yeah, she asked me not to tell you, but I told her pretty much the same thing and that you liked Tyrone and could probably talk to him and help him. I'd told her that I would keep Belan for as long as she needed me to."

"Well, I'm glad he felt comfortable enough to talk to me. I told him that he needs to slow up on the drinking. Get a handle on it before it gets out of control. I believe they will be fine, especially since Mr. George seems to be back on track. He wasn't drunk, either."

"That's great. So, can we talk about us?"

"Yeah," I said, then grabbed her hand and led her to the couch. When we sat, I continued as Belan held onto my goatee. "There is nothing I wouldn't do for you. So, seeing Oscar brought me to a dangerous level of rage. Knowing that he hurt you and had the nerve to show up here had me filled with rage. I literally had to get on my knees and pray. That was why I couldn't lay in the bed with y'all. I needed to get that negative energy off me, baby. I'm so sorry that I let that influence my interaction with you. That will never happen again."

"Thank you for that, Vance. I was starting to get nervous about us, thinking that maybe we moved too fast and didn't truly get to know one another like we should have. But what you're doing now is exhibiting kingly behavior. You're admitting your weaknesses to me and that couldn't be sexier. When you acknowledge your weakness, that means you aren't afraid to be vulnerable with me. So, I'm gonna keep it one hundred with you."

My heart increased in speed a lil bit, trying to prepare for what she had to say. Other than what happened today, our time together had been perfect, so hopefully she wasn't breaking things off. I sat back on the couch and she sat back as well, scooting closer to me and Belan. "I know that Meena has probably told you a lot about my past with Oscar, but I need you to hear it from me. How it all started. I don't even think Meena knows. We were already in a bad space when I met Meena."

She took a deep breath and continued as I draped my arm around her. "The first ten years of our marriage wasn't perfect. You obviously know that since you'd never met me. He'd told me not to come to the firehouse because that was his job and it didn't look right to have personal shit going on at work. So, I never went there... naïve and so trusting. When my mama died, I was crushed. Oscar was there for me, consoling me, but after the funeral, it was like he expected me to bounce back from that like nothing ever happened."

I kissed her forehead, knowing the devastation she probably felt. Both of my parents were deceased and had passed away at fairly young ages. "I fell into a slight depression because my mama was my best friend. We talked about everything from sex to fashion. Losing her made me feel alone. I didn't know how to navigate through life without her. That was when I first started gaining weight. After a year or so, I'd finally gotten the depression under control through a program I heard about at work. But by the time I got it together, I'd gained twenty pounds."

Shifting BeBe on my lap as she played with my beard, I rubbed Jennifer's hair and tried my best to make this moment easier for her to tell me about. "To make a long story short, Oscar started bashing me about my weight gain and he started staying out later and later. He became more volatile and began hitting me when things didn't go his way at home or when I 'talked back.' I'd just gotten some-what stable from the loss of my mother, but there he was, pushing me back into my feelings of inadequacy, uncertainties, and depres-sion all over again."

When she said that he'd hit her, I could feel my anger rising until she rubbed her hand down my chest. BeBe watched her, then began trying to do the same. My frown had turned into a smile that quickly. "After months of him belittling me and having sex with me only when he wanted to, I found myself sinking even more, gaining more weight and spiraling out of control. Whenever I looked in the mirror, I was disgusted with who I saw standing there. I was fat, unhealthy, and damn near immobile. I had to ride one of those scooter things in the grocery store just so I wouldn't be struggling to breathe from all the walking."

A tear left her eyes as she said, "I hated myself. There was nothing for me to live for until this ray of sunshine came up to my job, trying to find out what she had to do to get hired. Just talking to her gave me enough purpose to stay here in this world, because suicide had become a viable option. Being beat almost every other day began taking a toll on me and Meena noticed. By that time, she and Tyrone had moved next door. I'd told her about the house when they were on the hunt. She talked me into filing for divorce and believing that I was worth more."

I smiled slightly. Meena thrived on helping people out of self-pity and self-destruction. She was great at that and it was what made her an amazing social worker. "The final straw was when I'd called Meena over to look at a shirt I'd made. Before she could get here, Oscar had gotten home and went the fuck off on me because I hadn't cooked. I had the energy to make fucking t-shirts but couldn't make sure he had a home-cooked meal. He jumped all over me and Meena walked in on it. I begged her not to call the police, promising her that I would file for divorce the next week."

The trauma she'd been through on account of Oscar was enough for me to fuck him up for sure now. While I knew she didn't tell me everything, she'd told me enough. I didn't need to know all the details. Breathing deeply, I rubbed her shoulder. "For a whole year, I waddled in self-destruction, self-pity, and self-hate. I was tearing myself down just as much as he had. I felt like I didn't deserve love. But with Meena's help, I finally said enough was enough. I got on the right track and forced myself to do better. I joined a support group and started exercising. I'm still not the size I was when I met Oscar, but I'm happy where I am now."

"You're beautiful just as you are. I hate that you went through all that bullshit, but I'm also happy that it made you stronger as a woman. Strong enough to demand what you deserve. Strong enough to know that you don't need a man to attain the things you want. I'm just grateful that you want me."

Leaning over, I kissed her lips as BeBe reached for her NaNa. "On the contrary, Mr. Vance. I *need* you. I never thought there was such a place as nirvana, until I met you. You have become a part of my peace and tranquility. Vance... I'm falling for you. It's so damn soon, but I'm falling, and it seems I can't stop it."

"Why are you trying to stop it? I know I won't be far behind you. Just the way you claim me is far beyond anything I've ever experienced, even with Madelyn. I promise I won't ever let anything affect the way I treat you... I mean, unless you do something crazy to me."

She chuckled and I did, too. "You're my everything, Jennifer. I don't see myself ever being with anyone else."

"That's good enough for me, baby."

---

14

*J*ennifer

IT HAD BEEN a couple of weeks and Vance and I were finally able to go on our first official date. Our lives had been wrapped up with Belan lately and trying to make sure that Meena and Tyrone were good. Now that things seemed to be settling down and getting back to normal, Vance and I decided that it was beyond time for us to take time to enjoy ourselves. We'd gone to lunch a few times, but Belan was always with us. This would be pleasantly different. It was something I hadn't experienced in a long time and I was beyond excited.

As I stood in the mirror, applying my makeup, I couldn't help but feel a little lighter about telling Vance more about my past. I found my insecurities creeping in on me that day Oscar showed up at the house. Vance needed to understand me and know the bull-shit Oscar had put me through. It took a lot of self-love talks and determination for me to come out of the depression I was in. There was no way I would go back there for no one, including Vance. If he could understand why my mind was naturally trying to push him out by not calling or looking at his text message, then we would be fine, because I knew he didn't want to jeopardize what we had and what we could have in the future.

Thankfully, I hadn't heard a peep out of Oscar. I felt like he was trying to bluff me into thinking he would take the house from me. At this point, he could have this muthafucka. It wasn't worth my happiness. I had no one to leave this shit to. Whenever I died, it would belong to the city or whoever it went to. There was no family to take it, at least not close family. So, fuck it. If he wanted it, he could have it... after he paid for it, of course. Owning a home was a lot. The taxes alone were almost too much for me to handle, not to mention maintenance and upkeep and the insurance. I was feeling that way now, but I knew that things would probably change if he actually tried to take it. It was easy to talk about what you would do in certain situations, but until you were actually going through them, it was impossible at times to say how you would react.

That was why I had to get back to selling my t-shirts, bows, and other things. With my Cricut, I could do all sorts of things. The past couple of weeks, I'd profited a little over five hundred dollars. That money helped give me a little wiggle room. That was the only thing Vance and I didn't talk about: money. Although we'd been together a month and had moved quickly, that topic hadn't come up. Only that we were both retired.

After putting on my eyelashes, I took a deep breath and relaxed my hands. This shit was time consuming. I didn't see how some women fooled around with makeup and hair every day. This was special occasion type shit for me. Frankly, I didn't need it, but it only added to my already gorgeous face. Once they were applied, I looked at myself in the mirror and smiled. Vance was gonna be in awe of me tonight. This floral patterned, wrap dress was gonna turn heads. It exposed my cleavage, which was amazing since I'd been working out, and plenty of leg.

Turning around in the mirror, I knew that these big legs would be center focus, then my ass a close second. It was out there. Not only that, but the yellow of the dress looked so good against my bronzed skin. Walking to my bedroom, I sat on the bed to put on my nude heels. My dress nearly showed my ass when I sat, and I briefly thought about changing. I didn't want Vance to feel a way about that. I was no longer a single woman flaunting my weight loss. We were a couple and had been from jump. I'd ask his opinion once he got here.

I didn't have to wait much longer because he was ringing the doorbell. When I got to it and opened it, Vance stood there just staring at me as he held a bouquet of tulips. I smiled brightly at him and finally, he said, "Damn, Queen. You stole my breath. You look gorgeous."

"Thank you, King. Come in."

He handed me the flowers and kissed my lips softly, being sure not to smear my lipstick. "So, I need your honest opinion," I said as I put the flowers in a vase.

I turned to him to see him scanning my curves. It was like he was in a trance. "What's that, baby?"

"Do you think this dress is inappropriate? I mean, will you feel a way about me showing off my body? When I sit, it exposes a lot more."

"Come here, Queen."

I walked over to him slowly with my lips parted. The way he summoned me... the rasp in his voice... it had control over me and now, I was the one in a trance. His crisp, white shirt and navy pants looked amazing on him. When I stood in front of him, he licked his lips, then ran his palm up my thigh to my ass. After he touch my underwear, he lifted my dress to take a look. The dress was some-what thin, so I wore a thong. "Damn, baby. However you wanna dress this masterpiece is cool with me. Now if I wasn't with you to protect you from jackasses, I would prefer you not wear anything this damn sexy. But for tonight, I just pray we make it through the date without me having to get at'chu."

I held his face in my hands and I almost wanted to say fuck this date, but I needed it so badly. I needed to feel cherished by someone other than myself... desired and claimed openly. "Thank you, Vance. Let's get out of here before I put it on you. You look so damn sexy."

He smiled slightly, then grabbed my hand as I grabbed my nude-colored clutch from the couch. After locking up, he led me to his Blazer and helped me inside. I felt so sexy and Vance put that shit through the roof the way he admired my body. When he got in, he looked at my legs and licked his lips. Taking a deep breath and shaking his head slowly, he started the engine and we made our way to The Green Beanery. I'd never been, but from what I heard, it was extremely upscale.

When we got there, I realized that the things I'd heard about it were accurate. The entire menu was in French. Once the maître d walked away, I said, "Fancy."

"Nothing but the best for you, with your sexy ass."

My cheeks were so hot, I knew I had to be blushing like crazy. When I looked over at him, he licked his lips, then bit the bottom one. Dinner was gonna be amazing and I couldn't wait until afterwards to have him for dessert. He stretched his arm across the table and reached for my hand. I slid it into his slowly, looking into his eyes the entire time. "There's something I need to tell you."

Smiling slightly, I asked, "What's that?"

"Well, I was trying to think of a poetic way to tell you, so you'd know I was more than just some hood ex-con that didn't know how to express himself, but the proper words just seem to elude me right now." Taking a deep breath, he stared at me, baring his soul through his gaze. "I love you, Jennifer. You're everything I could have hoped for. To know you trust me as much as you do, makes me wanna give you the world."

I swallowed back the tears as I stared at him. "You love me?"

"Yeah. Is that a bad thing?"

"No. I... I just didn't expect you to say it. I feel it every time you touch me... every time we make love. Your every word exhibits the love you have for me and I felt loved from day two. I love you, too, Vance."

He kissed my hand and I could see the fire in his eyes. That old Rick James song, "Fire & Desire," came to mind. Some of the lyrics fit us. We were both cold when it came to love at some point in our lives... cold as ice. We turned on the fire in one another. It seemed as if it was just infatuation at first... like I was just lonely, and I was excited about what I thought I knew about him. But tonight proved that it was so much more. After only a month, but spending practically every day together, we were admitting to one another that we'd found our one.

When the maître d returned, he took our drink and first course orders, but I couldn't take my eyes off the amazing man sitting across from me. He ended up ordering for both of us. Once the waiter walked away, Vance said, "You keep looking at me like that, we gon' get this shit to-go."

I lowered my gaze to my lap, then brought it back up to his dark eyes. "I can't help it. Hearing you express how you feel about me is an amazing feeling that I never want to go away."

"I'm here to make sure it never goes away. I've never fallen in love this quickly, but man, you so perfect, Queen. Everything about you is perfect, even that light snore you have going on when you're asleep."

I giggled, then said, "You know you snore, too, and it ain't light."

He chuckled, then continued to stare at me until the waiter came back with our drinks. This glass of wine wasn't gon' hit on shit. When we left from here, I knew I would need something stronger. My inhibitions were usually down when I was with Vance, but if I was slightly tipsy, he wouldn't remember his name when I got done with him. I could tell he'd never gotten head where the woman truly loved the shit. I loved it so much, I practiced my technique even when I didn't have a soul to practice on.

Once the waiter returned with our salads and duck, the stare downs stopped, our gazes couldn't help but fall on our plates. I was starving, too. I hadn't eaten a thing since breakfast. In that aspect, love didn't affect me like it did years ago. When I fell for Oscar, I couldn't eat around him. *Fuck that!* I was on some grown woman shit now. Starving in the name of love was out. We ate in almost complete silence. It didn't feel awkward in the least bit. Our passion was on simmer right now, but it was gonna be explosive later.

By the time we finished eating and had gotten back in the car, before Vance could even crank up, he leaned over and put one hand on my thigh and the other at the back of my head, pulling me to him. The passion with which he kissed me with, had me melting in his leather seat. I moaned into his mouth and nearly chased his lips as he pulled away. "I been wanting to do that since I saw you. I didn't plan to tell you I loved you until tonight when I was gracing that pussy with the presence of my tongue, but shit happened the way it was supposed to."

"It did. I'm glad you told me when you did. Damn, Vance. Madelyn was a blessed woman, and now I am, too."

"I'm a blessed man to find love twice, both so different, but both powerful and passionate. Two queens that are amazingly compassionate, caring, and loving. It makes me wonder what I did to deserve that kind of love twice in my life."

"You're an amazing man, Vance. The lengths you will go to protect those you love has spoken volumes. Now, let's get out of here before you find out how happy I am all over your seats."

He chuckled, then said, "Well, damn. I don't give a fuck about them seats, but I'm gonna head home, baby."

He cranked up and we left the restaurant, holding hands. Vance lifted them and kissed the back of my hand. "Damn, I love you, Queen."

"I love you, too, King."

When we made it to his house, I didn't even wanna wait on him to walk around the car to help me out. I hopped out of the car fast as hell as he watched me with a frown on his face. "Woman—"

"I don't wanna hear it. Just get this damn door open. I need a drink."

He shook his head slowly, then approached the front door to unlock it. "The next time you do that shit, I'm gon' punish your ass."

"Don't wait 'til next time. Punish my ass tonight... as soon as I finish my Henny."

He shook his head slowly and pushed the door open for me to walk through first. Just as I was about to make a beeline for the kitchen, he yanked me back in his arms, then untied my dress. When it fell open, he pushed it off my shoulders. "Mmm. Now go get your drink."

He was unleashing the true savage in my ass. I believed she'd fully made her appearance as I slowly walked to the kitchen, giving him a show, crossing one leg in front of the other. When I got to the kitchen, I turned to see him watching me, holding his dick in his hand. When exactly he got undressed, I didn't know, because I didn't hear a thing. Nearly salivating at the mouth, I knew it wouldn't be long before I was on my knees, digesting all his babies. As I got the Henny down from the cabinet, I poked my ass out, making it jiggle a little before pouring me a glass.

What I didn't expect was for Vance to cross the room as quickly as he did. Standing behind me, he moved my thong to the side as he pushed me over to the countertop. He pushed inside of me as I sipped my Henny through a small straw I'd placed in it. "Fuck! You can't be teasing me, Queen. It brings out the beast in me."

I moaned as I listened to my pussy express her gratitude. When he pulled out of me, the release of the suction she had on him made a gushy-ass popping noise. I stood up straight and downed the rest of my Henny, then turned around to stare at him. When he lifted me to the countertop and pushed my legs up, I nearly came everywhere. He was so rough sometimes, but I loved that shit. Grabbing his head, I pulled him to my wetness, and he hit me with that hurricane tongue. "Oh shit, Vance!"

My legs were already trembling, and I could feel a lil buzz creeping up on me. This shit was about to be explosive. Lifting his head to stare at me, he allowed my juices to run down his chin and into his goatee. I held his gaze, but it felt like I was about check out any minute. My pussy was throbbing, and without him even touching it, I came. *What the fuck?* "Vance! Oh my God!"

This man was my undoing. Just staring into his eyes had pushed me over the edge. What kind of shit was that? He lowered his face to my pussy and slurped up all that shit like he was a damn Hoover. He hadn't said a word in acknowledgement of what had just happened. He briefly glanced at it when I first started cumming. I was so deeply in love with this man, he had control of me in ways I hadn't imagined. When he lifted his head once again, he scooped me from the countertop and brought me to the bedroom.

Lying me on the bed, he pulled my thong off as I unfastened my bra. After kissing my inner thighs, he went back in for a moment, licking and sucking my pussy like it was manna from heaven. As I tried to get away from him, he lifted his head and tapped my pussy with his fingertips. Tilting his head to the side, he stared at her like she was speaking to him. Then he slapped her a little harder and I came again... hard as hell. I could feel it leaking from me like water as my back lifted from the bed.

Vance went to his knees in front of me and pushed his dick inside of me. "Fuck!" he growled, then went to my breast.

He sucked my nipple as he toyed with the other one, stroking me as it still seized from feelings of satisfaction. My fingernails dug into his back as I moaned loudly. "This some king shit... for yo' ass. Fuck me, King."

He groaned and stroked me even deeper, feeding me all the

dick as I felt his balls hitting against me. I'd never wanted to experience pain with my pleasure, but God, if Vance didn't make that shit desirable. He bit my neck as he lifted my leg and dug into me. "King shit, huh? Show me some queen shit and cum on this kingly dick, then."

I'd already came twice, but my pussy was twitching like she wanted to honor his demand. Replacing his mouth with his hand, he choked me lightly as I wrapped my other leg around his waist. His lips landed on mine and he sucked my bottom lip into his mouth, causing me to moan loudly. Vance went to my ear and kissed it, then said, "I *said* cum on daddy dick."

My entire body shivered, and my fucking soul drained from my pussy. He had that shit forever as I screamed out, "Vance! Fuuuuck, I love you!"

"Mmm, I love you, too, Queen," he replied, then kissed me softly. "I swear this body do magic tricks."

When I'd calmed down some, my ass was feeling drunk and on some nasty shit. Pushing him away from me, he rolled to his back and I climbed on top of him, reverse cowgirl style. He palmed my ass as I slid down his dick, claiming it as being conquered before the shit even happened. The first roll of my hips, he said, "Mmm. Work that shit out then, baby."

As time had gone on, I realized he could go a lot longer without nutting. That excited me and worked my ass out all at the same time. Dropping my ass on him and making it twerk caused him to slap both cheeks at once. I glanced back at him to see he was propped up on his elbows, watching his dick disappear repeatedly inside of me. Thankful that the gym had been a friend to me for the past couple of years, I continued my bounce on him until he groaned, "I'm about to nut... fuck."

"Not yet, King."

I allowed his dick to slip out of me, then stood from the bed and had him scoot to the edge in a sitting position. When I went to my knees, he said, "Hell yeah."

I gave him a one-cheeked smile before I pulled him into my mouth, tasting how my juices had had their way with him. "That shit tastes excellent, huh, baby ?"

I moaned on him in agreeance with what he'd just said. My taste was definitely exquisite and of high quality, so I never minded indulging. Allowing his dick to check the back of my throat a couple of times produced that thick saliva I liked and he loved. Swirling my mouth around him, creating a vibration with the noise from the air getting into the suction, Vance grabbed me by the hair. "Oh, fuck! Let me cum in that pussy, baby."

After massaging his sack with my fingertips for a moment, I stood from the floor and he pushed me to the bed, on my stomach and said, "Toot that ass up."

When he entered me, I thought he'd killed me. Like on the cartoons, I saw my spirit separate from my damn body and attach itself to him. He slapped my ass repeatedly as he pounded into me, slaughtering my pussy with every stroke. He'd literally fucked the damn sound out of my ass. My whispered pants were loud and clear, but my voice was on hiatus. Vance clenched my ass as he growled loudly, "Fuuuuuck!"

His movements stiffened as he dropped his seed into me, giving me all of him as I gave him all of me. I'd came for the fourth time and I was so fucking drained, I didn't move another inch.

*V*ance

THIS LOVE WAS PERFECT, and I knew that God had chosen to bless me with someone special... again. Even after the wrong turns I made, He was still looking out for me. Jennifer was amazing and our date night had been everything I hoped it would be. In the past couple of weeks, we'd been on a few of them. All of them ending the same way the first one had. Sex with Jennifer was like nothing I'd ever experienced. I knew I'd hit the fucking jackpot. A woman that wasn't afraid to indulge in her own taste was always a freak in my book. She was my own personal freak.

She had a doctor's appointment today, so Belan and I were in the backyard, having fun. I'd gotten her a little swing set to leave here at Jennifer's house, so we didn't always have to go to the park. Since I'd parked behind Jennifer, I let her take my car. So, it looked as if she was here and not me. I figured that was why he had stopped and had the nerve to be at the door. I'd seen Oscar's face on my phone from the new doorbell I had installed. Had I not had Belan, I would have gone to the door. I couldn't risk losing my cool with my grandbaby here. It was probably a blessing that she was with me to begin with.

He stood there a little while longer, then dropped something in the mailbox and left. Grabbing Belan from the swing, I walked through the house until I got to the front door, then took it out of the mailbox... along with the other articles of mail. Going to the kitchen, I placed it all in the receptacle hanging from the wall, except for what he'd left. There was a note attached that read, *I'm sorry, Jennifer, but there were conditions on you keeping this house. I love you and I always have, but my love has conditions. Call me if you want this to go away.*

It was a good thing I didn't answer the door. I would have jacked his big ass up. Shaking my head slowly, I dropped it to the countertop. Looked like Jennifer was gonna have to call that lawyer after all. I couldn't stand a nigga that thought he had to assert his manhood by belittling a woman. He didn't realize that women were our strength and by killing a woman's spirit, he was killing him-damn-self. My hands were itching like crazy. Glancing at Belan in my arms, I closed my eyes, trying to take deep breaths, then kissed her cheek as she grabbed ahold of my goatee.

After going to the room to change her diaper, I heard keys hitting the countertop, then Jennifer say, "That muthafucka."

I picked Belan up and headed back up front. Jennifer had a deep frown on her face and tears in her eyes as she read over whatever he'd put in the envelope. She was so engrossed in what she was reading, she didn't hear us approaching until Belan belted out, "Na-Na-Na-Na!"

When she lifted her head, a tear fell from her eyes. Now I was really pissed. "Hey, baby. How was your appointment?" I asked as I hugged her.

"It was good."

"What did the papers say?"

"The only way I was allowed to keep this house was if I stayed single. No partners or even potential partners are allowed in the house. If I can't abide by that, then the house is to be put up for sale."

"Well put this shit for sale then. Move in with me."

"No! This is my house! I worked hard for this shit! His name is on it, but it was my money that paid for this! He can kiss my fucking ass! This my shit!"

I was stunned into silence. While I had thought that Oscar was the one who'd afforded her this house, it was the other way around. "Baby, I'm sorry. I didn't mean anything by that. I just thought that the two of you had gotten this house together."

"His credit was shot to hell and he'd just started the academy when I bought this house. I was stupid as hell for putting his name on it. This my shit, Vance!"

"Okay. Okay. Call that attorney you met in the grocery store. Was there any legal documents in what he left?"

"This letter is from his attorney."

More tears fell from her eyes and I literally wanted to go find him. Handing Belan to her, I said, "I'll be right back."

"No. You're not leaving me here. Vance, I don't need you to get in trouble. What will that do to help me? Huh? You are *not* leaving! Period!"

Belan had started to cry and was beyond pissed. Ignoring Jennifer's demands, I snatched my keys from the countertop and headed out the door. She ran behind me with Belan on her side. She was screaming for me to stop, but the last thing she said, got my attention. "You go to that firehouse and we're done! You hear me, Vance Etienne? I'm begging you to let me handle this the right way... legally. I refuse to lose you because you couldn't control your anger. Do you hear me? If you leave and go to that firehouse, that's it. I'm not putting myself through the stress of worrying about you and trying to fight his ass at the same time."

I turned to look at her. I couldn't believe she would throw in the towel for me trying to have her back, but I understood her point. That shit didn't stop me from getting in my car, though. I backed out the driveway as she stood there with a stunned look on her face. Oscar was trying to bully his way into her house, and I refused to stand for it. He thought she was weak, and he knew I was somewhat restricted. What he failed to realize, though, I'd done day for day. There were no stipulations placed on me. The only thing was that I could be convicted of something a lot quicker because I had a record.

By the time I drove up to the firehouse, I saw his car. He didn't drive the company vehicle home, apparently. I rolled my eyes and took a deep breath. Just as I was about to open the door, Jennifer's voice replayed in my head. *You go to that firehouse and we're done!* Was this worth losing her? What would I solve by being here? Not a damn thing. If anything, it would make this situation worse. My queen asked me to leave this alone. I ran my hand down my face, then put the car in gear and went back to her house.

When I got there, she was walking to her car with Belan in her car seat. I blocked her in, then got out and walked over to her. She rolled her eyes, then swiped a tear that fell. "Can you move, Vance? I'm going to the gym."

"Jenn, we need to talk."

"No, we don't. You made your choice and it makes me wonder if you did that for me or for yourself. I asked you not to leave. I don't need this kind of heartache and disappointment in my life. I refuse to go through a relationship where a man doesn't value my thoughts, views and requests of him. So, please leave. I told you I would be done and I am."

She put Belan in the backseat and after she opened her car door, I grabbed her arm before she could get in. "I didn't go in the firehouse, Queen."

Her eyebrows lifted and she closed the door, then started the car using her key fob. She stared at me, I assumed waiting for me to further explain. This was hard for me because I'd never been so vulnerable around her. Grabbing her hand, I said, "I'm afraid of losing someone I love again. Anybody that threatens what or who I feel belongs to me or is an important part of my life, brings out a part of me that I've come to embrace. Prison only brought him out more. I didn't become that way until Madelyn died. So, when that happened to Meena, I snapped. I couldn't lose my daughter, too."

She gently pushed me out of the way and opened the door so we could hear Belan. When she looked at me again, I continued, "I don't want Oscar to turn you into someone you aren't. The fact that he's threatening you to try to live your life as he would have it, pisses me off. But when I got to the firehouse and was about to get out, all I could think about was you saying we would be done. Those words pierced my heart. I never wanna lose you, especially not for something *I* did. I love you, Jennifer, and I just wanted to stand up for you, but I realized you were right. So, I didn't get out. I drove back here."

"You're telling me that you drove all the way downtown and didn't get out of the car?"

"Yeah, baby, that's what I'm saying. My ass didn't leave the leather cushion of my driver's seat. I'm sorry for stressing you out. Nothing I would have done would have made this situation any better. Plus, he probably wants to get a rise out of me. That would mean he won."

She wrapped her arms around my neck and hugged me tightly. "I never wanna lose you, Vance. But I was willing to let you go and that shit was gonna give me a heart attack."

I wrapped my arms around her waist and said, "I'm so sorry, Queen. You got me for life. Okay?"

She pulled away from me and nodded, then dropped her head. Lifting it by gently grabbing her chin, I kissed her pretty lips. "You forgive me, baby?"

"Yeah, King. I forgive you. Forgive me for giving you such an ultimatum in the first place. Leaving you would have killed me."

"Are you totally committed to going work out?"

"No. I was just trying to get my mind off losing you."

Wiping the tears from her cheeks, I kissed her forehead, then got BeBe out the car. "Pa-Pa-Pa-Pa-Pa!"

I smiled brightly and kissed her cheek. "Yeah, BeBe! You can say PaPa! Let's go back in the house. I need to make up with your NaNa."

"Ma-Ma!"

"Oh, you just saying all kinds of stuff today! Your mama not even here to hear it."

As we walked in the house, I rested my hand at the small of Jennifer's back and I could feel her slight tremble. She was worked up, but I planned to soothe her soul in just a minute. Taking Belan from her car seat, I put her in her playpen, then had Jennifer lay down on the couch. I straddled her and began rubbing her shoulders, doing whatever I could to help her release the tension. I knew Oscar's letter had brought her stress, but I felt like I'd brought her even more.

She moaned softly as I glanced over to see Belan gumming the hell out of her teddy bear. "Let me get baby girl's teething ring and I'll be right back."

"Okay."

As I got it from the fridge and was making my way back, the doorbell rang. Jennifer sat up and as I was about to answer the door, she said, "Let me get it, just in case."

I swallowed hard and nodded, then picked up Belan from her playpen. She held on to my goatee until she saw the teething ring in my hand. She quickly reached for it and the moment I gave it to her, it went to her mouth. Jennifer glanced back at me, then stepped outside. That let me know that it was Oscar's ass. I grabbed my phone and pulled up the app so I could hear what the fuck he had to say. That probably wasn't a wise decision, but at least this shit was recorded in case he said some fuck shit that Jennifer could use against him.

Sitting on the couch with BeBe on my lap still playing with her teether, the audio kicked in just as he was saying, "I hope you take heed to the letter in the envelope. Is Vance worth losing your house? You think I'm gonna just sit by idly and allow you to have another man in the house that was once ours?"

"Oscar, I don't give a fuck what'chu do. It's killing you that I'm happy, isn't it?"

"Yeah, it is. It's killing me that you're happy with someone else. Why can't you give us another shot? I love you."

"Because you a dirty dick bastard! An ignorant, lying sack of shit. Now, you delivered your letter earlier. There was no need for you to come back. Get the fuck off my porch."

I was itching to go outside. That muthafucka knew I was here. My car was in the driveway this time. I wanted to go knock his ass out. Just because he was the fire chief now didn't mean a got damn thing to me. As I watched, Jennifer opened the door to come inside and he said, "See you in court then."

"No, you won't. See you at arbitration. This won't go any further than that."

When she stormed back in the house, she immediately went to her purse, then made a phone call. "May I speak to Sidney Taylor?"

She walked back over to me and sat next to me with some fruit snacks for BeBe. She practically tossed her teething ring to get her snack. Jennifer began explaining who she was and why she was calling and evidently, the attorney remembered her from the grocery store. They weren't on the phone long. Jennifer agreed to go to her office tomorrow morning. Putting my arm around her, I said, "I'm sorry you're going through this. If you need it, your entire conversation was recorded through the doorbell."

"Good. I'm sure I'll need it. He's desperate to control me and I'm not sure what he gets out of trying to make me miserable."

"Nothing. Just the power to say he still has control over you. Just like he's trying to get a rise out of me, he's trying to get a rise out of you, too, baby. Don't give him the satisfaction. You hold more power than you give yourself credit for. Ignore his foolishness.

When he sees that he isn't bothering you, it'll piss him off and he'll stop."

"You think so?"

"Yep. You were right about calling the attorney, just in case. But like you said, this won't even go to court. I didn't hear the entire conversation, but from what I heard, he's only doing what he's doing because you're with me."

"He admitted that this was my house. That my money paid for this house, but because he was my husband, he had a right to it. And he said that I was a fool for putting his name on it. Dumb ass."

"You can bring that with you to the attorney tomorrow."

"You're not going to come with me?"

"If you want me to."

"I do. I need your support."

She laid against me. Oscar had better been glad that I couldn't own a gun. I would have shot his ass through the door. I rubbed her arm and tried to soothe her as best I could. Kissing her forehead, I knew that if this lawyer was worth her weight, Jennifer wouldn't have a thing to worry about. "You know, I originally thought that I wouldn't fight him for this house. That if he wanted it, he could just have it. But fuck that. This my shit and I'll be damn if I'm gon' let him have his way without a fight. Even though I would get half the money, I don't want that nigga to have the other half. It was all *my* money that paid for this house. I've given him enough over the years and allowed him to take shit that didn't belong to him... like my happiness. Not this time."

*J*ennifer

"HE HAS SOME NERVE, for lack of a better word. We can definitely use this recording against him. He's clearly admitting that the house should be yours and that he just wants to make you miserable. How stupid can a person be?"

Sidney Taylor was livid. She had another attorney in the room that was a divorce lawyer. Although we'd been divorced for over three years now, divorce lawyers specialized in the division of assets. The divorce attorney would be the lead and Mrs. Taylor would work with her. "Ms. Monroe... soon-to-be Rubin," Mrs. Childs said and smiled. "Don't worry about a thing. This is going to be easy to handle, especially with the recording. Despite that, if a judge ruled in his favor, you would have to sell the house and divide the money obtained from the sell."

"I understand," I said, glancing at Vance.

I didn't want to lose the house I'd worked hard to obtain. If I chose to sell it on my own terms, that would be different. Oscar Monroe was being an ass and that was why I made sure to fill out the paperwork to go back to my maiden name of Rubin, ASAP. "Ms. Jennifer, I want him bad! He's definitely gonna be called an asshole... sorry."

I chuckled at Mrs. Taylor's fiery temperament. She seemed to be a younger version of me. She had a winning record that spoke volumes, along with fifteen years of experience. "It's okay. I don't mind. I'm just ready for this to be over."

"I know. We're going to set a date for arbitration and I'm gonna do a little digging and reading through what you agreed upon from your divorce. From what I can see, you got the house and your car, and he agreed to let you have it, although the judge had suggested that you sell and split the assets. Now his ass wants to renege because you have a new man. These conditions he placed on there had to be overlooked by the judge. There's no way he can get away with dictating your life that way, especially for a house you paid for."

Mrs. Taylor was still pacing with my documents in her hand as she read them over. "As far as your retainer, we are going to demand that he pays all fees since he's the one that has you jumping through hoops to appease his ego. Chauvinistic bastard."

I smiled at Vance as Mrs. Taylor ranted. BeBe was sitting on his lap, knocked out. According to Meena, she had a rough night. Hopefully, it wasn't because of all the yelling I did at Vance yesterday. She was whiny the whole time he was gone. As Mrs. Childs and Mrs. Taylor gave us more information to get us ready for arbitration, she said she would call me if she needed additional information from me.

Having to tell her of my past with Oscar was hard, especially with Vance sitting there. I could have gone back to my old lawyer that knew our history, but something about this lady drew me to her. She was passionate and caring. Looking over her website, I could see that she wasn't hurting for business. So, that made me less leery of her. She was genuine and sincere about helping people.

When we finally left, we'd been there for almost three hours and I was just as drained as Belan. "So, what'chu think, Queen? It seems like they know their shit."

"Yeah, it does. I got a good vibe from her in the grocery store. It doesn't seem to be about the money for her. She finds joy in fighting for the underdog. Oscar thinks because he's the fire chief that he'll get away with this bullshit."

Vance put his arm around my shoulder as we walked out to the car. After getting Belan strapped in, we went to my house and I made lunch for the three of us. Belan was still cranky, so I gave her a bath in her lavender body wash and rubbed her down with her lavender lotion. Hopefully, that would soothe her crankiness. When I went back to the front room, Vance was sitting on the couch. After handing him his BeBe, I went to the kitchen to get dinner prepped. "Thank you for cleaning the kitchen, baby."

"You don't have to thank me for that, baby. We're a team."

I smiled as I seasoned the turkey wings, then put them in the oven. After washing my hands, I saw that Belan had gone to sleep while sucking her bottle. Vance laid her on the sofa on her blanket and came to me in the kitchen. He slid his arms around my waist from the back as I washed some rice. "So, I have to ask. Will you consider my proposition if you are forced to sell?"

He gently kissed my neck. Taking a deep breath, I stepped away from him to put the rice pot in the rice cooker. I turned to him and said, "I hope I don't have to sell, but if by chance I'm forced to, I've thought about your proposition. Most likely, I would move in with you. Since I love you so much, I don't see myself moving into an apartment or buying another house."

"I'm hoping everything works out for the best, but since you're my woman, you have to know at some point, we would progress to living together, right?"

I put my hand to his face and gently rubbed his cheek. "Yeah, King. I know."

He pulled me into him and caressed my back, causing me to rest my head against his shoulder. This bullshit was heavy, but I knew with the help of God, I would get through this like I got through everything else. Maybe God had placed Vance in my life for this very reason. I had options. Had I not had Vance, I could very well end up in an apartment. Then again, if I didn't have Vance, Oscar wouldn't be giving me such a hard time. "What type of beans do you want, baby?" I asked while still resting in his embrace.

"Whatever you decide to cook. It doesn't matter, Queen. Matter of fact, go rest. I'll cook the beans."

Vance kissed my forehead and lightly patted my ass. Before walking away, I kissed his lips. I had an amazing man that wanted to not only tend to me physically but tend to my heart as well. Emotionally, I was a wreck. I hated that I'd ever met Oscar. Thinking back on all the times I should have left him had made me angry with myself for being so weak, naïve, and gullible. I believed everything he said like a fool. *Significant others aren't allowed at this event. It's mainly for team bonding.* I heard that one at least twice a year. I was foolish to believe all his lies and was dumb to stay through all my disappointments. Most times, I ended up finding out the truth after the fact, but I still stayed. I was afraid to be alone and more than half the time, I was alone anyway.

This time, even though I was confident about my attorneys' abilities, I was still feeling defeated. I gave him that one-up on me. I was happy to divorce his ass, and when I saw that he wasn't fighting me for the house, I signed it and didn't read everything. I would have seen that bullshit then. Although, back then, I probably would have agreed to it. I was so broken. Standing from the couch, I walked back to the kitchen and embraced my man. "Y'all had to have thought Oscar's wife was stupid for letting him get away with the shit he was doing."

"I felt sorry for you. I saw all the bullshit he was doing. He brought numerous women to the firehouse. I was hoping that just one time, you would show up unannounced and bust his ass. We never thought you were stupid. But we did assume that you were a good woman. It was usually men like his ass that ended up ruining good women, tainting their view of what a man should be."

"At one point, I was afraid of him. I questioned him once about his whereabouts and he punched me in the eye. I never questioned his ass again. But I still got slapped for bullshit. I was afraid to leave and felt like I didn't deserve better. But he done fucked with the wrong one this time. I became a new woman... one that knows her worth, is strong, and confident. I made mistakes, thinking he loved me as much as I loved him. But I'm over that shit. I have a man... a king, that loves me for me. I don't have to do anything other than be myself."

Vance frowned slightly, then asked, "You do? What's his name? I might know him."

He had this serious look on his face that made me laugh. Here I was, trying to talk myself out of feeling down and upset when I had this amazing man that could pull me out of that with his amazing sense of humor. Pulling his face to mine, I kissed him passionately, then said, "You know who he is now?"

"Oh, shit! I think I do. His name is Vance Etienne. That nigga was something to talk about. He was a friendly guy who got along with everybody, then suddenly, when his daughter got hurt, that nigga snapped." His facial expression changed as he continued. "He shot a young man, killing him. Taking him away from his mama and family, while he pleaded for his life. That shit ate him up for a long time. In jail, he had nothing but time to think about what he'd done."

He turned and put the lid on the butter beans, then turned back to me. "What I'm saying is that we've all been through some things. I sank so low while I was in prison. It took me a long time to stop thinking about what I'd done. But just like you overcame that shit with Oscar, I overcame my past. I had an opportunity to write a letter to his mother and she chose to forgive me. I believed that was what freed me. But now, I find myself struggling with the man I've become in order to be the man you need me to be... that my daughter and granddaughter need."

Grabbing my hands, he continued, "I don't ever want you to struggle with who you are. You're a beautiful queen that deserves love... soul-stirring love. I consider it my obligation to be the man you deserve, that will love you like you need to be loved. It's never been hard for me to show my heart to a woman, but somehow, you exposed my soul. Everything about you is what I needed when I got out. I love you, Jennifer."

"I love you, too, King."

As he lowered his head to kiss me, there was a knock at the door. We both frowned, and before he could head to the door, I pulled him close. "I got it, baby."

"Jennifer, you don't have to be nervous about my temper. I won't do anything to risk losing you or my daughter again."

I nodded and suddenly felt horrible. It seemed as if I was holding his past against him. While I tried to convince Meena he'd changed, in certain situations, I found myself doubting that as well. When he came back to the kitchen, he had Meena with him. "Hey, Mama. How's my baby?"

"Hey, Meena. Baby girl was worn out. When we got back, I fed her and bathed her, then she laid on her PaPa and went to sleep."

"Aww. Well, let me get her because Tyrone is taking us to dinner tonight."

"I take it everything is still going well between you two."

"Yeees, Daddy."

Vance lowered his head, then looked back up at us. "I need to talk to both of you, ladies. Please."

He walked away and we hesitantly followed him to the couch where his BeBe was stirring. Meena sat next to her and picked her up, whispering in her ear. Belan said softly, "Ma-Ma."

I couldn't help but smile until I looked over at Vance. His expression was serious, and it wiped the smile from my lips. I swallowed hard as he began. "I went to prison because I first allowed myself to go into a fit of rage. I was angry and couldn't control my anger. I'd already lost my wife and I'd be damned if I was gonna lose my daughter because a muthafucka didn't know how to keep his hands to himself. I left the house, blinded by anger, hatred, and rage. At that moment, I hated Chad for everything he represented. In my mind, he was that drunk that beat his wife, telling her that he would kill her if she ever tried to leave."

I lowered my head, because Oscar had told me that a couple of times, so I knew exactly what Vance was speaking of. He continued, "My second reason for going to prison was that I grabbed my gun. Knowing that I was as angry as I was, I should have left it home. Having a gun in my hands at that moment was like sitting a poor man in a bank vault. It was impossible to avoid the inevitable. Thirdly, I shouldn't have left your side to begin with, Meena. I should have let the police do their job. Whether they would have arrested him or not, I didn't give them a chance before I took the law in my own hands."

He fidgeted a bit and I saw something I'd never seen in him: uncertainty. "I can't take back what I did that night, as badly as I want to at times. But because I did that, I feel like neither of you will ever trust me."

"I trust you, Daddy. With all my heart."

Vance held his hand up, halting Meena's words. "Why didn't you tell me that you and Tyrone were having problems? Had he not called me, I wouldn't have known. You think that anyone who I feel has done you wrong will suffer the same fate." Turning to me, he said, "I know I gave you reason to feel the way you do. I promise you, my temper is under control. I can't afford to lose y'all. I can't." Averting his gaze back to Meena, he said, "Meena, I love you, but I'm not the man you see me as. It feels like you think I'm a monster that will injure or kill at will. I've never been that man."

He stood from his seat and pulled Meena to her feet as the tears streamed down her face. "I won't ever leave you again, baby. I promise. You don't have to worry about me. I'm doing my best to transition from the past ten years. It's only been a little over a month. Give me time to get on track, baby."

"I'm so sorry, Daddy. I love you," Meena said as she cried into his chest. "I promise to do better."

Vance stretched out his other arm, requesting that I join them. I picked up Belan from the couch and went to his arms, too. "I'm sorry, daddy. I promise to do better, too."

Meena lifted her head and rolled her eyes, causing Vance to laugh, then lean over and kiss me. "I love you, Queen."

"I love you, too. You know that."

Meena went and grabbed Belan's bag, then came back and said, "Thank y'all for always keeping my baby. We gon' go before y'all decide to start saying more nasty stuff in front of me. Ugh!"

I laughed as she kissed her dad's cheek, then mine and allowed us to kiss Belan. We walked them out and watched them walk home. Turning to Vance, I kissed his lips and said, "I already know that everything will be fine, simply because I have you."

"Hell yeah. That's the confidence I wanna see."

After going inside, we checked on the food and held one another until it was time to eat.

"NA, WHAT NA?"

"They want to do the arbitration today. That is totally up to you. We're ready over here, but for them to pull this at the last minute, you can choose to make them wait."

"No. Let's get this shit over with. I'm sorry, Mrs. Taylor. I'm just sick of his entitled ass."

"I share your sentiments. Meet me here in an hour. They will meet us here since they waited 'til the last minute."

"Okay."

It was only eight-thirty in the morning. Thankfully, I was already dressed since I had Belan. It had been a week since Mrs. Taylor had called and introduced herself to his attorney, letting him know that she would be handling my case against Mr. Monroe. I was sure he knew exactly who she was. She was known nationwide for her work. Grabbing my phone, I called Vance. "Hello?"

"Hey, baby. You know that muthafucka tried to pull a slick one? I have to be to Mrs. Taylor's office in an hour."

"I'll hop in the shower right quick and come pick you and BeBe up."

"Okay, baby."

I ended the call and shook my head, thankful that we were about to get this bullshit settled. By the time I made sure Belan was cleaned up from breakfast and dressed, Vance was at the door. After opening the door for him, I combed Belan's hair up with lotion and put a cute bow on it. "You ready, baby?"

"Hell yeah. Let's go."

I got Belan's car seat out of my car and handed it to Vance to put in his car. Once we got her situated inside and had both gotten inside, we took the ten-minute drive to Mrs. Taylor's firm. My leg was shaking uncontrollably when we got there. It wasn't that I was nervous, I just hated being around Oscar's trifling ass. The quicker this was over, the better off we would all be. I could see myself slapping the shit out of his ass, giving him what he gave me for years.

Vance came around the car and opened my door, then got Belan from the backseat. "I don't know if I told you, but thank you for being here with me for support."

"Queen, your king should support you in everything you do. That's what I'm doing. I got'chu, baby."

I kissed his lips, then we headed inside. Oscar and his attorney hadn't arrived yet. The receptionist greeted us, then led us to Mrs. Taylor's office. "You made it fast. They just left his attorney's office, so they should be here in ten minutes. How are you feeling?"

"I'm okay. Ready to get it over with."

"Same here. He won't have a leg to stand on. You're going to leave here the same way you came. I promise." She turned to Vance and asked, "You wanna sit in the lounge?"

"Yes, ma'am. Thank you."

Vance leaned over and kissed me. "You're a queen. Walk in that shit. Show him how powerful you are. Make sure that crown straight and sit on your thrown, baby. He's just a jester."

"Thank you, King."

He kissed my lips as Belan said, "Na-Na-Na-Na!"

"NaNa will see you in a little bit."

They followed Mrs. Taylor's secretary to the lounge, and she led me to the conference room where Mrs. Childs was seated, looking over some documents. When we sat, Mrs. Taylor said, "First, let me say that pep talk was everything. I feel like I could conquer the world and he wasn't talking to me."

I chuckled as my face heated up. Vance was gon' get what he was begging for as soon as Meena picked up Belan. "They should be here any minute. We are about to play hardball. I think I know you enough to know that you won't be offended."

"Not at all."

Mrs. Taylor had her hair hanging loose and it was almost to her ass. I could tell it was her natural hair. She also wore noticeable makeup. She looked like she could have been a model instead of a lawyer, with the height to go along with it. As I sat, a woman's voice came over the intercom saying that Oscar's bitch ass had arrived with his attorney. Mrs. Taylor told her to send them back. She grabbed my hand under the table and so did Mrs. Childs. I wasn't sure what they were doing, but I went along with it.

When Oscar and his attorney walked in with smug grins on their faces, we all stared at them. Glancing at the two ladies next to me, neither of them smiled or stood. Oh, it was about to be some shit in here. That was probably why they grabbed my hands, to make sure I remained seated as well. They walked over to the table like they expected us to stand and greet them. Mrs. Taylor finally said, "Have a seat."

They both sat and she introduced herself as Oscar grinned at me. I rolled my eyes while other introductions were made. "Let's get on with this, shall we? State your demands," Mrs. Childs said.

"We are here to discuss what is clearly in the divorce decree in black and white. Ms. Monroe—"

"Her name is no longer Monroe. She's Ms. Rubin."

"Well, whatever. She signed the agreement that stated if she was to get involved with someone else, the assets had to be split."

"Is that all you have to say?" Mrs. Childs asked.

"That's more than enough, don't you think?"

She nodded at Mrs. Taylor and she began playing the recording as Oscar's eyes widened. "That's unlawful! I didn't know I was being recorded!" he said, standing to his feet.

"Sit'cho ass down, Oscar. It's a doorbell recording. You were standing on my porch and I have every right to record what the hell I want on my property."

He sat down with a frown on his face as he listened to himself state that I deserved to keep the house and how he didn't want Vance there. "Secondly, Mr. Monroe, I had a judge look at this and he said it would be overturned if we went to court. So, go ahead and waste all your time and money because you will lose this battle. You're already two grand in the hole with me now. I will drag your diseased ass through the mud. You do *not* want this battle with me. I have more footage than you can imagine of all the women you ran through that fire station. I fight dirty and I win. So, what are we here for again?"

"Are you threatening me, Mrs. Taylor?"

She smiled, then grabbed a remote and turned the TV on. When I saw him on that screen, bringing a woman to his office while wearing his wedding band, I wanted to throw up. He'd grabbed her ass and there was no mistaking what was about to go down. "Does that look like a threat? I don't make threats. When I present to a judge all your conquests during your marriage that Ms. Rubin couldn't prove at the time, you will be paying her for the rest of your damn life. Now, again, do you want this battle?"

Oscar flopped in his seat and nodded at his attorney, then stared at me like he wanted to kill me. My face was twitching in anger. "Vance ain't no better. He's gonna fuck over you, too."

I stood from my seat and slapped the dog shit out of him. "You will *not* speak on him. And don't look shocked. That's only a small piece of what I took from yo' ass over the years."

My attorneys had both stood, I assumed to keep me from going any further. I had no intentions of going further. I just wanted to slap the pause in his ass. I'd been itching to do that, but he hadn't given me a legitimate reason until then. Oscar's attorney handed Mrs. Taylor a check, then they both stood and walked out. "Did you see his face? He was stunned as hell!" Mrs. Taylor said. "Congratulations!"

"Thank y'all so much. You've been so efficient. Did he write the check for enough?"

"Yep. What we did was only fifteen hundred worth of work. I threw in that extra five hundred for you," Mrs. Taylor said. "Your time is just as valuable."

Mrs. Childs reached into a bank bag and handed me five crisp one hundred-dollar bills. "Wow. Thank y'all so much. This is amazing."

I hugged them both, then walked out to see Vance and Belan. He had a smile on his face, so I smiled back. "The way Oscar was cussing when they walked out of here, I take it things went well."

"Amazingly well. Let's go to lunch, my treat."

1 7

*V*ance

"Now Y'ALL done started the party right! These last two dollas!"

I laughed hard as hell. Mr. George was back in full-effect, singing and shit. We were having a barbeque at my house and I had made a blues playlist just for him. Everybody was back on track, so it was time to celebrate that shit. I'd just gotten back from an anger management class and had invited everyone over. It had been a month since Jennifer's dealings with Oscar and all was peaceful in our world.

Mr. George wasn't completely done with alcohol, but he only drank on weekends now and he limited himself to a six-pack. I noticed Tyrone had been doing the same. I stood at the barbeque pit, putting barbeque sauce on the ribs as Tyrone brought out the chicken. "I see he done got cranked up."

"Yep. I love when he enjoys himself."

"Me too."

Every song that came on, Mr. George acted like that was his favorite song. When "Someone Else is Steppin' In" came on, he grabbed Donna by the hand and pulled her to him to dance. They looked extremely happy and that made me happy. Seeing everyone happy and getting along was a great thing. Jennifer and I were doing well also. I spent nights with her and sometimes, she stayed with me. Most times, she stayed over on the weekends, so she could be home during the week for when Meena had to go to work.

After taking the ribs off, I got out of Tyrone's way. He'd done pretty good barbequing the chicken last time, so I let him work on that so I could go inside to check on my baby. When I walked inside with the ribs, she said, "Damn, that smells good, baby."

"I'm sure it taste good, too. Are the sides done?"

"Yep."

"Okay. When Tyrone gets done with the chicken, we'll be able to eat. Where's my BeBe?"

"Meena took her to your room to change her."

I nodded, then pulled Jennifer close to me and swayed to the music playing outside. I could hear Mr. George holla when he realized what song was playing. "I know you didn't put Marvin on the list!"

Jennifer and I laughed extra hard. He made our gatherings fun, that was for sure. "Please tell me you're staying over tonight."

"Yep. I have nowhere else to go or nothing else to do, except you."

I chuckled, then bit my bottom lip. "I can't wait, either. I haven't had you all week."

"I know. I'm sorry, King. I just try to make sure Meena and Tyrone get their time alone. Your BeBe was excited to be with us all week."

"That she was. So, you won't believe this, but the safety guy from the fire department called me. He wants me to update their manuals."

"Wow! Are you going to do it?"

"Well, lucky for me that I kept up with fire safety while I was locked up. I didn't have shit else to do, so I read up on every update to safety procedures and policies. I agreed to do it. Although it took me a while to accept it. I had to call him back."

"Why?"

"It was what I was doing when my life changed forever."

Her hands slid down my chest and she said, "I understand. It brought back horrible memories."

"Mmm hmm. But I realized that God is faithful. I didn't get paid for it last time because I didn't finish, so he gave me the opportunity now. I'm grateful to be able to just pick up where I left off it seems. But because I have you, it's even better than it was when I left."

My hands slid to her ass and I lowered my head to her neck as I heard, "Aww, *Lawd*! Can y'all go two minutes without touching and groping each other?"

"Jealous?" Jennifer asked, causing me to chuckle.

"Yes! Now, bye!" Meena said as she laughed and headed outside.

"Now, where were we?" I asked Jenn.

"You were just about to kiss my spot and make me take you in the bedroom to do some freaky shit to you. So, let's not go back to that just yet."

"You right. I'll hold out 'til later. If you get me cranked up now, we won't make it back outside."

"This I know."

"A'ight, baby. Let me go check on Tyrone."

I kissed her lips and grabbed her ass once more, then walked outside to see Mr. George still dancing to a Bobby Womack song. I laced that list to keep him entertained the whole evening. Chuckling slightly, I made my way to Tyrone to see him turning the meat. "Good job, son."

"Thanks, Eti. You want a beer?"

"Yeah, you can hand me one."

I sat next to him, watching Meena and Belan having fun on the swing set. She looked like her mother and Belan looked like she did as a baby. For a moment, it seemed I'd gone back in time, thirty years ago. I'd just gotten on the force two years before and had married Madelyn. She never worked outside the home. Only six months or so after we got married, she had found out she was pregnant with Meena. I was beyond excited to be a father. *Vance! Come swing with us!*

Madelyn's voice was clear as day as I sat watching Meena and Belan, reminiscing about Madelyn and Meena. Shaking my head and snapping out of it, I stared at my daughter and admired the amazing woman she'd become. She'd managed to apply a lot of her mother's teaching to her life and to motherhood. "She's beautiful, huh?"

"Which one?" I asked Tyrone.

"Well of course both of them, but I was referring to your daughter. I assumed that was who you were staring at."

"She's gorgeous, just like her mother. BeBe looks just like she did as a baby."

"So I've seen from the pictures."

A slight smile graced my lips as I watched Belan scream in excitement as Meena pushed her. They were my world and I was grateful to see the light of day again to be a part of their lives.

Once Tyrone finished the chicken, we all went inside to fix our plates, then made our way back outside. As we ate, I congratulated Tyrone on barbequing the chicken perfectly. We had to change the music to something else so Mr. George would calm down enough to eat. Meena had turned on Jill Scott, but that wasn't much better. He loved Jill Scott. We all laughed as he tried to sing along with her.

When we were done, I gathered trash and cleaned the table off, then winked at Meena for her to change the song. As Jennifer sat talking to Donna, I walked over to her as "Marry Me" by David Banner played in the background. I gently rubbed my hand down her arm to get her attention as everyone else looked on in excitement. They all knew what was coming. Jennifer was the only one in the dark, but not for long. When she turned to me, I went to my knee as her eyes widened. I allowed the song to play a little, so she could hear the words.

The tears had begun to fall from her eyes as she listened to the music, knowing what was about to go down. After a minute or two, I began, "From the moment I met you, I knew this moment would come. You are the woman God had for me. My transition back into society was so much easier with you by my side. Your love kept me... sustained me. Before you even really knew me, you cared for me. We've only been together for a little over two months, and here I am, on my knee, asking you to be my wife. That doesn't have to happen tomorrow or even next year. Just so long as you promise to one day be my wife. Let me change your last name to Etienne. Will you?"

She stared at me as tears streamed down her face. She took a deep breath, trying to gather her composure. I could feel the tremble in her hand as she struggled to release the words from her mouth. Suddenly, in what sounded like a gasp, she said, "Yes, King."

I slid the beautiful, three-carat chocolate diamond on her finger and stood, pulling her up with me and hugging her tightly. My lips found hers and I kissed her like no one else was watching. They were all applauding and whistling as I pulled away from her. My life was in shambles until I met Jennifer, but now it was just the way it was supposed to be. I had my queen... officially. "I love you, baby."

"I love you, too, King. I think a springtime wedding would be beautiful. What do you think? April sound good to you?"

"Seven months is more than enough time to prepare for what you want. If you wanted to get married next weekend, I'd be all for it. Like I said, it doesn't matter when, just so long as it happens."

"You're perfect, Vance... perfect for me."

EPILOGUE

*J*ennifer
      Seven months later...

"The wedding was beautiful. Even though it was outside in the backyard, it was more than I would have ever imagined. You transformed this place so much; I almost didn't recognize it. I had to look back at the house to be sure."

I laughed at Vance as we sat at our table, eating blackened catfish and shrimp etouffee. Meena and Tyrone were in the wedding as well, along with our BeBe as the flower girl. She was seventeen months old now, walking and getting into everything. It seemed her meddling had gotten worse ever since Meena announced she was pregnant last month. She was now about twelve or thirteen weeks along. Everyone was hoping for a boy this time since Meena assured us this one would be her last. She said she had to break the curse of only having one kid. Me, Vance,

Meena, and Tyrone... none of us had siblings. Tyrone's parents did, though.

Tomorrow, we would be leaving for Santorini, Greece, and I was so excited. To be leaving the country with Vance and soaking up one another's energy and love for an entire week was like a dream come true. He'd been working with the safety director at the fire station to teach new hires of procedures that were in the manual. They found it beneficial to not just leave it to them to go over the manual. They started a class. Although they only had a class once a month, Vance was extremely happy about it. He'd run into Oscar on a couple of occasions, but no words were spoken between them. I was extremely proud of him for getting his temper under control.

I'd begun selling my products again. I made t-shirts, bows, coffee mugs, wine glasses, and pretty much anything else that could be monogrammed. Once I added programs and invitations to my list of available services, I stayed as busy as I wanted to be. I literally had to turn down clients, so I didn't get overwhelmed. Meena was learning with me, so she could make extra money once she went on maternity leave.

I was so grateful for being at this point in my life. While I'd considered Meena as a daughter and Tyrone as a son for some years now, it was now official. The man of my dreams had swept me off my feet and shared his daughter and granddaughter with me. Several people had come from the fire department to witness our union along with a few neighbors and Tyrone's parents. We all had dinner together at least once every three months and our bond had become so strong. George and Donna's relationship had gotten even better as well.

After eating, Vance and I stood to have our first dance. We both enjoyed Stevie Wonder's, "Knocks Me Off My Feet," so we chose that song to dance to. I held his face in my hands and said, "I can't wait to spend this first night in the house as a married couple."

"Me either."

I'd moved in with him a month ago but opted to keep my house and turn it into an office for my business. I had consultations in it and did all my work there. That way I could keep it separate from my home-life, imposing office hours on myself. Vance loved that idea and had helped me come up with renovation ideas. "You know we may not get much sleep tonight."

"You don't say? I was hoping we didn't, King. We gon' have plenty of time to sleep on that long-ass flight."

"Hell yeah. I ain't never been on a plane for fourteen hours. But I know as long as you with me, it's worth it."

"Worth it indeed. Life has taken on a whole new meaning, baby, and I plan to enjoy it to the fullest, sharing it with you."

THE END

AFTERWORD

From the Author

This seasoned zaddy story was everything to me. The George Mills in the story was indeed a real person. He died back in 2013 and this was my way of paying tribute to his memory. He was always the life of the party, but only when he'd gotten lit. Otherwise, he wasn't a very talkative man. I hope you all enjoyed the journeys of Vance and Jennifer and how they overcame a lot of adversity and bad decisions... how they became stronger as individuals and even stronger as a couple.

There's also an amazing playlist on iTunes for this book under the same title that includes some great R&B, blues, and rap tracks to tickle your fancy. Please keep up with me on Facebook (@authormonicawalters), Instagram (@authormonicawalters) and Twitter (@monlwalters). You can also visit my Amazon author page at www.amazon.com/author/monica.walters to view my releases. Please subscribe to my webpage for updates! https://authormonicawalters.com.

For live discussions, giveaways, and inside information on

upcoming releases, join my Facebook group, Monica's Romantic Sweet Spot at https://bit.ly/2P2lo6X.

In Way Too Deep

You Belong to Me

The Shorts: A BLP Anthology with the Authors of BLP

All I Need is You (A crossover novel with Divine Love by T. Key)

Behind Closed Doors Series

Be Careful What You Wish For

You Just Might Get It

Show Me You Still Want It

Sweet Series

Bitter Sweet

Sweet and Sour

Sweeter Than Before

Sweet Revenge

Sweet Surrender

Sweet Temptation

Sweet Misery

Sweet Exhale

Motives and Betrayal Series

Ulterior Motives

Ultimate Betrayal

Ultimatum: #lovemeorleaveme, Part 1

Ultimatum: #lovemeorleaveme, Part 2

Written Between the Pages Series

The Devil Goes to Church Too

The Book of Noah (A Crossover Novel with The Flow of Jah's Heart by

T. Key)

The Revelations of Ryan, Jr. (A Crossover Novel with All That Jazz by
T. Key)

9 798657 296822